Pitbull's Enslavement

Ares Infidels MC # 3

by Ciara St James

Copyright

Editing & Formatting by Maggie Kern @ Ms. K Edits
Book Cover by Tracie Douglas @ Dark Water Covers

Photograph by Jessica Johnson Photography

Blurb/Warning

Pitbull:

He never imagines that he'll be captivated by a woman who comes into his bar to do something illegal, something he hates. His disappointment knows no bounds when he finds out she's not an angel. He finds he has to change his whole thought process when his actions have terrible consequences for her. He's determined to protect and claim her the next time they meet and to ear her forgiveness. She's not so sure that's the answer.

Luciana:

She's forced to do something reprehensible and against her morals, but she doesn't have a choice. When she's caught by a man who makes her heart pound, she's even more ashamed. No one will ever look at her as anything other than not worth anything. Her instinct is to protect him, which leads her to an ugly situation and an even bigger threat. She thinks the answer is to run.

Will they be able to destroy the enemies coming after her, including an enemy that is destroying her from the inside out? She's determined to protect everyone, including Pitbull. He's determined to love and protect her, because one thing is for sure, she's made him happy to live with Pitbull's Enslavement.

WARNING:
This book is intended for adult readers. It contains coarse language, adult situations, discusses events such as stalkers, assault, torture and murder that may trigger some readers. Sexual situations are graphic. There is no cheating, no cliffhanger and it has a HEA.

Ciara St James Books

Dublin Falls Archangel's Warriors MC

1- Terror's Temptress
2- Savage's Princess
3- Steel & Hammer's Hellcat
4- Menace's Siren
5- Ranger's Enchantress
6- Ghost's Beauty
7- Viper's Vixen
8- Devil Dog's Precious
9- Blaze's Spitfire
10- Smoke's Tigress
11- Hawk's Huntress
12- Storm's Flame

Ares Infidels MC- A Tenillo Guardians series

1- Sin's Enticement
2- Executioner's Enthrallment
3- Pitbull's Enslavement

Hunters Creek Archangel's Warriors MC

1- Bull's Duchess
2- Rebel's Firecracker
3- Ajax's Nymph – coming September 9, 2021

Please follow Ciara on Facebook, Instagram and TikTok. Also for information on new releases & to catch up with Ciara, go to www.ciara-st-james.com or www.facebook.com /ciara.stjames.1 or www.facebook.com/groups/tenilloguardians

Ares' Infidels MC Members

Kye Korbyn (Sin)- President
Connor Terrell (Saint)- VP
Slade Ashton (Executioner)- Enforcer
Deckard Hale (Phantom)- Secretary/ Hacker
Chase Bracco (Talon)- Treasurer
Asher Kendrick (Rampage)- Road Captain
Cole Landis (Pitbull)
Liam Dickerson (Wrecker)
Wyatt Carling (Torpedo)
Brayden Wilde (Boomer)
Drake Marshall (Cuffs)
Dash Nolan (Bullet) + Bk 3
Blake Price (Phalanx) + Bk 3

Pitbull: Prologue 1 Month Ago

I looked around at the party going on around me. It was another great day for the club. Not only were we welcoming a new brother into the fold, but we had also added two new prospects, Omen and Brennan. I was especially excited about Brennan joining, since he was a buddy of mine and I'd talked him into prospecting with us. If everything went well, we'd be welcoming them as brothers in a year or so. And we should be doing the same to Dash and Blake in a month or two. We were growing, and it was a fantastic thing for our club.

It had been one of the proudest days of my life, when I'd been patched in as a full member just over a year ago. Finding Sin and the Ares Infidels had been like a saving grace for me. I had no idea what would have happened to me after I left the Marines if I hadn't. I'd been twenty-nine years old and had no idea if I wanted to do something using my electronics background or go in a totally different direction. All I did know was, after serving ten years in the Corps, I no longer wanted to be in the Marines.

Don't get me wrong, I was proud as hell to have been a Marine. I'd served my country and I knew I helped to save lives, even if I wasn't serving on the front lines like some. I'd worked to maintain the all-important communication gear for my company—satellite, radar, and radio. It was a lifeline for Marines out in the field. There had been some sleepless nights and days when things went down. You had to get them back in working order as fast as possible. That meant if you had to stay up for twenty-four hours or more straight, then that's what you did.

Those had been exhausting and exhilarating times, but there were all the other things that had gone along with it that I wouldn't miss. The times when you knew that commanding officers were making the wrong choice, and you had to watch your guys go into situations they shouldn't have, and listen when those missions went horribly wrong. It had taken a toll and after ten years of it, I wanted out. Even if I had no idea where to go or what to do.

I'd been finishing out my terminal leave when I ran into a guy I knew. His name was Phantom, and he had been in a company or two with me over the years. We'd stayed somewhat in touch. He told me he was getting out too and was joining an MC in Texas. I was stunned. He was going to be a biker? All I could imagine is the guys you see on television—the guys who are into all kinds of illegal shit and go around stealing and hurting people. That wasn't Phantom at all.

When I expressed my astonishment, he'd laughed and explained how the Ares Infidels were different. That not all MCs were like what you saw on television or read about in books. This one was made up of all prior military guys from all the branches. The founder was a guy named Sin, who had been a Navy SEAL. I knew Sin. He and Phantom had been best buddies for years, and I'd met him a few times. Phantom explained that the club had officially started a year before that, and it was in Sin's hometown of Tenillo, Texas.

As we sat there that night drinking and talking, I started to get excited. Everything he was telling me sounded like something I could get behind. They had legit businesses and helped their community. They just liked having control of their own destinies. I really liked that idea. By the time the next morning came and the hangover wore off, I'd made up my mind. I was going to see if I could join the Infidels too. Phantom had given me the contact information for Sin. He said he was off to Texas that week to join them, and he'd tell Sin to expect my call.

When I got out three months later, I did the same thing. I'd been in contact with Sin and given him my information. He'd explained they would need to do a background check on me. No one got accepted as a prospect without one. After they completed it, he contacted me and offered me a position as a prospect. He explained what the prospecting gig would look like and how long it typically lasted, and he told me what the club would expect from me. None of it was outrageous to me. Maybe a little annoying to be the bottom man on the totem pole again and having to take shit, but I could deal with that any day.

The one bump, if you will, that I did run into, was explaining to my mom why I wasn't coming to Oregon to live close to her and the twins—my half-brother, Conner, and half-sister, Lily. I loved them, but it wasn't exactly where I wanted to settle—too damn much rain for me. Besides, they had their lives there, not me. Lily and Conner would be starting college in a couple of years, and we didn't exactly have a lot in common with the thirteen-year age difference. I felt more like their uncle than their brother.

I was happy that Mom had found my stepdad. My dad died when I was nine years old. We'd struggled for the next couple of years until she met Pete. They fell fast and hard for each other and before I knew it; she was pregnant with my brother and sister, and they got married. I'd gone off to the Marines as soon as I graduated from high school. Fast forward twelve years and here I was at another club party, watching as another guy found his place like I had.

However, this wasn't just a patch-in party for Drake and to welcome our new prospects. My brother, Executioner, had just given his woman, Skye, her property rag. He'd stunned us all when we found out he knew her, and they'd hooked up a little over two months ago one night in Fort Worth. He'd lost her by the next morning and had been frantic to find her, though he never told any of us. One day, he'd walked into the flower shop in town on club business and there she was. That was it. He pursued her with single-minded purpose. Now, they were not only together, but expecting a baby. Fuck, that blew my mind.

As I watched him holding her and talking to her mom and some of the Time Served guys, I could see how damn happy he was. I mean, really, deep down in your soul, happy. I wondered what that felt like. Not that I was unhappy, I wasn't, but to feel like that, I had no idea how it would feel. Or if I'd ever experience it like he and Sin were, or for that matter, Boss and Hook from the

Time Served MC. You could see the happiness and love on their faces every time they looked at their women. That would be something else to have, though I didn't think everyone got that lucky in life.

A hand on my arm had me looking around. It was Brea, Hook's best friend. We'd been introduced to her today when she came with them. She smiled up at me. "You look like you're deep in thought over here. Care for some company? I know we just met, but I'm a good listener if you need an ear." She held up a beer. I took it.

"Just thinking about how different things have grown in the last two years, and how lucky some of my brothers are. They're like Boss and Hook. Makes me wonder who might be next."

"Maybe it'll be you. Have you ever thought of that?"

I laughed and shook my head. "No, I wouldn't count on that. It would take a brave woman to take me on. I have no idea what kind of woman it would take to have me looking and acting like them." I pointed at the couples.

"I think you'll find someone who's perfect for you, Pitbull. And when you do, she'll knock you for a loop, and put that same look on your face. I wouldn't be surprised if you meet her sooner rather than later. Something tells me, your life is about to change."

I laughed again, then steered the conversation away from my imaginary woman. Because I knew that was all she was, imaginary. Though deep down, a part of me wanted what Brea said to be real, more real than I would ever admit to anyone. I spent the remainder of the night trying to forget our conversation and my thoughts about having a woman of my own.

Prologue: Two and a Half Weeks Ago

I looked at the guy in disgust. He and his buddies thought taking women and selling them or forcing them into prostitution was alright. It made me want to do more than cut out his eyes like I'd threatened. He'd been crying like a bitch. He hadn't cared about the women who'd cried and pleaded for their freedom and lives. Why in the hell would he think we'd care about him?

I watched with satisfaction as he was dispatched to hell. The pain and torture were more than earned for daring to lay hands on Sis, Brea's daughter. Brea was a close friend of the Time Served MC, and she was now Chef's lady. I'd have done it to anyone who did what he did, but to know the victims, that made it even sweeter. As they decided what to do with the remains, I thought more about the women. We knew that more women had been taken just days ago. The number was beyond alarming. We had to find out where they were going and put a stop to it. The women of Tenillo and the surrounding areas needed to be able to walk down the street without fearing they'd be snatched up and never heard from again. Our town was counting on us to figure this out and make them safe again.

Prologue: A Week Ago

Things needed to slow the fuck down, and the danger to our friends and family had to stop. It was bad enough we were trying to protect our community, but shit kept coming back on us. Specifically, shit kept happening to the women in our club and our Time Served buddies' ladies.

After Sis had been abducted, it was only a week later when Skye and her mom, Jackie, had been taken hostage by extortionists in the flower shop. We'd been working to find them and take them out of business for a while. A man had gotten the drop on my brother, Torpedo, and knocked him out. Something had set off Omen's freaky Cajun mojo. He'd told Executioner something was wrong and to get his ass to the flower shop. That shit right there was scary and awesome as hell. Omen had some kind of second sight, or some shit, he claimed. Not sure if I totally believed it, but after what I saw, I had to think it might be real. I'd take anything he had to say seriously.

That day, we caught two of the extortionists. Before the day had passed, the final one had found a way to get his hands on Skye's brother, Tanner, and she'd gone after them. A wild ride later and we'd found all three extortionists who had been harassing our town, got a tad more information out of them, then killed all of them. Now, Executioner and Skye were planning their wedding in August. God, my head whirled, thinking about all of it.

I hoped things would settle but wasn't holding my breath. On top of all that, we'd explored a bunker Sis and Pop had found on Pop's property over a week ago. They'd found a big metal door going down into a concrete pad. It had been hidden by brush and when it was removed to make room to build more houses, they'd found it. My brothers and I were the ones to go down in it, because it was likely part of the old Air Force base next door. If we were caught trespassing, we'd be less likely to go to jail than Boss and his guys, who were all ex-felons.

We'd found that it was a long narrow bunker, and it led to another bunker underground on the actual Air Force base. A passageway connected them. Beyond the second bunker was a longer passageway that led under the highway and came out behind the shitty bar and truck stop across the freeway. They were both hell-holes and nowhere someone decent wanted to hangout, though the truckers, junkies, lot lizards, and other low-lives seemed to love it. We found the exit was inside of an old shack out behind the bar, the Liar's Lair. This raised more questions. Why was it hidden in a shack? What was it being used for?

We knew it was in use, because even though it was empty when we explored it, there were signs that the dust had been disturbed more than once. In order to find out who was using it and for what, Phantom and Preacher had set up cameras and recording equipment, which would activate when they detected movement and sound. We were waiting to see what that got us, then we could figure out what to do about it.

We knew it had to be nothing good. Otherwise, why hide it? It did help us and the Time Served guys to figure something else out—why Pop had been shot on his own property a couple of months back. They knew it was most likely some guys who'd wanted access across Pop's land. He'd told them no and right after that, someone had cut his fence. He had seen them coming across his property and gone after them to confront them alone, and they'd shot him. Suffice to say, they'd sealed their fate once they're caught. Pop was the pseudo father to Boss and his guys. He was their mentor and the guy who got them on track when they'd gotten out of prison. They'd make them bleed for almost killing that old man when they found them. All I wanted was for us to get that figured out, along with the missing women and the drug dealing we suspected was happening at the gym and laundromat before anything else went wrong. Was that too much to ask?

Pitbull: Chapter 1

Damn! Our bar, the Hangout, was hopping tonight. Not a surprise on a Saturday night in Texas, but it seemed to be even busier than usual. Thank God, we'd hired Blue, Brea's friend, to work for us three weeks ago. Blue had announced she was staying in Tenillo and was looking for a job. I snapped her up immediately. She had a lot of bartender and barback experience and had been able to hit the ground running. Our last bartender had just up and disappeared on us. He gave us no warning and no notice. If I got my hands on him, I'd beat his ass to teach him some manners. Didn't anyone have a work ethic anymore?

As I watched the security monitors from my office, I saw the waitresses running around like mad as well. Maybe I should think about staffing another one on Saturdays if this was going to be the new norm. We had people wanting to work for the Infidels. I flipped to the monitor that overlooked the front door where the bouncers were standing and checking IDs. They had strict orders that no one got in without one, and if the ID looked like it might be phony, then the person was turned away as well. No way any of us wanted to be caught breaking the law and allowing anyone who was underage in our bar.

While Texas law said we could allow anyone in the bar as long as they weren't drinking, we didn't. Nor did we serve alcohol to minors who were with their legal guardian or parent, even though that was legal, too. It was better to keep it at twenty-one and above. A few people had left pissed, but we didn't care. We didn't want to run the risk of getting closed down.

I was about to check the dance floor when I saw a young woman come through the door. I stopped and stared at her. She looked young, probably no older than twenty-two or twenty-three. Way too young to be catching my eye, but she did. And it wasn't just because of her age, it was her looks and her demeanor.

She looked like she wasn't comfortable being in here. She looked around and acted nervous when the bouncer said something to her. She handed him her ID. I saw Franco ask her something, and she nodded. He gave back her ID and waved her inside. She stepped into the main part of the bar like she was going to her doom. This had my curiosity piqued. Why was she so reluctant to be here? Was she meeting someone she was afraid of or didn't want to meet? All kinds of thoughts raced through my head.

As I watched her slowly walk around the bar, I thought about how she looked. Even if she was young and I shouldn't look, she'd caught my fucking attention and made me take notice. She was tiny, which for me wasn't what I typically liked in a woman. At six feet, I looked for women more in the average height range. I estimated her to be maybe five feet. She had on a pair of jeans, a tank top, and a jacket—standard wear around here. They clung to her tiny body, showing off a tiny waist and rounded hips. She wasn't sporting a huge rack or anything, but her body seemed to fit her. I bet I could span that waist with both of my hands. My hands almost itched to try it.

Her skin was a light tan color. She looked like she might be partially Hispanic, probably Mexican, if she was from around here. Her hair was up in a ponytail, and it hung below her shoulder blades. It was hard to tell what color it was, but it was dark, and I could see what looked like lighter streaks in it. Her eyes were too far away to see the color, no matter how I zoomed in. Her face looked delicate and the expression of sadness on it got my attention.

For the next hour, I watched her seemingly move aimlessly around the room. She'd stop once in a while and chat with different people. Those conversations never lasted long, and then she'd move on. Sometimes people would come up to her. Every time, I saw she looked like she wanted to be anywhere but here, and she was always checking around her. A few times, I saw guys trying to get her to stay with them and she'd hurry off. A few had grabbed her arm. I'd almost come through the monitors when I saw those. Who in the hell were they to touch her?!

I was about to go out and see if I could see her up close and maybe talk to her when I noticed her coming down the hall to the bathrooms, which was just up the hall from my office. She went into the ladies' bathroom and then, a few minutes later, she came out. I'd just stood up to go out when I saw a woman come up to her and say something. Then I saw a slight movement of the mystery woman's hand touching the other woman's. Something small flashed between them.

I stiffened. I recognized what was happening. She was fucking dealing drugs in our bar! Rage tore through me, along with disappointment. She was nothing but a lowlife dealer, probably a damn junkie herself. I kicked my chair into the wall as I stormed to the office door and tore it open. It banged off the wall as I came out into the hall. Even over the loud music, people heard it hit. They looked around at me in surprise.

I saw her eyes go round when she saw me barreling down on her. She turned to run, but I got a hold of her arm before she could. The woman she'd just given the drugs to ran. I yanked her to me and dragged her to the office. She struggled to get away, but I tightened my grip and slammed the door closed behind us, making sure to lock it. I pushed her down on the couch. She scrambled into the corner and huddled in it with her knees drawn up to her chest.

Even though I was pissed and disappointed, it bothered me to see her scared of me, but that wasn't what I needed to worry about right now. I leaned down and got close to her face. She flinched. Up close, I couldn't help but see she was even more gorgeous than on the security monitor and her eyes were a startling amber color. "Give it to me," I growled at her.

"G-give you what? Why did you bring me in here?" She stuttered and her voice quivered with fright. I stomped down on my need to protect a scared woman. She was a dealer. I needed to remember that.

"Don't play stupid with me. I know what you've been doing all damn night. Give it to me, now!"

"I don't know what you're talking about. I came out of the bathroom and then you were coming after me like a crazy person. I think you must have mistaken me for someone else."

"Bullshit. I've been watching you. You've been all over the bar. At first, I had no idea what you were doing, then I saw you slip something to that woman outside the bathroom. You're fucking dealing drugs in our bar! Do you have any idea who owns this bar?" I snarled at her. She was now trembling and shaking her head.

I turned enough for her to see the back of my rag. Her eyes got even bigger, and she shook harder. "The Ares Infidels MC owns this bar. You were dealing in our place. I'm not going to ask again. I want the fucking drugs!"

She looked like she was about to faint, but she tried one more time to deny she had any. "I-I don't have any drugs. This is a mistake. Please, let me go and we can forget this happened." I didn't ask her again. I grabbed her jacket and tore it open. She slapped my hands, but I ignored her. I felt inside the inner lining until I found the opening. I pulled out several small bags of white powder. I flung them down on the couch at her feet. I pushed her away from me in disgust.

"Oh, so what is this, my fucking imagination? I should call the cops and let them see what you don't have." She was sobbing now. When I threatened to call the cops, she fell off the couch on her knees. She put her hands up like she was praying and began to beg.

"Please, please don't do that. Please. I swear, I'll never come here again. You'll never see me again."

"Who are you and who are you dealing for?"

"My name is Luciana. No one, it's mine. I just needed to make some cash. I've never done this before. I promise I'll never do it again."

"You expect me to believe this is all you and that you've never done this before? How dumb do you think I am? I want to know who your dealer is!" I shouted at her. However, no matter how scared she got, or how loud and mean I got, she never gave me a name. She kept swearing it was hers and she just needed to make some money.

After a solid half hour, I had to make a hard decision. Did I call in the club and we push this further? Or did I call the cops? Typically, I would've just called my brothers and we would've tortured the information out of the person, but I couldn't bring myself to do that. We were taught to protect women and children. That was how my mother raised me. The idea of hurting her made me sick. I knew none of my brothers would want to do it, though if it was necessary, we would.

So, with a heavy heart and a knot in my stomach, I decided. I pulled her to her feet and ran my hands down her body. I took off her jacket and searched the rest of her. She was slapping my hands again and trying to get away. I made sure to keep it impersonal, but I wanted to find all the drugs and money. When I was done searching her and her clothes, I had ten baggies of powder and a wad of cash. I held them up.

"These are mine. Call it payment for you dealing this shit in our place tonight. I want you to get the hell out of here and I'd better never see you in here again. Do you understand? If I do, the cops will be the last thing you have to worry about."

The fear on her face had me almost taking those words back. She looked at the drugs and money, then back at me. I swore I saw despair in her eyes, then she shrank away from me. She grabbed her jacket and went to the door. As she unlocked it, I watched her closely. She opened it, then looked back at me.

"You'll never see me again," she whispered. As she hurried out the door, I went to it and hollered after her.

"I'd better not see you again." She never turned to look back at me, but the people standing in the hall did. I could see them staring at me in shock. I slammed the door shut and went back to the monitors. I watched as she ran out the front door. In the parking lot, she got into an old beat-up car. I couldn't make out the license plate. As she did, I fought the feeling of disappointment in my gut. The one woman I'd felt some kind of spark for, and she was a fucking dealer. God, I needed a damn drink. Then I'd have to confess to my brothers that I'd let a drug dealer walk. They just might beat my ass.

⟵▷⟵▷⟵▷⟵▷⟵▷

Monday night and I was off from the bar. I needed a night off. Ever since Saturday, I'd been thinking almost nonstop about Luciana, and about my anger at her dealing and the disappointment that she was a dealer. I'd confessed to the guys on Sunday what I'd done. None of them were happy, but they also agreed that hurting a woman for information wasn't something we wanted to do unless we had no choice.

That didn't stop me from berating myself for letting her go, and for not finding out her last name. When Phantom ran her ID, it came back fake. Who knows what her real name was? My anger didn't stop me from thinking about her and what she'd looked like, what being close to her had done to my body. The whole time I was yelling and trying to intimidate her, she'd had my body reacting to her. The scent of her had been like flowers mixed with something sweet. She should have smelled like smoke, sweat and maybe alcohol after being in the bar for so long.

I was still trying to figure out why she'd been driven to deal. I'd flushed the drugs and then gave the money to the food bank in town. At least something good would come out of it. Now, I was sitting in the common room of our clubhouse, having a beer, trying to forget her. Some of the guys were hanging out after work, but I'd told them I wanted to be alone. The door opening had me looking up and Wrecker and Cuffs walked in.

They were my brothers on the police force. They were just getting off work by the looks of their clothes. Cuffs was a detective and Wrecker was the deputy chief of police to Boss. They headed straight toward me. I sat up. They looked serious. When they got to the table, they pulled out chairs and sat down heavily.

"What's up?"

"Pitbull, we need to talk to you. Can we go somewhere private?" Wrecker asked. The seriousness on his face and the tone of his voice was off, making me frown.

"Private? Why do we need to talk in private?" As I asked, the main door opened again and in came Sin, Saint, and Executioner. They came straight to my table and stood there with their arms crossed. Shit, something was very wrong. The three main officers in the club stared down at me. I stood up. "Sure, where do you want to talk?"

"We can use my office," Sin said. I followed them down the hall. I racked my brain to think what this could be about. Once we were inside and the door was closed, they got started.

"Have a seat. We need to ask you about Saturday night," Cuffs said. I took a seat at the table. Cuffs and Wrecker sat across from me. Sin, Saint, and Executioner remained standing.

"What about Saturday night?"

"About the woman you caught who was dealing drugs. We need to go over what happened."

"I told you what happened. Why? What's this about?"

"Just humor us and tell us again," Wrecker said. I quickly took them over the details again. When I was done, Wrecker and Cuffs looked at each other. I was starting to get pissed.

"What the fuck is going on here? Did she come to

the station and file a complaint on me? What? And why are these three standing here like guards?"

Wrecker sighed and Sin, Saint, and Executioner took a seat. "We had to ask, Pitbull. We don't think you did anything to her, but we needed to be sure there wasn't something you forgot to tell us. We asked these three to be here since it involves the club."

"Why would you say you didn't think I did anything to her? Did she say I did?" I was getting more pissed. The bitch had lied and went to the cops saying I did something. I might have yelled at her and searched her, but that was it.

"No, she didn't say a word about you, but when we started to investigate, we realized she was the one you told us about—the one dealing at the bar last Saturday."

"What in the hell happened? Did she get busted?"

Cuffs looked at me and then down at the table. When he looked up, I saw the sadness in his eyes. "No, she didn't report you or get busted. We were called to the hospital today, to take a statement from a young woman. That young woman said her name was Luciana Ramirez. That got us thinking it might be the same woman. When we questioned her, she didn't say a word about being at the bar Saturday night."

"Why is she in the hospital?" A churning sensation started low in my gut.

"She was found beaten and unconscious early Sunday morning. She'd been thrown out in an abandoned field out by the Haven area. A couple of kids out playing ball found her and told their parents. They called an ambulance."

"Beaten? How badly is she hurt?" I couldn't help but ask. The thought of that tiny thing being beaten made me sick. Even if she was a dealer, no woman deserved to be abused.

"She just woke up this afternoon. The beating was severe. The doctor was worried she might not wake up or might have permanent brain damage when she didn't regain consciousness at first." I stood up and walked over to the door, then back.

"Who beat her? Why?"

"She's not saying. She said she doesn't know, but I know she does. I could see it in her eyes. She's fucking terrified. As badly hurt as she was, she tried to get the doctor to discharge her. Said she'd be fine. She can't even walk!" Wrecker spat out. His fist slammed down on the table in anger.

"I want to see her."

"Pitbull, you can't. She's in ICU and they're only letting in family and us. We just needed to see if you might have remembered something else or seen something. Someone who might have paid too much attention to her or might have left right after she did. We'll need to see the security tapes, talk to some of the other people who were there that night. That beating had to have happened not long after she left. You said it was midnight when you kicked her out. The doctor estimates she was beaten sometime between two and four that morning," Cuffs told me.

I sank back down in my chair. A horrible thought went through my mind. Had I done something to get her hurt? "Did she get beaten because of me? Because I took her drugs and the money?"

They both looked uncomfortable. "Taking those drugs was the right thing to do. Did it get her hurt? We don't know. It's possible. If she was lying about not having a dealer and she came back without the drugs or cash, then it's very possible. Drug dealers aren't usually the most understanding people, but you had no way to know that, and you couldn't have sent her out of there with them." Wrecker tried to reassure me. It didn't help. I knew that it was because of what I did.

"How bad is bad? You said she just regained consciousness. What was done to her?"

They both shifted in their chairs. "We can't legally tell you that, Pitbull," Cuffs said.

"I'm not asking you as cops. I'm asking as your fucking brother. What was done to her?" I yelled as I slammed my fist on the table.

"Okay, settle down. She was severely beaten all over her body. There are lacerations too. Her ribs are bruised, and a couple are cracked. Her left arm is sprained. There's what looks like belt marks across her back, and her head was beaten off the ground or something hard." I was about to puke listening to them. They paused and then Cuffs finished softly. "And she was stabbed in the side and choked. We think the choking is what made her assailant or assailants think she was dead, and they dumped her body."

I stood up and rushed over to the trash can beside Sin's desk. I stood there fighting not to puke. All I could see was her beautiful face and then an image of her being beaten. The knowledge I'd been the one to cause this made me sick. I could cut up a fucking man and not blink, but this made me nauseous. Oh God, I'd fucking almost gotten her killed! It was my fault! When I stopped dry heaving, Sin handed me a bottle of water and a piece of gum. I took a drink then fell back in a chair.

I looked at them. All five were staring at me with concern. I wasn't the one they should be concerned about. She was the one. I took a deep breath and asked the one question I dreaded the answer to the most. The one that might send me completely over the edge. "Was she raped?"

Wrecker shook his head. "No, the doctor said she wasn't raped, thank God. But there was a lot of rage behind that beating. Whoever did it wanted her to suffer. I don't think they meant to kill her, but the choking likely made them think they had. She had surgery to repair the stab wound. The other things will heal with time. They don't think she'll have permanent damage," he added, like that was supposed to make it better. The only thing that would make it better was to find whoever was responsible and wipe them off the face of the earth. I was going to make them bleed.

"I'm going to see her," I told them as I stood up. Executioner slid in front of the door. I eyed him. He might outweigh me and stand a half foot taller, but I wasn't called Pitbull for nothing. I'd take his ass on, and the way I was feeling, I'd win.

"Executioner, I say this with love and respect, but if you don't get the fuck out of my way, we're gonna have a problem," I told him softly. Sin got between us. He held up his hand.

"Calm down. There's not gonna be any fighting. I understand you're upset. You can't go over there and cause problems. They told you, only family."

"When has that ever stopped us? I'll tell them I'm her damn husband if I have to. I have to see her. You don't understand. I need to see with my own eyes what was done to her and to find out who did it. I sent her out of there without a single thought of what might happen to her if she had a dealer and came back empty handed! She could have died. I scared the hell out of her. She had to know she was walking into a deadly situation. Why didn't she tell me?" I whispered the last part. I knew why. Because I'd scared her more than her dealer. I should have been nicer and talked to her gently. Maybe then she would have told me something and I could have protected her. I stared hard at Sin. Finally, he stepped away.

"Let him go, but we're coming with you. We need to find out who did this. We need to make sure she's okay," Sin told them. I didn't wait to hear more. I tore out of the office and down the hall. I was gonna get on my bike and go. In the end, the five of them went with me. We roared through town on our way to the hospital. Time seemed to be moving too slow as the miles sped by.

Luciana: Chapter 2

After the two officers left, I thought about what I needed to do. They didn't look like they had believed my story. I had to get out of here. No way was I staying. Not only could I not afford it, but if Juan found out I was alive, he'd drag me back there. No way was I going to go back. This was probably my only chance to get away. No way in hell was I going to blow it.

I waited until after dinner and they'd given me more pain medication. It would be hell to go without, but I would endure it. I had rung the nurses' station and told them I was taking a nap and not to disturb me for a while. They assured me they would leave me alone for two hours, but then they'd have to do a check. That would be enough time.

It took me a couple of minutes to get my feet over the edge of the bed. I was sweating and the pain in my whole body and especially my side was terrible. It throbbed with spikes of intermittent pain as though I was being stabbed with a knife. I took a couple of fortifying breaths, then I stood up. The room whirled around me. I clung to the bed rail and waited for it to stop. When it did, I shuffled my feet over to the closet. I knew that had to be where my clothes were, or what was left of them.

I didn't remember all of what happened Saturday night, but I recalled enough to know I had come in wearing something. When I swung open the door, I saw a pair of jeans and my tank. There were no other clothes or shoes, but they would do. I grabbed them and turned to shuffle to the bathroom. I needed to pee and then get dressed.

I was halfway to the bathroom, when my door opened and I heard a deep voice that I recognized growl, "What the fuck are you doing?" I whipped around too fast and lost my footing. I was falling and there was nothing I could do about it. I watched as the man who'd taken my drugs and money came racing toward me. I screamed and threw up a hand to protect my face and threw the other out to break my fall.

Before I hit the ground, I was swept up into strong arms and held against an even harder chest. My nightmare stared down at me with his light brown eyes blazing at me. I cringed and tried to get away from him. I had no idea what he'd do to me. I couldn't take another beating.

"Please, don't. Let me down. I can't take it again," I whispered. I hated to beg but I would. He sat me down on the bed and then stepped back to look at me from head to toe. His face was a mask of fury. I shrank back into the pillows. He was pissed again. What would he do this time?

"Don't do what?"

"Don't hurt me. I can't take it right now. I didn't go back to your bar. Why're you here?" I asked as I tried to figure out how he knew I was here and why he'd be visiting me. It was then that the other men with him registered. Two I didn't know but could see they wore leather vests like him. The other two were the officers I'd talked to earlier, only this time they had on vests too. Oh my God, they were bikers! I panted to get more air into my lungs. I was hyperventilating. They were going to kill me. Maybe they knew Juan and he had sent them to finish what he'd started.

"I won't tell. Tell Juan I won't tell. Please, I'll go far away, and no one will ever know," I pleaded with him. His face registered surprise, then more outrage.

"We're not here to hurt you! Why were you up, walking alone and holding your clothes?" The one who had identified himself as Deputy Police Chief Dickerson asked. I saw his vest read *Wrecker*. The other one who had introduced himself as Detective Marshall was frowning and his vest read *Cuffs*. I had the insane urge to laugh. Cuffs was an appropriate nickname for a cop, but I wasn't sure if Wrecker was.

"I'm leaving. I don't need to be here." Their eyes widened and their eyebrows inched toward their hairlines. I tried to smile and act like it was no big deal. The one who had taken my stuff, the one who was called Pitbull, leaned closer. I fought not to flinch or pull away. It seemed to make him more pissed.

"Like hell you don't need to be here. You're fucking black and blue all over! You can barely move. Your ribs are messed up and so is your arm. You were unconscious for more than a day. You need to keep your ass in that bed. Let them control your pain and help you heal," he barked at me. I could see why he was called Pitbull. He wouldn't let go and he barked out orders. I'd usually take exception and say something smart back, but I wasn't feeling up to it. I tried a different approach.

"You're right. I should rest. I'll do that." I waited for them to leave. They didn't. They stood with their arms crossed, looking like big hulking guards. I looked at the two cops. Surely, even if they were in this gang, they had to do things right. Didn't they?

"Officers, did you need something? I thought we talked about everything earlier."

They didn't answer me, Pitbull did. "Who's Juan?"

I blinked and then made my face go slack. I had to bluff my way out of this. If they had no idea who Juan was, then I couldn't let them find out. If I set the cops on him, he'd know I was alive, and he'd hunt me to the ends of the earth for certain. I knew what was in store for me if I went back. It would be worse than this beating. In my mind, it was worse than death.

"Juan? Who's Juan?"

"Don't play dumb. You mentioned him when we came in. You thought he'd sent us. Is that who beat you? Who is he? Where can we find him?" Pitbull fired off one question after the other. I tried to breathe nice and easy.

"You must have misunderstood me, or I said something in confusion. I don't know anyone named Juan. I told these guys earlier. I don't remember who beat me. The doctor said it's likely I might never remember because of the head trauma. I'm sorry you came all this way for nothing. Now, if you don't mind, I think I'll get some rest like you suggested." I pulled the covers up over me.

Pitbull walked over to the others and murmured to them. They seemed to argue for a second or two, then they headed for the door. I breathed a sigh of relief until I noticed he wasn't going with them. I wanted to call them back. Were they going to stand guard while he took care of me? I started to shake even though I was fighting not to do it. I was tired of being afraid and people knowing it. It made you look weak. I could be strong.

He came back to the bed and sat down in a chair sitting on the right side. He pulled it right up to the rail. I bit my bottom lip. He stared into my eyes. They flicked down to my mouth when I bit it and then back up. His eyes were lit from within by something burning, it seemed.

"Luciana, you need to listen to me very carefully. I know you remember who did this. I know you remember why they did it. I want to know who Juan is and if he is the one who beat you. I want to know why you were beaten and where I can find him. I'm not leaving until you tell me. Your pretty little ass is staying right here in this bed so they can treat you." This time he said it softly, which made him scarier.

"I can't tell you. And threatening me isn't going to make me. If I got this for not coming back with the drugs or money, what do you think I'll get for siccing the cops on the person who did this? I escaped death and I'm not tempting fate again. I need to disappear," I told him, deciding lying wouldn't work.

He took my uninjured arm into his hand and gently ran his fingers up and down my hand and lower arm. It was soothing. "So, you were beaten because of me. Tell me who did it. We can protect you."

I laughed and it wasn't a humorous one. "You can't protect me. No one can. I have to get out of town before he finds out I'm alive. Hell, he might already know. Please, if you want to help me, then help me leave. I don't care where I go, as long as I disappear and I'm safe," I pleaded. I didn't think it would do any good, but I had to try. I was desperate. I couldn't continue to live the life I'd been living for the last few years.

He stood up and leaned over me. I flinched. I couldn't help it. His hand came up and he traced a finger from my temple to my jaw. "*Cariño*, I can protect you. We can make sure he never gets his hands on you again, but he can still hurt someone else. Tell me."

I shook my head. I couldn't. Though a part of me wanted to tell him so he could make Juan pay. There was a tiny part that felt all warm and glowing because he'd called me honey. A tear ran down my cheek though I tried to stop it. "I can't," I whispered back. He sighed and then shocked me by laying a soft kiss on my lips. He didn't do more than touch them and then he drew back. He went to the door. I thought he was leaving, but he only opened it and spoke to his guys outside. I couldn't hear what they were saying, but after a few minutes, they all nodded, and he closed the door. He came back to the bed and sat down again.

"Here's what we're going to do. When the nurse comes back, we'll ask her to call the doctor and see how soon we can get you out of here. When he says it's safe to do so, we'll get you out of here and somewhere safe. Somewhere you won't have to worry about the man who did this. But until then, you have me and my brothers as your personal guard detail. You'll never be alone."

"I don't need you to guard me! I just need to leave. The longer I stay, the more likely it is he'll find out I'm here."

"Then let him, and when he comes for you, I'll fucking kill him," he growled. I stared at him in astonishment. He would kill Juan. Why?

"Why would you do that? You don't know him." Or at least I didn't think he did.

"Because he dared to lay a finger on you."

"You grabbed me at the bar," I reminded him. He sighed and looked uncomfortable.

"I did and I shouldn't have. I'm sorry. But I didn't hurt you nor did I intend to hurt you. He did. He choked you and left you for dead, Luciana. I don't think that was his original intent, but he ended up doing it anyway. For that, he'll die. One day, I'll find out who he is and then he's done."

"Why do you care? You don't know me. You don't even like me," I argued. The idea he'd want to kill someone just for hurting me made no sense. I could see it if I were his family, but I was a stranger. A stranger who'd sold drugs in his bar. Something I wasn't proud of doing.

"No woman deserves this. I don't know you yet, but I will. And I don't dislike you, *cariño*. Why don't you lie back and try to get in a nap while we wait for the nurse? I'll be here and one of my brothers is outside the door. You're safe."

I wanted to argue and tell him to leave, but the idea I might be able to sleep and truly rest without the danger of someone waking me up, or ordering me to do something I didn't want to do or to hurt me, was too tempting. I hadn't slept peacefully in years. As we sat staring at each other, he took my hand and began to rub it again. I felt my eyes grow heavy and my breathing slow down as the tension oozed out of me. The last thing I remembered before I fell asleep was him humming a song as he rubbed my arm.

⟨─▷⟨─▷⟨─▷⟨─▷⟨─▷

"*Where is it? Where's the fucking money and the drugs, Ana? Tell me!*"

"*I told you, some man took them. I don't have them, Juan.*"

"*Bullshit. You're hiding them. You think you can use it to get away like she did. Well, that's not going to happen. Not ever. I control what happens to you. I will decide your fate!*" he screamed, his face looking demented. He landed the first blow. Then he was like a tornado, hit after hit, kicks, and even his belt.

"*Please, Juan, please stop! I swear I didn't steal it. A*

guy did at one of the places I went to sell. I couldn't get away from him," I sobbed. I wasn't about to tell him who the man was. If he ended up believing me, he'd probably go there and kill the guy. He flipped me over onto my back. I groaned as pain shot through my whole body. He grabbed my head in both hands and began to bang it off the floor.

"Fucking tell me where it is!" I could tell he was high. Maybe he won't stop this time. Maybe he'd kill me, and my nightmare would be over. As the room began to whirl, his hands wrapped around my throat, and he started to squeeze. I couldn't breathe. I tried to get his hands loose, but I was too weak. As things got darker and darker, I heard him laugh. "You know what I'm gonna do. You've forced me to do this, Ana."

I came awake, gasping for air and gripping my own throat. Hands were prying mine away. I opened my eyes to see gorgeous brown ones staring down at me in concern. It was Pitbull. I looked around and realized I'd been dreaming. I was in the hospital. Juan wasn't here, or at least he wasn't here yet. Pitbull slowly let go of my hands.

"You're alright, Luciana. You're safe. It was just a nightmare. Were you remembering the night you were attacked?" I nodded. I reached for the glass of water on the table next to my bed. He got it and held it, so I could take a drink from the straw. The water felt good on my parched throat. When I'd had enough, he sat it back down. He took my hand. "Tell me about it."

"What's there to tell? I got my ass beat. And I told you, if he finds out I'm still alive, he'll be coming for me. Did the nurse or doctor come in while I was asleep? Can

I go?" I asked him hopefully. He frowned then shook his head.

"No, they didn't. You haven't been out long. And I told you, we can protect you. Tell us who did this and where he is."

"No. Stop asking. It's not your concern anyway. Why're you here? If you're hoping to get in on his business, forget it. I'm not telling you shit. There's enough of that poison floating around Tenillo." I hissed at him. I hated that our town was being flooded with more and more of it, and that Juan was a part of it. But nothing I said or did would make him walk away. It was easy money, he said.

Pitbull gave me a scowl and pulled away to pace around the room. I could see I'd made him mad. I watched him closely to see what he'd do. As he paced, I let myself look at him and recall what he'd made me feel the night I met him. Even though he'd terrified me, I couldn't help to notice he was sexy and handsome.

He was significantly taller than me, which wasn't hard for almost everyone. I took after my mom and was only five feet tall. The bane of my existence—never could reach shit without a stool. He was probably six feet. His skin was tan but not like mine. His tan was from being out in the sun. He was older than me, maybe thirty or so. His face was slightly square, his jaw covered in a short scruff of darker brown hair that matched the hair on his head. He kept that in a short, almost crew cut style. His light brown eyes were intense, and his lips had drawn my attention more than once. They were full and had made me want to put my lips on his. Something I'd never had the urge to do to a guy.

But all of that still was nothing compared to his body. He obviously worked out a lot. He had big arms with prominent veins running down them. Those muscles that run from your back to your neck, *trapezius*, I think I recall them called that from school, were big. I could see he had tattoos all over his arms and the back of his neck. His muscular chest tapered down to a smaller waist and then to his thick thighs. All of that had made me aware of my body, even while he'd been scaring the hell out of me. What a thing to think about, and here I was doing it again. Something must be wrong with me.

I snapped out of my daydreaming when he came back over to the bed. "Let's get something straight. We're not in the fucking drug business! We never have been, nor will we ever be. We want to stop this shit from being sold all over our town. Kids are fucking overdosing and dying. My brother Sin's old lady almost got killed because of it. But we can't do anything if people like you keep selling it for a quick buck." His voice expressed his anger and disgust. I sat up fast and choked back the groan of pain. I pointed my finger at him.

"You have no idea what causes someone like me to sell those drugs, so don't act like you do. You know nothing about me, Pitbull. You have no idea what would happen if I didn't sell that shit. You live in your perfect little world where everything goes the way you want. Well, that's not my world. You think I wanted to be out there selling that poison? Helping people ruin their lives and their families lives? Fuck you. You don't know me." I said harshly then rolled over, presenting him with my back. I closed my eyes. Hopefully, he'd leave and then I could get on with my escape. Time was slipping away. I needed to get gone.

Even though I fought it, a tear ran down my cheek. I wanted to go back five years to when things hadn't been like this. To when I'd been happy, and I was loved. Suddenly, a big body squeezed into bed behind me, and a strong arm wrapped gently around my waist. His lips grazed my ear. "Then tell me, *cariño*. Tell me why you're doing it if it's not what you want to do. Let me help you," he whispered softly.

A sob shook me as the tears fell. It felt so nice to be held like this. To have someone care, even if I knew it wasn't real. I let myself bask in it for a few minutes —enough to hopefully last me for a lifetime because I'd probably never get to experience this again.

Pitbull: Chapter 3

I held her as she cried. It was tearing me up to hear it. She sounded like she was in pain. I let her cry as I thought about what she'd said. She'd been so mad that I thought she was selling drugs because she wanted to sell them. She'd called them poison and expressed disgust at how they destroyed lives. If that was the case, why was she doing it?

I kept kissing her cheek and neck as she cried. God, she felt so damn perfect in my arms. She fit like she'd been made for them. She was soft and her skin gave off this sweet scent and was so warm. She made my whole body relax and want to never move. I pulled my lower body back to make room between us. I didn't want her to feel the erection I was getting from holding her, but it was a fierce one. As inappropriate as it was, all my body wanted to do was stretch her out and make love to her.

I tried to distract myself by thinking of reasons why she was doing it. The one that came to mind was she was being forced to do it by this Juan guy. But how was he forcing her? What hold did he have over her? Was he her boyfriend or husband? That thought made me want to howl in rage. I didn't want him to be someone who had a claim like that on her. It would make it harder to get her free of him, harder to have her forget him and be with someone else.

I jerked as that thought flitted through my head. Was I seriously thinking about her and me together? That I'd take this man's place in her life? That was nuts. However, the more I thought about it, the more I liked the idea. I wanted to protect her and make her smile. I wanted to hold her, kiss her, and make love to her. Even in the middle of this mess and being angry with her, she'd captured my attention like no woman ever had. I wanted to know her for more than a couple of nights.

Her sobs had quieted down. I kissed her hair. "*Bebé*, I'm sorry. You're right, I don't know. But I want to, so tell me. Who is Juan and why does he have a hold on you? One that makes you do this if you don't want to sell the drugs."

"I can't. Just leave it alone. If you want to help, then help me get out of town. I have somewhere I can go if I can just get there. He won't be able to find me and bring me back. I'm tired, Pitbull. I'm so tired of living this way. I just want to rest, any way I can." Her voice slipped off at the end. I looked down to see she'd fallen back to sleep. It scared me how she said the last part. Any way she could. Did she mean suicide? My whole body tensed in denial. No way was I going to let her kill herself to get away from this bastard, Juan. I eased out of the bed and went out in the hallway.

Wrecker and Cuffs were still there. I guess the other three had gone back to the compound. They looked up with looks of hope on their faces. I shook my head. "She won't tell me who he is, but she's not selling those drugs because she wants to. She more or less confirmed she hates them and is doing it against her will. I don't know what hold he has on her, but she wants to get out of town. And she's tired and wants to rest, any way she can."

Both of them stiffened when I told them the last part. "You don't think she'd kill herself, do you?" Cuffs asked with a frown on his face.

"God, I don't know. But she's close to the end of her rope, I think. She just cried herself back to sleep, after waking up from a nightmare. I'm positive she was reliving the night she was beaten and left for dead. But there's something I don't understand. He beat the hell out of her, but never touched her face. Why?"

"Fuck, who knows, but we need to get her out of here. I think she's right to be scared. If he finds her, he might try and finish the job. We didn't put out anything at the department on her as being found or as a missing person, no use helping him to find out. But she's too exposed here," Wrecker said as he texted on his phone.

I was interrupted from saying anything else by a nurse coming up to us. She looked us up and down. I could see she had a look of interest in her eyes. Her mouth curled up in a suggestive smile and her eyes sparkled. At any other time, I'd be happy to see it. She was attractive and might be fun. But this time, I had no desire to find out. The only woman who had my interest was lying in the bed in that room almost beaten to death, and something was telling me, that would be the only woman who'd have my interest for the rest of my life. Maybe Wrecker or Cuffs would take this nurse up on her silent offer.

"Can I help you, gentlemen? You know only family should be in the ICU," she purred.

Wrecker and Cuffs pulled out their badges. Her eyes got bigger and then she looked at me. "And are you a cop too, handsome?"

"No, I'm her man." She stepped back as I glared at her. "I want to know how soon she can get out of here. She needs to be at home where she can rest and heal."

"I don't think being at home is the best thing for her. She didn't get in this condition by herself." Her snotty words made it obvious she thought I'd beaten Luciana. I looked at my brothers.

"Can you believe this? She thinks I beat Luciana and you guys are just going to let me take her home. Damn, doesn't say much for her belief in the cops, does it?" They were both scowling at her now. She glanced around flustered and started to stutter.

"I-I'm sorry. I didn't think. I mean, of course, they wouldn't let you see her if you were the one who hurt her. Let me go talk to her doctor. I'll be right back." She hurried off down the hall like her ass was on fire. I couldn't help but laugh.

"Well, I think she's lost her chance to get in your pants," I told the two of them.

"What about yours?" Cuffs asked with a smirk on his face. I shook my head.

"Not gonna happen, even if she hadn't accused me of beating the hell out of Luciana."

"You know, you have this look on your face," Wrecker said with a smile.

"What look?"

"The same damn look I see every time I look at Sin and Executioner, hell, even Boss, Hook, and Chef. Like you can't see anyone but her. Are you taking the plunge, Pitbull? You don't know her at all."

"I know she didn't do this freely. The rest I can learn. And yeah, I think you might be right. Our brothers and friends might just be on to something." They both groaned but clapped me on the back at the same time.

"What do you need us to do?" Cuffs offered.

"Just help me get her out of here as fast as we can. She's gonna need some help at home. I think Lyric and Skye, as well as Sara and Jackie will do it. I'm worried about her pain. Pills might not cut it. She's on IV pain medicine right now. She's probably gonna need that for a while until she starts to heal. Do you know how we can get some?"

"Maybe. Let me ask Saint. He's got a medic background. He might know someone. I figure he can give it to her if she needs it. He's put in lots of IVs and shit. If not, maybe home health could come out. We'd have to swear them to secrecy, but they shouldn't talk about their patients anyway," Wrecker mumbled. I had no idea how he knew that, but I didn't care. If it was how we kept her comfortable, then we'd do it.

Movement down the hall caught my attention. It

was the nurse we'd scared off. She was coming down the hall with a man in a white coat and another man. He was dressed in a suit. Hmm, wonder what this was about? She came to a stop but didn't say anything. The man in the white coat stepped forward. "I'm Dr. Norris. I'm caring for Ms. Ramirez while she's here. I need to ask you to come with us."

"Sorry, doc, not happening. She's not going to be left alone. Someone beat the hell out of her and almost killed her. I'm not giving them another chance. You can talk to us right here," I told him. The guy in the suit shifted from foot to foot then cleared his throat.

"I'm Mr. Sutton. I'm the hospital's administrator. We don't generally let people stand in the halls of the ICU. I don't know what your connection is to Ms. Ramirez, but this isn't allowed," he said in a pompous voice.

Wrecker stared at him and then said in a bored voice, "I can always call Police Chief Barnes down here, though he might not be too happy. I'm Deputy Chief Dickerson, his right-hand. This is Detective Marshall. We're investigating Ms. Ramirez's case. This is Mr. Landis. He's her boyfriend. He's her only family, so he should certainly be here. She's in danger of being targeted again by whoever did this to her. We won't be leaving her alone. What we need to do is find out how soon she can be released. She needs to be moved into protective custody."

"W-well, she's still very sore and healing. She was stabbed and we had to do surgery, which makes her at high risk for an infection. She needs to be monitored to make sure she doesn't get one. We're giving her antibiotics as a preventative measure, and there's the pain. She's not able to take pills yet," Dr. Norris said in a hurry.

"If she had someone who could monitor her and administer her meds, even if it's in an IV, would she be able to leave?" I asked.

The doctor and the administrator stared at each other for a minute then looked back at me. The doctor was the one to answer me. "Maybe. It would have to be someone with medical training, and she'd need to follow up with her regular doctor to be sure she was healing."

"And there's the question of her bill," Mr. Sutton snapped. I gave him a cold look.

"What about her bill?"

"She doesn't have insurance for this stay. And if she gets home health, she doesn't have the insurance to pay that either. We're going to transfer her to the state hospital down near Fort Worth. They take indigent cases." Anger ripped through me. Since she couldn't pay, he was going to ship her off to some hellhole hospital?

"Like hell you are. I'll pay the goddamn bill and for anything else she needs, but you're not transferring her anywhere. Besides her wound and the pain, is she at risk from the head injury or any of the other injuries she sustained?" I asked the doctor.

"Her brain scan came back fine, and the others just need to heal. But that's—"

I cut him off. "Get the damn paperwork together and whatever we need to get her set up at home. She's leaving. You have until tomorrow to get it figured out." I stared at them. They looked at Wrecker and Cuffs like they would help them. They were both standing with their arms crossed like I was. The three of them gave up and hurried away. They had their heads together talking as they did.

"Well, that leaves us a few hours to get things ready at the compound. I'll ask Sara if she can get a room close to yours set up for her. Saint texted back that he has a way to get her the meds she'll need, and he can do her infusions," Wrecker told me as he stared down at his phone.

"I appreciate Saint doing it. I'll let him know what she's on and the dosages. It's on the bags hanging in her room. As for the room, I'll ask Sara if she'll make sure my room is cleaned. I want a new mattress on the bed and new sheets. She needs to go out and buy whatever Luciana needs and I'll pay her back. Hell, she'll need clothes too. I'll send her sizes and stuff. Maybe Lyric and the others can help get whatever girly stuff women use," I said as I ran through the lists in my head, trying to think of what all she'd need. Their silence had me glancing at them. They both stood with big grins on their faces.

"What in the hell are you two grinning about?"

"Your room, huh? New mattress and shit and clothes. Sounds like you're planning for her to stay. And that you're gonna keep her, brother," Cuffs said as he smirked at me. I flipped him off.

"Fuck you. And yeah, she's staying if I have anything to say about it, and it'll be in my room. Now, do you need anything else, or can I get inside and make sure she's still asleep?"

"Sin is sending Omen to stand the first shift outside this room as her guard. I assumed you'd be staying in the room with her," Wrecker said. I gave him a look. He just laughed. "He'll be relieved in four hours. We'll keep it up until she's released. I'll talk to Sara. You just send the medicine information to Saint and the sizes to Sara. We'll make sure everything is in place when you bring your girl home."

I loved the sound of *your girl* and *home*. It felt right, which was insane, but I wasn't going to resist. I gave both of them a half-hug, back slap. "Thanks, I appreciate it."

"No thanks needed. We help our family. Call us if you need us," Cuffs said as they both waved and took off down the hall. I watched them turn the corner then slipped back inside her room. It was time to get the show on the road. Luciana Ramirez was coming home with me. I'd make sure she was safe from this Juan and anyone else who might hurt her. She'd become my main focus.

She was still curled up on her side sleeping. I quietly moved around the room, checking the bags hanging from her IV pole. I texted the names and instructions to Saint. He texted back almost immediately that he'd get things ready. Then I went back to the closet where I'd thrown her clothes earlier. I looked at the sizes. Jesus, she wore a size four jeans and a small top. She was tiny as hell. There were no shoes, but we could get those later. I sent those over to Sara and thanked her for helping. She responded that she was happy to do it and not to worry, she'd have everything ready.

With those out of the way, all I had left to do was sit and watch her sleep. As I did, I daydreamed about what I was going to do to Juan when I found him. Because make no mistake, I would find him. I didn't care how long it took or who he was. He was going to pay for forcing her to sell drugs and for almost killing her. I wondered what else he'd made her do or did to her.

It was over an hour later when she woke up. It was after midnight. Omen had come and was standing outside her door. I switched on the bedside light when I heard her moving around. She gasped and then relaxed when she saw it was me. I gave her a drink of water. She grimaced when she moved.

"You need anything, *bebé?* How's your pain?" She gave me a startled look.

"Why do you keep calling me baby and honey?"

"Don't you like to be called those?" I countered. I didn't want to scare her off by telling her that she brought those words to mind whenever I looked at her. She felt like my baby and my honey. I didn't go around using those words with women, ever.

"I guess they're okay. I've never had anyone call me those. It's just weird to me. My pain is a little much."

I knew she was trying to divert us to something else, and I let her. "If you push this button, it'll dispense some pain medicine. You can push it as often as every fifteen minutes. The dose is tiny, so no worries about taking too much. You need to keep on top of it. Hopefully, in a few days, you can switch to pills." She nodded and pushed the button.

"Do you need to go to the bathroom?" She hadn't been to it since I got here, and she'd been on her way there when I came in. She blushed and then nodded.

"Yeah, I need to call a nurse. I don't think I should walk alone." I lowered the bed rail and bent down. She pushed against my shoulder. "What are you doing?" she asked in alarm.

"I'm helping you to the bathroom. What does it look like?" I teased her.

"I said a nurse can help me. Besides, I can walk. I'm just not that steady."

"Well, if I carry you, then you don't have to worry at all about being unsteady," I said as I swooped her up and walked her into the bathroom. I sat her down. She glared up at me. It was funny as hell to see this tiny thing trying to intimidate me. I gave her a kiss on the end of her pert little nose. "Do your business then call when you're done. Don't try and walk without me, Luciana," I warned her.

As I went out and closed the door, I heard her mutter, "Asshole." I laughed. I stood outside, waiting to hear her call for me, or for the water to come on. A couple of minutes later, I heard the water. I opened the door. She swung around to look at me. She wavered on her feet. I wrapped my arms around her.

"I told you not to get up alone. You need to listen, woman. Wash your hands." She huffed and washed them. I handed her a towel to dry them, then swept her back up. She didn't say a word this time. Once I had her back in bed, she spoke.

"Pitbull, did the nurse come in while I was asleep? Can I leave?" She seemed eager to be gone.

"We talked to the nurse and the doctor. They're working on when they can discharge you. I'm hoping later tomorrow, well, today, I guess. We're just getting things in place. You said you wanted help to get out of town. Where do you want to go?" I was curious as to where she thought she could go and why.

"You get me to a bus station, and I'll worry about the rest. Though..." She looked hesitant.

"Though what?"

"I need to ask another favor. I need to borrow some money. Just enough to get me to where I'm going. I promise I'll pay it back. I just don't have any and what little I did have. I can't get to it." She hurried to tell me. She looked so uncomfortable asking me to help her. It hurt to think that she had no expectation of anyone being willing to help another person in need.

"I'm not worried about the money or anything else. We'll make sure you're safe. That's all you need to worry about. I'm gonna ask one of the prospects to go get some food. Do you want anything?"

"It's the middle of the night! You're gonna wake someone up to go get you food?"

"Yeah, I am. Prospects know they have to do this kind of thing. They don't care. I didn't get my dinner, and I know what you probably had for dinner in here sucked. Tell me what to get you."

"I'm fine. Get whatever you want. Is one of your guys standing outside the room?"

"Yep, Omen is. He's a prospect but I'll send one of the others. He needs to stay here. Why don't you get a salad?"

She gave me a pissed look. "A salad? Why? Do you think that's all women eat or should eat? I might be tiny, but I eat real food, you know! Chicken and potatoes and stuff like that. Jeez, why do guys think we have to eat lettuce?" She grumbled. I hid my grin and sent a text to Brennan, giving him the order. He texted back saying he'd be there ASAP with the food. I also told him to check with Omen to see if he wanted anything.

"Okay, while we wait, why don't we get to know each other better? I'll go first. You know I'm in the Ares Infidels. I've been with them just over two years, since I got out of the Marine Corps. I'm thirty-one. I've never been married, and I live on our club's compound with my brothers."

She hesitated and then answered, "I grew up here in Tenillo. I've never been anywhere but here. I've never been married. I'm twenty-one."

God, she was ten years younger—just a baby—but that wasn't going to be enough to deter me. I was going to do everything in my power to make sure Luciana was mine. If she wanted to travel or do other things, I'd make it happen. I had the money to do it.

"I have younger half-siblings, a brother and a sister. They're twins. Conner and Lily live in Oregon with our mom and my stepdad. They're starting college in the fall. They're eighteen."

She didn't answer. I thought it was telling she wasn't sharing anything about her family. Did she have any? I didn't think so. Not if she was planning to leave. "Do you go to college?"

She looked away from me. "No, I wasn't able to. Your brother and sister are lucky. Do they know what they want to study?" I could see that it hurt her to admit she didn't go, and the eagerness in her voice made me think she had secretly wanted to attend college.

"Not yet, so they'll take general study courses until they decide. If you'd been able to go, did you have something you wanted to study?"

She hesitated, then said quietly, "Nursing. I always wanted to be a nurse."

"It's not too late. You're young, Luciana."

"Maybe. I'll have to see what life brings, I guess. You said you live with your brothers in a compound. Those are the guys in your club, right? How many are there?" I let her change the subject.

"Counting me, there are eleven of us who're full members and four prospects. Though, Dash and Blake are close to becoming new members. Cuffs just got patched in a few weeks ago."

"Patched in? Prospects?"

I went on to explain to her what those meant. She seemed to find it interesting. When I was done explaining, she sighed. "That sounds nice, to have that many people you have things in common with. Enough to feel like they're your family. Are there any wives or kids? Or are those not allowed in an MC?"

"They're allowed. Until recently, we only had Sin, our president's mom, Sara, as the only woman. Then Sin met his old lady, Lyric. They're getting married on July Fourth. Then my brother, Executioner, met his woman, Skye. They're getting married at the end of August and are gonna have a baby. Sara is happy as hell to have more women around. She says it helps keep us in line." I chuckled. She laughed.

"I guess it is a little too much testosterone for one woman. It's nice she has them. Why do you call them old ladies? That's not nice. I hope you don't say it to their faces."

"*Cariño*, it's not derogatory. In an MC, that's a sign of respect. You claim someone as your old lady, she's more than your wife. You'll do everything you can to protect her. A lot of the women will refer to their man as their old man. Age has nothing to do with it."

"Oh, I guess that's okay then. Just seems weird. You said it's more than a wife. Does that mean all bikers don't marry their old ladies?"

"A lot don't because being an old lady is seen as more binding. However, my brothers want both."

"How can cops be in an MC?"

"Just luck of the draw, I guess. The police chief, Boss, is actually the president of the Time Served MC."

"But don't you do, you know, illegal stuff?"

"We're not angels, but we don't make our money off of illegal shit. We own legitimate businesses all over town. The Hangout is one of them. I manage it for the club. We own the Harley dealership, Tenillo Cycles, the tattoo shop, Infidels' Ink, a welding business, Ares' Forge, an electrical and plumbing business, Ares' Voltz, a custom garage, Infidels' Custom Motors, and a gun range, Infidels' Armory. Executioner's woman, Skye, owns the flower shop, Blossoms, with her mom."

"Wow, I recognize all those places. I had no idea your club owned them. Those must keep you all really busy."

"They do, but we still find time to have fun. What do you do for fun?"

"I haven't been able to do it in so long, I don't remember," she said very softly. I got up and leaned down over her. I tipped up her chin with my finger.

"I promise you'll have a lot of fun again. Soon." I lowered my mouth and kissed her. It wasn't like the touch of the lips I gave her earlier. I made sure to press hard and to nibble on her bottom lip. She gasped, and I took the opportunity to get my tongue inside. As I teased her tongue with mine, she got a little bolder and teased back. Just that much had me hard and wanting more, but she wasn't in any condition for us to get carried away. However, once she was, I'd show her just how much fun we could have. We were pulled apart by a knock on the door. I drew back and gave her a smile.

"Just a little something to think about." Her face was flushed. "Come in," I yelled. It had to be Brennan with our food.

Luciana: Chapter 4

I looked around my hospital room. It was daylight and I was getting ready to leave. It had been a long and confusing past eighteen hours, and the main reason for it was standing there by my bed. Pitbull hadn't left my side since he came into my hospital room yesterday evening. And that whole time, he'd been confusing the hell out of me. He'd teased me, ordered me, been gentle with me, and kissed me. The kissing was what had taken me the most by surprise.

Last night after he'd kissed me and said it was something for me to think about, he hadn't touched me again. He kept talking, sharing stuff about himself, but no more kisses. I wanted to say it was for the best, but I'd be lying. I wanted more of those. I'd never felt anything like what that kiss had made me feel. I was sad to be leaving. I'd never get another one, but it was the safest thing to do.

Not only would Juan find me if I stayed, but there was no way a guy like Pitbull wanted a woman like me. I was an uneducated woman who was going nowhere. He would end up with a woman who was someone one day. Someone he could be proud to have on his arm. I could dream for a night, but it was time to face the real world. Mine didn't include good men like him.

I checked the room one more time. I'm not sure why. The only things I had with me were the clothes on my back. I'd have to work on getting a new ID and stuff after I was safe. Mine were still at the house unless Juan had destroyed them. I knew enough to know you could find someone to forge papers, as long as you were willing to pay the price. I usually hated what the last five years had taught me, but in this case, it would come in handy.

A nurse came in pushing a wheelchair. "Ms. Ramirez, we need you to let us push you downstairs in this. It's hospital policy." I didn't argue, I just sat down. As she pushed me out into the hallway, Pitbull brought up the rear. I saw three more hulking bikers standing out there. Damn, I guess they were serious about helping me get out of town.

When we got to the front lobby door, an SUV pulled up. Pitbull pushed me over to the passenger side and lifted me out of my wheelchair and into the front seat. The guy behind the wheel smiled at me and then got out. Pitbull shut my door and walked around to the driver's door and got in. I heard several bikes roar to life. As soon as they pulled up beside us, he took off. I stayed quiet and watched the scenery flash by. I didn't feel like talking. I just wanted to get on a bus before I broke down in tears.

"Do you want something to eat, Luciana?"

"No, I'm fine. I'm not really hungry," I mumbled. I closed my eyes. It shouldn't take long to get to the other side of town where the bus station was... maybe fifteen minutes. The rhythmic thumping of the tires on the road started to become hypnotizing. When we came to a stop later, I opened my eyes reluctantly. Only when I did, it wasn't the bus station I saw. It was a big building made out of concrete blocks. I looked around.

It looked like we were no longer in town. There were a few houses sitting farther away, and I saw a tall, solid wall and a big gate. The bikes were pulling in front of the same building to join several others already there. I swung my head to look at Pitbull. He was calmly looking at me. "Where are we?"

"At the Ares' compound."

"Why're we here? We were supposed to go to the bus station."

"I never said that. I said I'd make sure you were safe. That's what I'm doing, *bebé*." He watched my face as he said it.

"I'm not staying here! Pitbull, take me to the bus station!" I half-yelled in a panic. Maybe he was helping Juan, and this was their plan to get me away from witnesses. Before he could say anything or even move, I tore off my seat belt and pulled the door handle as I threw myself toward the door. I heard him swear as I tumbled out of the SUV. I caught myself before I hit the ground, though the jarring sensation made me cry out in pain. I saw black spots for a couple of seconds. I scrambled to my feet and took off.

I didn't get far before strong arms were around me, lifting me off the ground. I screamed and kicked. "Let me go! I said I wouldn't tell." He held me close.

"Luciana, calm down. I'm not going to hurt you," he growled, but I was past hearing him or believing a word he said. I tried to bite down on his arm. He swore and his grip tightened. A flash of pain streaked through me, and I screamed. As I did, my vision got hazy and started to go dark. Right before I passed out, I told him, "I hate you. You're just like him—a liar."

When I regained my senses later, I was lying on a bed in a room I didn't recognize. Pitbull was pacing the floor. I groaned in pain. He spun around and came hurrying over to the bed. He kneeled beside it and took a hold of my hand. I tried to pull away, but he held tight. "God, *cariño*, are you alright? You scared the fuck out of me. Here, let me call Saint. He'll give you some pain medicine."

"I don't want him or you to give me anything. Where is he?"

"Who, Saint?"

"No, Juan. Where is he? Why isn't he here? Does he think he can torture me more? I'm over it! I'm done being scared. Just get it over with. I don't care what he does to me!" I screamed. The door to the room crashed open and several big guys filled it. I swung my fist at Pitbull's face. He ducked and then he was on the bed with me, wrapping me up in his arms. His legs and arms were curled around me as I struggled. The pain was building but I didn't care. I was dead or as good as any way.

"Oh God, stop, *bebé*, stop. No one is going to hurt you. Juan isn't here. I wouldn't do that to you," he whispered hoarsely. The guys all moved back out of the doorway.

Before it closed, one of them said, "Let me know when you want me to start her medication." He closed the door behind him. I was shaking as I sobbed. Pitbull was whispering nonsense and kissing my cheek, ear, and hair.

"I'm sorry. I didn't know that you'd think by bringing you here, I was taking you to him. I swear to God, I'd never do that. I only want to protect you, Luciana. Running when you're in this shape isn't going to be good. You need medication and help, not trapped on a bus going, Lord knows where."

"I can't stay here! Don't you understand? He'll find out. And when he does, it'll be worse than if I'd gone back. I know what he said he was going to do. If he does, then I'll wish I was dead. I might as well blow my brains out now."

He turned me over and hovered over me. His eyes blazed. "Don't ever talk about killing yourself. Do you hear me? Never! If he finds out you're here, so what? I'm gonna kill him, Luciana. He's a dead man. He just doesn't know it. Why are you protecting him? Is he your boyfriend or your lover?" he growled.

I felt my mouth drop open in surprise. Without thinking I blurted out, "No, he's my brother." I clapped my hand over my mouth as I realized what I'd told him. His face registered his surprise then anger bloomed across it.

"He's your fucking brother. He made you deal drugs and beat you almost to death! Other than killing you, what more can he do?"

"He can sell me. And I'd rather be dead than that. Selling those drugs was the lesser of the two evils. When I came back that night without the cash or the drugs, he made sure to tell me as he beat the hell out of me, that he was done. He was going to sell me," I whispered. I was too tired to keep hiding the truth. My own brother hated me. He didn't want to protect me or love me.

"Jesus Christ! He's gonna sell you? Oh *cariño*, like hell he is. Not while there's a breath left in my body will he sell you, hurt you, or kill you. Fuck, I need Saint in here." He let go enough to pull his phone out of his pocket and text. I didn't care. I was sobbing. A minute later, the door opened and in walked the guy from earlier. He had a syringe in his hand. He held it up.

"Hey there, beautiful. I have something here that'll take that pain away. You look like you need a break. It's like what you were getting in the hospital. I made sure it was the right dose. My name is Saint. I was a medic in the SEALs." He came over and pushed up the sleeve on my right arm. They'd left in the IV port from the hospital. He cleaned the end with an alcohol prep then injected the medicine. I felt it take effect almost immediately.

"That's better isn't it, sweetheart?" he whispered as he smiled down at me. Pitbull growled at him.

"You don't need to be smiling at her and calling her beautiful and sweetheart, Saint. She's already taken." I gave him a confused look. Saint just laughed and held up his hands. "Tell Sin I need to speak to the members ASAP. Will you see if Sara or one of the other ladies can come sit with her? I don't want to leave her alone."

Saint nodded. "All four are out in the common room. They're dying to meet her. I'll tell Sin and then send one back." He left the room. I looked at Pitbull.

"Why do you need to talk to them? Is it about me?"

"It is, but only so we can figure out the best way to keep you safe. I want you to rest. After you take a nap, we'll get you something to eat." A knock at the door had him calling out for whoever it was to come in. The door opened, and four women came in. Two were older, and the others were not much older than I was. He got up off the bed.

"Luciana, these are the ladies I told you about. This is Sin's mom, Sara. This is his fiancée, Lyric, and this is Executioner's fiancée, Skye. And this is Skye's mom, Jackie. One of them will stay with you while I'm in my meeting. If you need anything, let them know." He turned to them. "If she needs to go to the bathroom, don't let her walk alone. She's not steady, and she might fall. She just had a pain shot, so hopefully she can rest. She's due soon for her antibiotic, but Saint will give it to her when it's time."

The one he introduced as Sara smiled at me kindly and then patted his arm. "You go do whatever you need to do. We'll take good care of her." He came back to the bed and leaned down. He searched my eyes.

"I'll be back as soon as I can. Don't stress or worry. You're safe," he whispered, then he kissed me. It was like the one he'd given me last night. I got lost in it and didn't surface until he pulled away. He ran his thumb along my bottom lip then left. I looked at the women. They all had smiles and expectant looks on their faces. Oh God, what had he left behind for me to face?

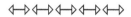

Pitbull:

I held onto my rage until I was away from Luciana. I'd been afraid if I'd let it go, I'd scare the hell out of her. Once I was outside the clubhouse, I roared my rage to the sky. I wanted to beat something or better yet, someone. My brothers all came outside and stood around me. They waited for me to regain control before they said anything.

"What's wrong, Pitbull?" Sin asked once I'd calmed down a little.

"I need to talk to you all in church." They nodded, and we filed back inside and down to our meeting room. Inside, after we all were seated, Sin gestured to me.

"You all saw how Luciana reacted when she got here." They nodded. "Well, she thought I was taking her to turn her over to Juan. That I'd lied. When she woke up from passing out, she let loose, and she told me who Juan is, and why she's so afraid of him." I took a deep breath to control my anger.

"He's her fucking brother! Her own brother forced her to sell drugs and then beat her almost to death!" I snarled. They all looked at me in shock. "And that's not the worst. The only reason she sold the drugs was because she said it was the lesser of two evils. The worst being, if she didn't, he was going to sell her. When she came back that night, before she lost consciousness from the damn beating, he told her he was done and was going to do it."

Swearing and yells burst out of all of them. When they calmed down, Sin asked me, "Do you think he's behind the other women who've gone missing around here? The one behind the guys who grabbed Sis?"

"I don't know. I didn't ask her. She's hanging on by a thread. Saint had to come in and give her pain meds. She's barely forty-eight hours from regaining consciousness. Her body is beat all to hell. Her mental state has to be delicate after her brother beat her so savagely. I didn't want to push her and ask. I think it's possible. Or he might know who's behind it."

"Phantom, see what you can find out about Juan Ramirez. I assume they have the same last name. Surely, with both their names, you can find out something about them. I want to know why she's with him and everything else you can find. Since she was running, I think he might be her only family, but we need to make sure." Phantom nodded to Sin.

He swung back to me. "Brother, I know you want to help her, and she sure as hell needs the help. I can have her moved over to the house with me and Lyric. She might be more comfortable there. You don't have to give up your bed."

Saint, Wrecker, and Cuffs all laughed. Sin gave them a confused look. "I don't think you'll be able to get her out of his room and bed without having to shoot him,

Pres. He seems to have formed a slight attachment to her," Saint said.

"You're goddamn right I have. She stays with me, though I wouldn't mind having her somewhere more comfortable. I don't need any of you Casanovas getting any ideas." I stared at Saint. The bastard just laughed at me.

"Ah, so this is about more than just protecting a woman in need?" Sin asked with a smile.

"Hell yeah. It's about me protecting the woman I want to be mine. And I'm gonna be the one who kills her filthy scumbag brother when we find him."

"Deal. Okay, so we need to see what Phantom can dig up. We need to let her rest a bit and then question her about her brother. I hate to rush her, but we need to do it soon. Every second we delay, another woman could be taken. Wrecker, I'll let you and Cuffs update Boss. I'll bet my last dollar they'll want to be in on this. Chef is frothing at the mouth to get the ones behind Sis's abduction. That's if Brea and Blue let him." He laughed again.

All of us recalled how Blue and Brea had gone nuts on the guys who'd taken Sis when they caught them. Blue had hit one with her car and then shot another. Brea had beat the hell out of the third one even as he was choking her. None of it compared to what Chef did. He was like a crazed grizzly, tossing people around alongside the damn road that night. It was kind of fun as well as terrifying to watch.

"In the meantime, we keep Luciana here and out

of sight. Hopefully, he has no idea she's even alive. He might be waiting to hear news of her body being found."

"Do you think Boss would be alright if we reported one was found? It might prevent Juan from getting nosy and buy us time. I'd think he would be lying low just in case," Cuffs asked Wrecker.

"I think Boss might go for it. I'll ask him when we update him. For now, we keep it quiet that she's here. The women need to know not to talk about her to anyone outside of here."

"Okay, then we'll get these things in motion. Pitbull, if you need anything for her, let us know. She needs to know she's safe and we'll do whatever is necessary to keep her that way. And congratulations," Sin said.

"Congratulations on what?"

"On finding your old lady and your happily ever after. You're joining a select club," he teased as the other guys laughed. I spent the next couple of minutes being teased, but I didn't care. I'd gladly let them do that if it got me Luciana. Because Sin was right, she was what I needed to get my happily ever after. Brea had been right that night when she said it would happen sooner than I thought. Maybe she was related to Omen and had the Cajun mojo too.

Luciana: Chapter 5

I didn't know what to say to the women who stood smiling and looking at me expectantly. Was I supposed to do something? Pitbull had told me to rest and let them know if I needed anything. All I wanted was to be alone with my thoughts. Thoughts that centered around that second kiss he'd just given me. Why had he done it? What did it mean? Or did it not mean anything? He was a biker after all. He probably kissed women all the time. I was making it into something it wasn't.

Sara came over and sat down on the edge of the bed while the others sat on the chairs and the desk in the room. Sara took my hand. "Alright, honey, don't let us scare you. That man just threw us at you and ran, but he's right, we're here to help. We just were so excited to get to meet another woman. We need all the ladies we can get here. The guys outnumber us by too many. It's the power of the 'P'—pussy." My mouth dropped open. She laughed along with the others.

"Oh, but I'm just here temporarily. You'll have to find someone else to be a member of your... whatever you call it."

"How about the pussy posse? I know Jenn, Paula, and Brea would love that. They can be members too.

Lord knows they need a posse with that bunch over there," Sara said as she looked at the other women. I was lost. Who was she talking about? My confusion must have been written all over my face.

"Sorry, we're confusing you more. Brea, Jenn, and Paula are the old ladies to the guys in the Time Served MC. We're all friends. They have a bunch of testosterone-riddled alphas running around over there too. They think they run things, but we know the truth. Pussy rules the world." I couldn't help it, I laughed. She was nothing like any mom I'd ever met.

Jackie shook her head. "She's going to think we're nuts, Sara. I'm Jackie, Skye's mom. Nice to meet you, Luciana. I have to say, I wouldn't count on you being here temporarily. Not after that kiss we just saw." The other three all nodded enthusiastically.

"That wasn't what you thought it was. He's just being... I don't know, nice or something. Pitbull and the club are helping me out until I can get somewhere safe."

"Bullshit! Mom, did he kiss you like that when he met you? How about you, Sara? I mean, he wouldn't have me or Lyric unless he wanted to lose his head, but you ladies are single," Skye asked as she grinned at me.

"Nope. And if he does go around doing it to all the single ladies, then I have a bone to pick with him," Sara said with a mock frown on her face. I decided not to say more on that topic.

"You know, you don't have to babysit me. I can get to the bathroom myself. He's just being overly cautious. The medicine seems to be helping the pain."

"If you want to sleep, go ahead, but no way are we leaving you alone. One of us will stay. Hopefully, they shouldn't take too long in their meeting. They need to go plan their attack, pound on their chests, measure their dicks, you know, strategize," Lyric added. "If you're not sleepy then why don't we get to know each other?" I couldn't help but let my jaw drop again as she and the other ladies laughed. I decided I'd leave that statement alone too.

"Sure. What do you want to know?" I wondered if they wanted to ask about my brother. While I'd told Pitbull he'd done this to me, I wasn't ready to have that conversation with anyone else yet. It hurt that the big brother I'd worshipped had turned into a man who could do something like this to anyone, let alone his sister.

"Obviously, you live here in Tenillo. Did you grow up here? I came here a little over two years ago," Lyric said.

"I was born and raised here. I've never even left Texas. What about the rest of you?"

"All three of us are from here as well. Besides Skye, I have a sixteen-year-old son, Tanner, and a fourteen-year-old son, Tyson," Jackie told me.

"Do you have any family, Luciana? By the way, I love your name," Skye said with a smile.

"Thank you. I think you and Lyric have pretty names too. My parents are gone. I have a brother but that's all."

"Won't he be worried about you?" Sara asked with a frown on her face. When I didn't say anything, she got a look of realization on her face. Her hand came up to cover her mouth as she gasped, and her eyes got round. "Oh my God. Did he do this to you, Luciana?"

I swallowed the lump in my throat and nodded. All of them cried out in outrage and the others came over to sit on the edge of the bed and touch me. They were offering me comfort. Something I hadn't had in years. Tears formed in my eyes.

"Honey, I don't know why he did this, and you don't have to tell us, but be assured he won't be putting his hands on you again. No way Pitbull will allow that, or any of the guys," Sara whispered.

"That's what worries me. Why would they involve themselves in my family drama further? I'm a stranger. I asked them to help me, but only to help get me out of town. Instead, he brought me here. I don't want to bring anything down on anyone else. If my brother finds out I'm alive and that I'm here, it's only going to cause more trouble for people."

"Why do you think Pitbull brought you here?" Lyric asked with a funny look on her face.

"Because he has some kind of hero complex, maybe. I don't know. At first, I thought he was going to turn me over to my brother. When that didn't happen... I don't know what to think."

"Maybe that kiss should have told you something. He's interested in you, Luciana," she said patiently.

"There's no way in the world a man like him would be into me. I'm an uneducated, young woman with no future. Guys like him are for the ladies who are making something out of themselves. Besides, I'm not into the 'have sex with strangers then leave' thing. No way he can't find that in any bar or business in town if that's what he wants, and from women who know a helluva lot more than I do," I blurted out.

"Wow, you have no clue, do you? I saw his face when he looked at you and after he kissed you. He's definitely thinking of more than sex with a stranger. It's going to be fun to watch him at work," Skye added.

"Look, can we talk about something else? What do you do? Do you work? How long have you been with your guys?" I asked out of desperation to get them off the topic of me and Pitbull. Thankfully, they let me.

"I work at the Harley dealership with my son, Sin. And of course, I try to corral these boys. I was so damn glad when Sin had the smarts to fall for Lyric," Sara said with a smile as she looked at Lyric.

Lyric gave her a hug. "I've been with Sin for a couple of months. I came to them looking for help. I'm a high school teacher and I knew something bad was going on at my school. No one would believe me, so I came to the club to see if they would. I was right. There was stuff going on."

"I run the flower shop in town, Blossoms. I met the club when they came to talk to me about these guys who were extorting money from business owners. That was a couple of months ago as well," Jackie added.

"I met Executioner when we were both in Fort Worth and had no idea who the other was or that we lived in the same town. A month later when he came to the shop, we met again. He stuck to me like glue and refused to go away, so I said yes to marrying him. Oh, and we're having a baby in November." Skye laughed as she ran her hand over her flat stomach. I shook my head in amazement.

"So, all of you except Sara have only known the club for what, three months? Wow. Hasn't one of them snapped you up, Jackie?" She blushed and the others laughed again.

"There seems to be a couple of guys who might want that job," Skye teased her mom. Jackie was an attractive woman, who didn't look like she should have a daughter Skye's age. Jackie didn't say a word.

"Sara, are you hiding a man somewhere?" I asked.

She grinned. "If I am, he'll have to stay hidden because Sin might lose his mind. Now, enough about us. You said you have a brother and he's not someone we want to meet. What kind of work do you do?"

I realized they had no idea Pitbull had caught me selling drugs in their bar. What do I tell them? If I told them the truth, they'd stop looking at me with kindness and treat me like the lowlife I was forced to be, but I couldn't run from it either.

"Until three days ago, I was a drug dealer for my brother. That's how I met Pitbull. I went to the Hangout to deal, and he caught me. He took my drugs and money and threw me out. When I got home, my brother lost his mind and didn't believe me at first. Then he wanted to know who the guy was. I refused to tell him. He went crazy and started to beat me with his fists and then a belt. He even kicked me. Finally, he choked me, and I passed out. He must have thought I was dead, and he dumped my body."

All four of them sat there with their mouths hanging open in disbelief. Then I heard Pitbull's voice. "You mean you fucking got beat because you tried to protect me?" He practically shouted from the doorway. I whipped my head around to stare at him. I hadn't heard him open the door. A few of his brothers were standing with him. I wanted to crawl in a hole and disappear.

"I-I—" I stuttered.

He cut me off. "Ladies, thank you for watching her. I'll take it from here." They all got up reluctantly and gave me a hug or a hand squeeze before they left. The closing of the door sounded like the closing of my only escape route. I stared down at my hands. The bed dipped as he sat down beside me. He raised my face with a finger under my chin.

"Did you protect me from your brother?"

Slowly, I nodded. "I couldn't tell him your name. He would have killed you, Pitbull," I whispered.

His hand slid to the back of my head and then he was kissing me. It was another mind-blowing kiss that had me thinking thoughts I shouldn't. My body heated up instantly, and I could feel my nipples get hard and the crotch of my panties dampen. He lowered me slowly back on the mattress and devoured my mouth, his tongue and mine twining together. When I thought I might die from lack of breath, he raised his head. His eyes were fiery, his breath coming out in little pants like mine.

"Don't you ever fucking protect me again. Do you hear me? It's my job to keep you safe. I can handle your brother and anything he and his lowlife buddies throw at me. You aren't going to be a buffer."

"Pitbull—"

"We're alone, *bebé.* Call me Cole when it's just us. Cole Landis is my name."

His request that I call him Cole melted my insides. "Cole, you can't ask me to do that. It's bad enough I had to stand by and let him hurt other people because there wasn't anything I could do to stop him. In your case, I could. I just didn't expect him to go off like that."

He maneuvered himself around, so he was sitting with his back to the headboard and he had me gently wrapped in his arms. He was cognizant at all times of how hurt I was. "I need to ask you some questions about your brother. Are you up to it, or do you want to rest first?"

I sighed. I might as well get it over with. "What do you want to know?"

"First, has he always been like this? Violent and living on the wrong side of the law?"

"No, when I was younger, he was the best big brother you could ask for. He would take me places and watch out for me."

"When did he change?"

"He got into high school, and he met a new group of friends his junior year, I think. Anyway, he began to stay out all night. He got drunk, then my parents found weed. They grounded him over and over, but nothing seemed to work. They took away his car and his phone. He kept getting worse and worse. Dad finally kicked him out when he turned eighteen, but he still would just show up unannounced and cause trouble."

"How did you become under his control?"

"When I was sixteen, my mom and dad were killed in a home invasion. Someone broke into the house one night."

"Were you there when it happened?" His whole body tensed up.

"No, I was staying at a friend's house. I didn't know anything until the cops showed up at their door with my brother hot on their heels."

"Why in the hell did the court give you to him? They had to know what he was like," he growled.

"Honestly, I think the judge was dirty. By then, Juan was dealing and doing other things for some gang, I call them. He bragged he could do whatever he wanted in this town, and no one could touch him."

"You said you're twenty-one. That's five years with him. Why didn't you leave when you turned eighteen?" I pushed away from him and sat up. He gently grabbed my arm to prevent me from getting up.

"You don't think I tried? I was lucky he let me finish high school. Those first two years, he was content to have me cook and clean and wait on him. I packed my stuff and was ready to go on my eighteenth birthday. He caught me at the bus station with my friend. He made it clear to me if I ever tried to run again, he'd hunt down anyone who was my friend and kill them." I felt the tears running down my face.

"Shh, it's okay. Just a little more, then we can drop it. Is that when he had you start selling drugs?"

"No, he'd send me to deliver packages. I suspected what was in them, but I had no choice. He cut off my only way to escape—the bus. I didn't know of anyone I could go to who could do anything about it. I did that until six months ago. Then he got weird and started saying he needed me to deal and if I didn't, I'd be sorry."

"He was going to sell you?"

"Yeah. I hated selling those damn drugs, but the idea of being sold to some man to be raped and maybe used by more than one man... I couldn't do it. I thought about killing myself, but I was too chicken to do it. I was raised that suicide is a mortal sin and your soul will be condemned to purgatory," I confessed.

He picked me up off the mattress and onto his lap. He rocked me in his strong arms as he rubbed softly up and down my back. His mouth was in my hair. "*Cariño*, it makes me sick to hear you talk about killing yourself. If you had, I'd have never met you, and that would have been a travesty."

“Cole, why are you being so sweet to me? I came into your bar and sold drugs. I have no job, no education, and no future. Is this something you like to do? Swoop in and rescue sad cases like me? I don’t need you to rescue me other than to help me get out of town. Once I am, I have a place to go. I just have to get away first.”

He pulled my face around to look up at him. He had a fierce look on his face again. His lips were tight with anger. “I’m not fucking doing this because I’m looking to play hero. I’m doing it because our town needs to be cleaned up. Your brother and his friends are part of the disease that seems to be living in the underbelly in Tenillo. And even more importantly, I need to help you, Luciana. Because from the instant you walked into the bar, I haven’t been able to think of anything but you. It damn near killed me when I found out you were dealing. I wanted to punch something. However, that was nothing compared to what I felt when Wrecker and Cuffs told me you’d been beaten and left for dead. That almost stopped my damn heart. I know we just met, and we know nothing about each other, but I’m convinced we could have something really special between us.”

I was speechless. His lips grazed across mine. “Say something, Luciana.”

“What do you mean, something special? Like we can have an affair or something?”

“God no. I mean, special as in you and me together for the next several decades. Living together, making love, and having a family, kind of special. I’ve never felt anything like this for a woman. I’m not willing to let you slip through my fingers. And no way am I going to let Juan or any of his associates hurt you."

His admission had my head whirling, and I couldn't think what else to say. So, I did what my body said to do. I kissed him and I put all the pent-up feelings I had for him into that kiss. As he took me down to the mattress, I let the sensations take over.

Pitbull:

As she kissed me, I let all the desire and feelings I was having loose. Hearing her say she protected me and took a beating had pissed me off. Then to find out she'd thought about killing herself and hearing how hopeless it was for her, I had to tell her what I was feeling. Walking into my room and seeing her there felt like I was coming home.

I loved my life, and I was happy, but I did sometimes feel like there should be more. With her here, I finally knew what it was, her. As I ravished her mouth, I was careful not to press too hard, but I had to touch her. I traced down her arms and across her stomach. My body tingled like tiny flames were lapping at the edges of my nerves. All I wanted to do was sink into her depths, to fill her with me and make love to her for hours; however, that would have to wait. She needed to heal and get to know me more. I fought to bring my desire back under control and to get my cock to settle down. It was hard and desperate to be inside of her.

As I pulled away, I ground my cock into her core lightly. She whimpered. Her face was flushed, and her eyes were glazed with passion. "That's only the start of what I want, Luciana. We can get to know each other, but I know we're meant to be together. A fire like this is a once-in-a-lifetime one," I whispered. She traced her fingers along my jaw and lips. I shuddered as my eyelids closed. Her hands were so tiny and soft.

"Cole, what if—"

"No what-ifs. We'll make this work. I plan on giving you everything you want and need. Now, a couple more things and then I'm getting you some food. We need to know your address and where we might find your brother, if he's not there."

She tensed up. I could see the instant rejection of that idea in her eyes. "*Bebé*, we need to know. We're going to talk to Boss, and you know Wrecker and Cuffs are cops. They'll help us with this. They need to be stopped. Do you know who Juan works for?"

She shook her head no. "All I know is he gets a call sometimes and he leaves. When he gets back, he has more drugs. One time I overheard him tell one of his guys he had to go meet H."

He could be anyone, but it did make me wonder, could his contact be Officer Hannigan? We'd been following her, and she spent a lot of time at the gym and laundromat. She'd go to other places and there were always a lot of people around. She could be making drops and we didn't see it. I got up and went to my desk. I got a pen and a piece of paper and handed it to her. She jotted down three addresses.

"The first one is our apartment. The other two are places he goes to a lot and hangs with his buddies. Anyone you find there. I can promise you is involved in his business."

"Do you know if he's involved in selling women? He had someone he was going to sell you to. Is that also part of his business?"

"I don't know. If it is, he kept it real quiet, though he did threaten me with it several times."

"Did he ever say who he would sell you to?"

"He only said there was a guy who wanted me in the worst way. That he was protecting me from him and if I didn't do as I was told, he'd let him have me." She collapsed crying. She'd had enough. I curled up with her and held her as she cried herself to sleep. I laid there, plotting on what I was going to do next. I'd protect my *amada*, my beloved.

Pitbull: Chapter 6

It had been four days since I brought Luciana to the compound. We'd settled into a routine of sorts. We'd moved from my room at the clubhouse and in with Sin and Lyric. I didn't want to impose, but it was more comfortable for her. Of course, I couldn't let her stay there without me. Something compelled me to be with her whenever I wasn't working. By some miracle, she allowed it.

We slept in the same bed at night, but other than some kissing and very mild petting, we kept things clean. She was starting to heal, and the bruises were fading. She'd moved from IV antibiotics and pain medication to taking pills. Saint kept an eye on her wound and said it was healing nicely. She joked she'd never wear a bikini again. I was determined she would wear one, at least for me. Though it was hell to lie with her and not make love to her, I wasn't willing to sleep alone. I'd found I loved waking up to her beside me. God, I'd fallen like a ton of bricks just like Sin and Executioner.

The ladies had welcomed her and were helping to get her to relax. In fact, they'd arranged for the ladies from the Time Served crew to come over today. While they did lady time, we'd be updating Boss and his guys on what we'd discovered in the last two days.

I watched as they all came through the door. Kerrigan, Lyric's best friend, had come earlier. She'd been told that she couldn't mention Luciana to anyone. She swore she'd keep it on the down low. We knew we could trust her. I saw that not only had Jenn, Brea, and Paula come but also Brea's daughter, Sis, and Paula's friends Frankie and Blue. Frankie was a doctor but had grown up in a mafia family. She knew how to keep her mouth shut. Blue worked for the club and knew the MC and prison lifestyle. She'd keep her mouth shut.

I was standing with our ladies when they saw us. They made a beeline for us. As she drew near, Blue came up and flung an arm around me. She bumped her hip into me. "How's it going, boss man?" I laughed at her. Then I saw Luciana frown and turn to say something to Sara. Her body was humming with tension. I grinned as I pulled Blue by the hand over to her.

"Hey, *bebé*, I know you haven't met the other ladies yet, but let me introduce you to Blue. She works at the Hangout. You probably saw her that night you were there." Luciana gave her a nod.

"Hi," is all she said.

"Blue, this is my Luciana. I want you to make her feel welcome, and don't get her into trouble. You and your crew of ladies are nuts." Blue laughed as I tugged Luciana into my side. I kissed her mouth.

"I make no promises, Pitbull. Luciana, it's great to meet you. Any woman who can put up with him, needs a medal, or maybe her head examined. Does insanity run in your family?" Her teasing manner made Luciana relax, and she laughed.

"I'm not sure about the insanity, but it might. Nice to meet you, too. I remember seeing you at the Hangout." This broke the ice, and the others came over to be introduced. As soon as they were settled and talking, the men and I went into church. Sin had cold beers waiting for all of us.

"Boss, thanks for coming over and bringing the ladies. The ladies want to socialize, and we can't go out on the town yet. Luciana is still hiding, as you know," Sin said.

"No problem. It's all we could do to keep them away this long. Keeping her out of sight is a must. So far, we've had no one coming to claim the body of the young woman we found 'dead' in that field. We made sure it was in the paper and everywhere around town. We left her as a Jane Doe, but her brother has to believe it's her. He doesn't want to claim her and have us ask him questions. Hopefully, he'll stay blissfully unaware of her being alive until after we catch him."

"Yeah, we don't know where the bastard is hiding, but he's not at any of his usual haunts. We've been keeping an eye on those along with your guys. Thanks." I nodded to Chef, Stamp, Bug, and Kitty from the Time Served guys. They even had help at times from the guys who worked at Pop's wrecking yard—Soda, Chewie, and Fish.

"Not a problem. We want to catch these scumbags as much as you do. And find out if they're involved in the disappearance of those women too," Chef growled.

He wanted a piece of those guys in the worst way after what they did to Sis.

"There's one who apparently wants Luciana bad. She doesn't know his name. Phantom has been digging into Juan Ramirez. He's as dirty as the day is long. He's mine when we catch him," I growled. I still couldn't get over the fact that her own brother had done that to her and then threatened to sell her like she was an object.

I wasn't naïve enough to think human slavery didn't happen all over the world. Everyone likes to think it only happens in third-world countries, but they're wrong. It was just the run-in over Sis and now Luciana had been the first that hit close to home. We had to assume the missing women were all taken and sold as part of that or prostitution rings.

"How's Luciana doing? She seems to be moving around better. Sure looks better than when she arrived at the hospital," Boss asked.

"Physically, she's on the mend. Mentally, she's still scared that Juan will find out she's not dead and will show up here. She doesn't say it much, but I see it in her eyes when she seems to stare off into space. I'll be honest, I'm worried she'll try and leave."

"Does she have some place to go? I mean, if she does, maybe that would be a good idea," Stamp suggested.

"Like hell! She's not going anywhere. She's staying here," I snarled at him. He looked at Kitty.

"I told you. You owe me twenty dollars, pay up." He held out his hand. Kitty rolled his eyes and grumbled as he pulled out his wallet and slapped a twenty in his hand. The other guys laughed, even my brothers.

"What the hell is that about?"

"I bet him that you were already gone on her and that there was no way you'd let her leave. He said it was too soon. I won. But in all seriousness, does she have some place to go?"

"She said she did, but I have no idea where that would be. She doesn't have anyone to go—" Phantom clearing his throat made me look at him. He was frowning. "What?"

"I just found something out. I waited to tell you now when everyone was here. Not sure if this is who she would have gone to, but it's the only person I can find who it might be."

"Spill it."

"It seems that Juan had a girlfriend. One who up and left him three months ago. No warning and no one seems to know where she went, including Juan. Word is, he was on the warpath searching for her. He accused Luciana of helping her to get away. It was after she left that he got even more out of control. He's using all the time now."

"Did she mention this woman, Pitbull?" Sin asked.

"Nothing."

"Then we need to find out why. It looks like the girlfriend had been with him for a couple of years and then she suddenly leaves? How did she get away? Luciana told you she tried, and he had her watched. If that's true, why wouldn't he have had his girlfriend watched too?"

I could hear the speculation and maybe a bit of distrust in Saint's voice. As much as I hated it, he was right. If it was too hard for Luciana to escape, how did the other woman? "What's the girlfriend's name? I'll go find out right now."

"Her name is Lila Garcia. We're not accusing her of anything, brother. We just need to know everything. The tiniest thing could be important," Phantom added. I knew he was trying to defuse the tension in the room. I got up and left the room without saying another word. This couldn't wait.

I found her in the common room, laughing with the ladies. She looked so happy and relaxed. I hated to disrupt it, but I had to know. I walked up to her. When she saw me, she smiled and then looked around puzzled. "Where are the rest of the guys?"

"I need to talk to you. Come with me." I took her arm and tugged her to her feet. She gave me a shocked look and then she stumbled after me as I hurried her down the hall to my room. Inside, I pointed to the bed. "Sit." She sank down on it as I closed the door.

"Cole, what's wrong?"

"Did you tell me everything?"

"Everything about what?"

"About your brother and your situation."

"Yes, I did. Why?"

"You wanted us to help you get out of town. You said you had somewhere to go if you could get away. Where? And was there someone there you knew?" I watched her eyes go blank.

"I don't understand why you're asking me this. Did something happen—"

"Answer the question, Luciana," I said a little harshly. Had she been lying? Was she playing me for some reason? She stood up and marched over to me.

"I don't like that tone. I haven't done anything wrong."

"Tell me about Lila Garcia." Shock blossomed across her face for a second and then she masked it.

"Who?"

"Don't fucking play with me! You heard me. Lila Garcia. You remember, your brother's girlfriend? The one no one has seen in three months. Is she who you were going to go stay with? And if she is, how is it she could find a way to get away from Juan, but you couldn't? You're covering shit up and I want to know why. I'm putting my neck on the line for you. My whole club and the Time Served MC are, too."

"No one asked you to put your neck on the line! I wanted to leave town, remember? You were the one who wouldn't let me. Lila isn't your concern," she snapped.

I gripped her arms and tugged her to her feet. "Like hell she's not! What are you hiding? Is this some game?

Did Juan really do this to you, or was it someone else?" I snapped back and instantly knew I was way off base. "Fuck, I'm sorry, Luciana, I—" I didn't get to finish because she slapped me.

"How dare you accuse me of lying and playing a game. Do you and your brothers think I'm setting you up or something?" The door to my room opened and there stood Sin and some of the others.

"I said I'd take care of this, Sin."

"Oh, I need to be taken care of, do I? Fuck you and your club, Pitbull. I have nothing else to say. Why don't you send me back to Juan, since it seems I'm lying and using you? I think I'd rather be there than here." She jerked out of my hands and stomped to the doorway. When she got there, she glared up at them. They slowly parted and let her pass. I took off after her.

She stormed down the hall to the common room. "Luciana, come back here. You're not going anywhere!" She swung around and stopped. The anger in her eyes wasn't a surprise, but the pain made me feel sick.

"You want to know what the big secret is? I'll tell you. All of you listen up because I'll only say it once and then that's it. I didn't tell you about Lila because I'm protecting her from Juan. Yeah, she was the one I was going to stay with. The reason why she could get away and not me isn't because he didn't watch her. It's because I distracted him and his guys so she could run. And I paid for that, believe me, but there's no way I'm gonna let him find her."

"What do you mean, you paid? What did he do to

you?" I asked, fear churning in my stomach.

"You want the details, do you? Hell, why not? It's not like I need any privacy. He had me stripped naked and pictures taken. Ones that he said he'd give to the guy who wanted to buy me. He threatened to do it if he found out for sure I helped her leave or if I gave him any more trouble. I knew what was in store for me the night I went home without the cash and the drugs, but I won't tell him or you where she is!" she yelled. Her face was white, and she was shaking.

"Oh God, *bebé,* I'm so fucking sorry," I told her as I tried to take her in my arms. She shoved me away. Tears streamed down her cheeks. The old ladies all stood around quietly, watching us. I saw the pissed looks on their faces.

"Don't touch me or call me, *bebé.* I'll die before I tell anyone where she is. My niece or nephew will have the life I won't. One that's happy and safe." As she cried this out, she ran out the front door.

"Jesus Christ go after her," Sin said with a pained expression on his face—one that was on everyone's face. I was already on the move. Jesus, what had I done? I caught up to her on her way to the gate. I didn't waste time or my breath. I swung her up in my arms and turned toward Sin and Lyric's house. She screamed at me, her fists beating on my chest. She was swearing at me.

"Put me down, you bastard! God, to think I thought you were different. You're just as much of an asshole as most men. You're good. You acted like you cared and this whole time you were thinking I was lying, and you were using me to get to Juan. What do you want? To take over his drug trade for yourself, after all?"

I took the front steps two at a time and then sat down on the swing on their porch. She tried to get up, but I held her on my lap. "Listen to me! No one wants to take over his drug trade. I'm sorry that I asked it like I did. We just need to know everything. Please, settle down and talk to me," I pleaded with her. She glared up at me.

"Screw you! Do whatever the hell you want. I don't care. I was ready to die before this. Send me back. It'll be a fucking relief."

I roared out my rage at her words and gripped her face between my hands. I made sure not to hurt her. I looked her deeply in the eyes. "I'm never letting you go back to him! Never. I'm an asshole who had one second of insecurity. I knew as soon as I said it, I was wrong. We only want to help. We don't want to take over his business. We want to stop it." As she laid there not saying anything, I ran my hand down her side. She flinched. I jerked back my hand, realizing I was right over her stab wound. Something wet smeared on my hand. I held it up in the light. There was blood on my palm. I tore up the bottom of her shirt. Fresh, red blood was seeping out of her wound onto the bandage. She gasped in shock and pain.

"Shit! Let me get Saint. You tore something, Luciana." I held on to her with one arm and fished out my phone. I dialed him with shaking hands. Had I done some kind of damage to her in the struggle? What if she was bleeding internally?

He answered immediately. "Is everything alright? That was quick."

"Get over to Sin's house. She's torn her incision or something. There's blood."

"Fuck, I'll be right there. Keep her still." He hung up. I rocked her in my arms.

"Lie still. He's coming. God, I never meant to hurt you, *cariño*. Not with my words or physically," I whispered. She was crying. I couldn't tell if it was in pain or just emotion, but it was tearing me up to hear it and know I was the cause. I heard the sound of running feet and glanced up to see the whole club, the Time Served guys, and the ladies running from the clubhouse. Saint was in the lead. He beat the others to the porch by a couple of steps. He raced up them and came over to us. He kneeled next to us.

"Hey, Luciana, sweetheart, you need to let me see what you did." She shook her head. "Please. You might have done more than pulled a stitch. I need to make sure. Otherwise, my brother, Pitbull, might lose his damn mind. He's looking kind of sick." She sniffed and looked at me. I let her see the fear in my eyes. She slowly nodded and pulled up the bottom of her shirt. The blood was still leaking out, and the spot on her bandage was bigger. He pulled back the bandage. Blood was all over the incision, so I couldn't tell how bad it was.

"Get her inside and lay her down on the bed. Will someone go get my kit? It's in the treatment room." Omen was the one to run back to the clubhouse. I took her inside to the room we'd been sharing. I laid her down on the comforter. Most of the others stayed outside in the hall, but Lyric and Sara came in with me, along with Saint, and Sin.

"Let me wash my hands and then I can help Saint if he needs it," Sara said. She went into the bathroom along with Saint.

"How do you feel, Luciana?" I asked her as I held her on my lap and kissed her temple. She hissed in pain.

"It's stinging and pain is shooting across the incision. Ow, it hurts," she whispered as Saint came back out.

"Can you give her something for the pain?" I asked him urgently.

"As soon as I get my kit, I can give her what I was putting in her IV before." He barely answered before Omen came through the door with his bag. He handed it off and then went out in the hallway. I watched as he opened packages of gauze, cleaning solution, and then put on his gloves. He gently removed the old bandage and cleansed the area. When he got the blood cleaned away, I could see two stitches had torn loose. He palpated around there. She hissed but that was it. I held back from yelling at him. He took off his dirty gloves and got out a syringe and a vial of medicine. He drew up a dose.

"Sweetheart, I need to put this in your hip. Can you roll to the side for me?" I shifted her and pulled down the back of her stretch pants far enough he could give her the shot. With that given, he got out another package. It was a suturing kit. Shit, he had to sew her. He put on more gloves. Sara held open the packaging. Luciana held up a hand.

"It's going to hurt like hell. Let me do it." He gave her a shocked look.

"Excuse me?"

"Suturing hurts. I have a better pain tolerance if I do it myself. I can reach it. It only needs a couple of stitches."

"Sweetness, there's a special way you need to stitch a wound," he explained to her patiently.

"I know. I've done it before. Here, give me some of the antiseptic gel and a pair of gloves." He glanced at me as if to ask, *what do I do?* I nodded. As we watched, she calmly put three stitches in her wound. They looked like a doctor had done them when she was done. She bit her lip as she sewed, but that was it. When she finished, she spread antibiotic cream over the incision and then covered it with a clean bandage.

"Luciana, we'll need to keep an eye on it and be sure it doesn't get infected. Luckily, you're still on antibiotics. You need to stay still and not fight anymore."

She rolled her eyes. "No promises. I'd like to take a nap if I can." Sin and Saint nodded and headed for the door, along with Sara and Lyric. I was torn. I wanted to stay with her. She sighed. "Pitbull, I need you to leave, too. I'm too tired to talk right now. Just let me get some rest."

I swallowed. "Okay, but I'll be right downstairs. Call

if you need anything." I gave her a kiss. She didn't let me kiss her lips, but she didn't fight the kiss on her cheek. I eased her onto her back and then got up. Her eyes were already closed. I gave her one last look before I went out into the hall and closed the door.

Only Saint and Sin were waiting. They shook their heads. "Damn, that was messed up. She's pissed. Can't say I blame her. She was only trying to protect her family. It's all our fault for putting it out there like that to you. We're sorry, man," Sin said as we walked downstairs. The others were all gathered in his kitchen and living room. I sat down on a stool at the island.

"I screwed this all up. I made it sound like she was hiding shit. I hope she can forgive me." The thought that she wouldn't made me feel physically ill.

"She will. Lyric forgives shit with me all the time. We came to tell you that Phantom found something else. He discovered where Lila is. She's living in Oklahoma City. She went to a doctor and used her real name."

"Shit, we need to make sure no one else can find her. I have no idea if he has that ability or not. Maybe when this is all over, she can come back. Luciana will want to see her niece or nephew grow up."

"Yeah, she will. I'll work on covering her trail," Phantom assured me.

"When we find him, I want him and the guys who stripped her and took those photos. And every one of those photos will be found and destroyed," I growled as the anger came back. She'd been stripped. It wasn't rape, but it was almost like a form of it. Strange men had seen her naked body, and she'd been vulnerable. They could have done anything to her. I snapped my head up.

"You don't think they raped her, do you?"

"Hell, I don't know, brother. I hope like hell he didn't let that happen." Wrecker grunted.

"We need to find out. I'll let her rest for a while. In the meantime, I'll get to work on finding a way to get her to accept my apology and to not demand to leave. If she does, I can't let her, and that will probably make her hate me more." They all nodded and murmured their support. I watched as they left. I didn't know if Boss and his guys would stay or leave. Right now, Luciana was my priority.

Luciana: Chapter 7

I realized I had slept after all. I'd told Pitbull I wanted to, just to get some time alone. I was feeling battered and alone. After a two-hour nap, I woke up knowing I'd overreacted to his questions. He and the club didn't know me. They had no reason to take everything I said as the truth. Just like I didn't know them.

The last few days had been like a dream here at their place. I hadn't worried about being sent out to do something I hated, or worried that today would be the day Juan snapped and sold me. A few times he'd said he should just kill me and get it over with.

If I accomplished nothing else, I got Lila away from him and his life. She'd been the best thing to ever happen to him, only he destroyed her love for him like he did everything else. She'd gotten tired of the shit but was afraid to leave. However, when she found out she was pregnant, she knew she had to try. That's when she came to me, and we made our plan.

I squeezed my eyes tighter, trying not to remember the fallout and how those men had looked at me and touched me that night. I guess I should be thankful Juan didn't let them rape me. I sucked in a shuddering breath. When I did, I heard movement. I snapped my eyes open and flipped over in bed.

Pitbull was sitting in the corner in a chair. He looked tired. As soon as our eyes met, he was up and over to the bed. He sat down beside me. His head lowered and he rested his forehead on mine. "I'm so fucking sorry, Luciana. I was a total jackass. I never meant to scare you or hurt you."

I slid out from under him and sat up. "You don't need to apologize. I overreacted. Where's everyone? Did they leave? I'm sorry I put such a damper on the day."

"You didn't. They're at the clubhouse, I think. I don't know. I've been here with you."

"You didn't need to stay here with me! I'm fine. Go have some fun. I think I'm gonna just rest some more." I flinched as I twisted. A fiery sensation shot across my incision, causing me to hiss. He was on me in an instant.

"Is it your side? Let me see. Shit, you scared the shit out of me when that started to bleed again. Why don't you take a pain pill? Or I can get Saint to give you another shot." He went to stand up as if to leave. I grabbed his hand.

"Stop. It's not that bad. I'll take a pill in a little bit. It might take it a little longer to heal."

"*Querida*, how did you learn to suture wounds? You said you've done it before. Why? On whom?"

"It's not like Juan and his guys can go to the doctor every time they get knifed or shot. I've sewn them up a lot and dug out a few bullets too. Though this is the first time I sutured myself. Even as a kid, I preferred to treat my own boo boos rather than let someone else do it."

"Shit, your life has been hell, hasn't it? That's why you got Lila out of here. You didn't want that life for your nephew or niece."

"No, I don't. She's safe and that's all I care about. I think maybe it's a good idea that I leave town after all. It sounds like Juan believes the story that my body was found. He won't be looking for me."

"You can't, Luciana."

"Why not?"

"Because I don't want you to go." His face was so sad with his eyes downcast and a slight frown.

"Cole, these last few days have been great, but it can't go on forever. You have a life. You need to live it. I want a chance to have one," I whispered, even though saying it hurt like hell. If things had been different, I might have had a chance to have a life with him.

He took my hands in both of his and kissed my knuckles. He scraped gently along them with his teeth. He was staring deep into my eyes. "I want a life with you. I believe we can be happy, *bebé.* We just need to make you safe."

"You don't know me! And contrary to the latest mess, I don't need someone to rescue me."

"No, I need someone to rescue me. Someone I can come home to every night. Someone to love and hold, to build a life with."

"And you can have that. There are plenty of women who'd jump at a chance to be with you, Cole."

"Just not you."

"I'm not the kind of woman you need. The woman for you is a warrior. Someone who can fight beside you and make you proud to be with her."

"Yeah, you."

"God, Cole, I'm the sister of a damn drug dealer and who knows what else! No one in this town will look at me and see anything other than that. You'd grow to resent me. I've watched one person I loved grow to hate me. I won't do that again."

"Hmm, so you think you could love me?" He asked as he teased the corner of my mouth with nibbling bites. I fought not to whimper. He was turning my body into a mass of quivering sensations.

"Any woman could love you. Don't let it go to your head."

"As long as you're the one, I don't care about other women. I'm not letting you go. I have plans, Luciana."

"What kind of plans?" I whispered as he kissed down my jaw and neck to the sensitive hollow between my neck and shoulder.

"Ones that include you falling in love with me, becoming my woman, and eventually having my kids." He sucked on the flesh. I cried out. He was kissing me, and I got lost. All I could think about was his mouth. He consumed me in a fiery world of raw passion. His hands massaged my breasts through my top, his thumbs finding my hard nipples and strumming across them.

When he drew back, we were both breathless. "That's just the beginning of what I feel. When you're ready, I'll show you the rest, but we can't get carried away. You're still healing."

"But—" He laid a finger across my lips.

"Do you want a life with me? Just answer me that much. If we could have one, would you want it?" he asked. I hesitated and then nodded.

"Good, then that's what we'll do. I need to bring you up to date on something." He sat back. I tensed.

"Phantom found Lila," he said. I cried out. "Shh, she's safe. She had to use her real name at the doctor's office for some reason. He's working to make sure he covers the trail to her. I don't know if Juan or his associates have that capability or not."

"Cole, he can't find them! He has no idea she's pregnant. If he did, he'd go even more nuts. He's been rambling lately about having someone to pass on his business to. I know that's why she panicked when she found out she was pregnant. If he finds her, he'll never let her get a chance to get away again," I told him in a panic.

"He won't. We'll send guys to watch her if we have to, but you realize, Luciana, there's no scenario where your brother walks away from this. Even if he went to prison, he'd still be able to pull strings."

"I know. I gave up trying to save him as soon as he let those men do what they did."

"*Querida,* God, I need to ask. Did they do more than strip you and take photos?" he asked. I squirmed. I didn't want to talk about that. He swore and jumped up to pace the bedroom.

"I fucking knew it! They're dead, Luciana. I'll make it hurt before they die," he promised.

"No! No, Cole, they didn't rape me. He wouldn't let them go that far," I hurried to tell him. He looked like he was about to lose his mind.

"But they did more than take pictures, didn't they?"

I closed my eyes and nodded. "They made sure to touch me and made crude comments about what they wanted to do. They kept cupping themselves and telling me all the things they'd do to me. They begged Juan to let them have me. I don't know why he didn't." I broke down and sobbed. That was when the last ray of hope for my brother died–when he let them do that.

He got back on the bed and took me in his arms. He rocked me and murmured soft words as I cried. I felt like all I did was cry. That had never been me. I was the one to look you in the eye and not shed a tear, no matter how much you hurt me. The last five years had beaten that woman down. I wanted to get her back.

Pitbull:

Luciana had fallen back to sleep after we talked, and she broke down crying over what had happened to her at the hands of her brother and those animals. Men like that had no reason to be allowed to breathe other people's air. I sent a text to Sin.

I'm staying the rest of the day and this evening with her. She's upset and hurting. She needs rest, and I couldn't leave her.

He responded right back. *Understood. The Time Served guys and ladies have just left. They said to let her know they'd come back and finish girl time soon. Did you get things ironed out?*

Seems like it.

It was an hour later when there was a quiet knock at the door. I got up, making sure not to disturb her sleep. I opened the door to find Lyric and Sara. "We're going to bring in some dinner. Do you want us to bring some for you guys or will you be coming to the clubhouse?" Lyric asked.

"Text me when it gets here. I'll see what Luciana feels like doing."

"We can go to the clubhouse. I've laid here long

enough," came her sleepy voice from the bed.

"Okay, we'll see you there," Sara smiled at her and then they left. I closed the door and went to the bed. Her hair was tousled from sleeping and I thought it looked sexy as hell.

"Do you want to take a shower or anything before we go? Are you sure you feel up to it? No one will care if you'd rather stay here."

"I do want to wash my face and brush my teeth and hair. I need to move. I'm getting sore lying here. Give me five, maybe ten minutes." She slid off the bed. I made sure she was steady before I let her walk to the bathroom. While she was getting ready, I changed my shirt. I had brought a few of my things over from the clubhouse.

She was done and back out in less than ten minutes. Her hair was pulled up in a messy knot on the top of her head. Even without a scrap of makeup, she looked beautiful to me. I wrapped my arm around her waist and led her to the door. She was quiet on the walk over to the clubhouse. When we entered, I saw that everyone was there. They all shouted out greetings. I felt her relax when they didn't act differently toward her. I took her to one of the tables where Sara, Lyric, Jackie, and Skye were seated. I went to get us drinks at the bar from Blake. Hers was a Coke and mine was a beer. As I sat them down and took my seat, Phantom came over.

"Luciana, I wanted you to know that I put in some backstop stuff to cover any trail that might lead to Lila Garcia. She should be as safe as possible. I'll be keeping an eye on her and set up some flags to alert me if anyone starts digging into her."

Her smile was blinding. "Thank you. Thank you so much, Phantom. I can't tell you how much that means to me. Juan and his buddies can't ever find her. I don't know how I'll ever pay you all back for what you've done for me and now her."

"Hell, sweetness, the stupid lovesick look on Pitbull's face is enough payback," Saint said with a wink at her. I gave him the middle finger which made him laugh, along with the others in the room.

"Laugh it up, but I think most of you here are still single. Paybacks are a bitch. You're just jealous," I told them. Luciana gave me a startled look. I leaned over and whispered in her ear, "I told you what I wanted. I'm already half in love with you, *bebé.* I have no intention of not winning your heart for mine."

She traced her hand down my face and then gave me a tiny kiss on the mouth. "It won't take much, Cole," she whispered back. My heart leaped at her admission.

"Hey, enough of that! It's bad enough we see Sin and Lyric, and Executioner and Skye doing that all the damn time. Give us a break," Boomer groused. They all burst out laughing when Luciana gave Boomer the finger. His shock was funny as hell.

Saint broke up the laughter. "I hate to be a downer, but how're you feeling? Do you need a shot? Is the pain too much?"

"No, it's bearable. I have a high pain tolerance. The

incision burns, but the pills should be enough. I'm waiting until bedtime to take another one."

"Don't push it. If you need one now, take it. I've got to say that the stitching you did was impressive and a badass move. I know grown SEALs and Marines who couldn't do it. How did you learn to do that? Do you want a job?" he teased her.

"I've had to patch up my brother and his guys more than once. Bullets are the tricky ones. I've always wanted to be a nurse and blood and stuff doesn't bother me, so it was natural for me to be the go-to for that kind of thing."

"A nurse? Have you looked into taking the schooling?" This was Talon. She shook her head.

"I couldn't afford it and besides, Juan would never have let me do it."

"Well, that's not a problem anymore. As soon as we take care of this little problem, you should start taking classes. You'd be great at it," Talon told her. She looked shocked.

"Oh, I don't think I could—"

"*Querida*, you're only twenty-one. There's lots of time to get your education. I think you should definitely think about it. If it's what you want to do, then do it. I'll support you however you need me." This got a lot of ahhs from the peanut gallery. She gave me a heart-melting smile. I couldn't resist, so I kissed her. I made sure it was a deep, hungry one.

This got the rest of our evening started. The food

came from the local pizza place, and we laughed, ate, and then ended up watching movies in the common room. By the time I saw her yawning, it was already eleven o'clock. I stood up. "Time to get her to the house and into bed. I'll see you guys later. Let me grab something from my room and then I'll be ready," I told her. She nodded.

I quickly grabbed more clothes and some personal care shit from my room and shoved it into a bag. I was back up the hallway and at the mouth of the hall where it opened into the common room. I groaned. The bunnies had shown up while I was in my room. So far, I've kept Luciana clear of them. I didn't want them to make her uncomfortable. I knew from Lyric and Skye that they made old ladies feel insecure. I thought that was crazy. Anyone could see they were a totally different breed of women.

Vonnie had gotten her ass kicked out when she wouldn't stop causing trouble. So far, Barbie, Shy, and Tabby Cat have stayed more or less on their best behavior. I wasn't holding my breath that it would last forever. I headed for Luciana. She was watching the bunnies with a frown on her face. Crap!

I'd almost made it to her when Barbie shouted out, "Why, Pitbull, where have you been hiding, stud? I've been lonely." I closed my eyes for a second and tried not to lose my cool. When I opened them, Luciana was looking at Barbie then back at me. Her eyes got round and then she stood up. She said something to the ladies and then went rushing toward the door. I took off after her. No way was a bunny going to set back the progress I made with her.

As I passed Barbie, she reached out to touch my arm. I jerked it away from her. "Barbie, enough. I'm not interested. See that woman who just left? That's my lady. Don't do that shit again," I growled. Her face registered her surprise then she narrowed her eyes. She looked at Shy and Tabby Cat.

"What the fuck is going on here? Another one has picked one of them instead of us." She sounded pissed. I wanted to go after Luciana, but I needed to say this first.

"No one ever told you we'd want any of you for more than sex. No offense, but that's what you're here for. Did you think that would go on forever? That we wouldn't want to settle down and start families? And when we do, it's not with someone like you. I'm sorry."

"Settle down? You're gonna make her your old lady and have kids with her?" she shrieked. I looked at my brothers.

"Explain it to her, will you? I need to go talk to Luciana." They nodded and I left them there. I hurried over to Sin's house. I raced up the stairs to the room where we'd been staying. I took a deep breath then opened the door. Luciana was sitting on the edge of the bed, staring out the window into the darkness. I went over and sat down beside her. I tried to take her hand, but she pulled away from me.

"*Cariño*, please. Let me explain. Barbie and the other women—" She stopped me with a hand over my mouth. When she looked at me, I saw what looked like fear in her eyes. What the fuck?

"I know what those women are, Cole. I'm not stupid or naïve. I know you're a man with a man's needs. I want to know, are they here because they want to be, or because they're forced to be?"

My mouth dropped open. "Forced? God no, we don't force them. They're what is called a bunny in the biker world. They service bikers in exchange for protection, a place to stay, and money. But we don't force them to do it. They come to us seeking that. Their reasons are their own. I won't pretend I'm a saint, but I'd never have sex with someone who didn't want it." It hurt that she thought I might.

"That's all I need to know. I'm sorry. After my brother, I'm sensitive about this. I never thought he'd do what he's doing. I know he's forced women to have sex with his men and him. Do you think you'll still be using them for sex?"

"No, I won't! I told you, you're who I want," I told her angrily.

"That doesn't mean you won't still have sex with other women. Most men do, I've found. They have wives and girlfriends, but then sleep with prostitutes and other women. Some women do the same thing. If that's what you want, then we need to stop this now. I can't be in that type of relationship, Cole. It would kill me," she whispered. I heard the pain in her voice. I gently pushed her to lie back on the bed. I leaned over her.

"Luciana, I would never cheapen us by doing that, just like I expect to be the only one for you. Yes, I've been with them and other women. I'm not a virgin."

"What if I can't give you all that you need?"

"Why couldn't you?" I asked her, puzzled why she would think that. She flicked her eyes away from mine. Her hands were curled up into fists. I eased them open. "Look at me and tell me why you'd think that?"

"I'm not like them."

"I know. Why would you think I'd want you to be?"

She shifted on the bed and then looked up at me. She took a deep breath. "I mean, I'm not like them at all, Cole. I don't have any experience. They know what they're doing. I don't."

I froze as her words sunk in. Was she saying what I thought she was saying? "Are you telling me that you've never had sex?"

She nodded. A look of embarrassment and a little unease was written all over her face. My heart jumped and I latched onto her mouth. I kissed her deeply and thrust my tongue into her mouth to wrestle with hers. The taste of her and the feel of her body against mine had me hard. I took her hand and slipped it down between us. I pressed it to the zipper of my jeans.

"Does that feel like that turns me off? I'm fucking amazed that you haven't and that I'm gonna be the only man to ever be inside of you. And make no mistake, when I take you, you're mine forever, Luciana. We can explore what you like and what I like together and discover even more. That makes me happy as fuck," I told her. She gasped, then she kissed me. Her hand tightened just a fraction on my cock. I fought not to come in my jeans.

We got lost for I don't know how long. I realized at some point I'd pushed up her top and had her breast in my hand. I'd pushed the cup away and her tight nipple pressed into the palm of my hand. I broke away from her mouth and sucked it into my mouth. She gasped and her hips came up off the mattress. I flicked back and forth over it, making it tighten even more.

Her hands fumbled at my belt. I stopped her. "No, we can't. You're not ready. You need to heal. God knows I want to. More than you can fucking imagine, but not until you're ready. I don't want our first time to be in the heat of the moment," I said, though it was probably going to kill me. My cock was shouting at me to shut the fuck up.

She whimpered and then dropped her hand. "Okay, I understand."

"Don't think for a second it's because I don't want to. It's gonna kill me not to be inside of you, but I need to make sure you're okay. And you need to be safe. You need to get on birth control. I need to get tested, though I've always worn condoms."

"Tested? Why? If you wear condoms—" I cut her off.

"Because I don't want to wear them with you. And you need time before we have kids. You're young. You need to have some fun and get that nursing degree you want so much." Her mouth gaped open in surprise.

"Kids? Degree?"

"Don't you want kids? I assumed you did. It's okay if

you don't—"

"I do! I do want them. I guess I thought guys didn't care too much about that. And I can't go to school, Cole."

"Yes, you can. I'm gonna make sure you do. While having kids won't prevent it, it would make it harder on you. I can't carry them though, I'll be hands-on when we do have them. So, how about we go see the doctor and get you on something and I'll have a test done?"

"The test is fine, but I don't need to see a doctor. I'm on birth control shots already. I was scared to death Juan might—." She stopped and I saw her swallow.

"That he'd sell you or force you to sell yourself. Jesus Christ, I hate that. I promise one day, you'll be able to look back and see this all as a distant memory. Enough about him, I'll go tomorrow to the doctor, but make no mistake, as soon as you give me the green light, we're gonna make love and someday have those kids. Okay?" I kissed her tenderly.

She nodded and kissed me back. "Deal." I sank back into our kissing. I just needed one more, then we'd stop.

Pitbull: Chapter 8

Almost another week with no progress on finding Juan and his buddies. It was killing me not to be able to hunt him down and end the danger to Luciana, as well as the other women in this town. We were more than certain now that he had heard about a body being found, and that he hadn't figured out she was really alive. The watch at their old apartment and his two main haunts was happening twenty-four seven.

Luckily, Phantom and Preacher had come up with a way to give us a bit of a break. They installed hidden cameras one night when no one was around at those three locations. If Juan or anybody were to come back, we'd be alerted and send some guys over to intercept them immediately. They were like the ones they'd put in the bunker and tunnels. We were antsy, waiting to get a break in something.

As promised, first thing Monday, I went to the doctor to have a test run to make sure I was clean. When the time came, I didn't want anything to be in question. I wanted to be able to make love to her anytime and anywhere without worrying about if I had protection. Her being on birth control only mattered because I wanted her to have a chance to get her degree and have fun, like I told her. I could wait a few years to have kids.

The last two days had been a struggle. She was becoming more mobile. The pain was better and even though she'd torn the incision, it looked good. Saint said she had great healing abilities. She'd told him she always took vitamin C and Zinc. Come to find it out, that helped with healing wounds. I didn't understand it all, but the two of them had talked about it. Though I trusted Saint's opinion, I wanted to have a doctor's opinion too.

We'd been invited over to Boss and Jenn's place to have a cookout, but first the ladies were going to have some kind of clothing show. Not sure what the hell that was about, but as long as Luciana got more clothes, I was happy. Sara had told me about the plan, and I'd made sure they would have things for her.

So far, she'd been wearing the few clothes Sara had picked up for her before I brought her home, but she needed more, including more than the flip-flops she'd been wearing. She never complained or asked for anything. I'd tried to get her to shop online for more stuff and she kept waving it off. Well, she couldn't today, because the old ladies had a list of what I wanted her to buy.

While the ladies had their fun, we'd hang with Boss and his guys, maybe check out what he'd done to their meeting room in the basement part of the wellhouse. I also wanted to introduce Luciana to Tonya. She was a damn tiger that Hook had as a pet. She lived at the house with him and Paula. That shit there terrified me. They seemed to act like it was just another day at home. Being a vet gave him a bunch of odd creatures, which somehow found their way over at Boss' house too.

We were getting ready to head out when I heard Luciana scream. I whipped around to find her pinned to the wall by Zeus. He was Sin's huge-ass Caucasian Shepherd. He looked like a bear and was almost the size of one. Next to him was Bear, Lyric's twenty pounds of pug terror. He was the ruler of those two. To see them together, you couldn't do anything but laugh, especially when Zeus followed Bear around.

Zeus had taken one look at Luciana and decided she was his, like she was a puppy or something. I teased her that it was because she was tiny and not much bigger than Bear. She'd given me the dirtiest look; however, the damage had been done. The guys had taken to teasing her the same way.

"Zeus, I swear, if you lick off my makeup, no more head rubs for you!" she told him sternly. I swear the damn dog understood her, because he got off his rear paws, which made him taller than her, and sat back on his hind quarters. He gazed at her adoringly. Bear, on the other hand, gave her a mildly interested look and then walked away.

I walked over to stand by Zeus. He had her cornered even if he wasn't trying to lick her. She glared at me. "Are you gonna get this nut to let me go or just stand there grinning like a fool?" she asked me exasperatedly. I smiled more.

"Well, I don't know. What do I get if I do save you?"

She glanced around, then she gave me a smirk and ran her hands up her sides and cupped her breasts. It pushed up her breasts, making her cleavage deeper. She licked her lips. I fought back the groan that wanted to explode out of me. I was instantly hard. She'd been getting bolder in our make-out sessions. I was hard pressed not to give in and make her mine.

"Maybe I could think of something, but if you don't want to, I could see if someone else might help me." I knew she was only teasing me, but I instantly got a flash of jealousy. I stepped up and pushed Zeus on the head. He harrumphed and then walked off, like I'd denied him his favorite toy. He looked back with sad doggy eyes at her. I pressed her against the wall with my body and held her arms above her head with one of my hands.

I ground my cock into her, being careful not to rub her incision. She gave a low, breathy moan. I nipped her ear and whispered, "If you try it, I'll have you stripped and under me with my cock inside of you so fast, you won't know what happened. I'll fuck you until you can't think of anyone else. Ever. Again."

Her eyes were burning. She pressed into me. "Promise? Because if you do, I'll do it right now. I need you, Cole," she whispered back.

I closed my eyes. "*Bebé*, God, I want to, you know that. But you're still healing." I pleaded with her. Her head moved and she latched onto my mouth. We hungrily kissed each other, letting our tongues do what other parts of us were desperate to do. When we parted to pant, she smiled at me.

"If a doctor said I was okay to do it, would you accept that? I can't wait for us to be together for another month, Cole. I might just burst into flames. Unless you want to go somewhere and stay away for a month?"

"Fuck no, I'm not leaving," I growled.

"Good, because that could kill me too. So, will you?"

I sighed. "Yeah, if a real doctor said it was okay then I'd be all over you in a heartbeat, but until one does, you're gonna have to give me a break."

"Okay, I will. Now, are you ready to go?"

I nodded. A whistle ripped through the clubhouse. I turned to find all my brothers standing there, looking at us with shit-eating grins on their faces. Jackie, Sara, Lyric, and Skye were with them doing the same.

"You two ready or are we about to see a live sex show," Saint asked as he wiggled his eyebrows. Before I could say anything, Luciana did.

"No, we're not giving you a show, you perv. I swear, Saint, I pity the woman who gets you. She'll need to smack you in the head at least five times a day." She said it with a smile and a twinkle in her eyes. The two of them had gotten close, but not in a way that made me jealous. He treated her like a kid sister. He was always checking on her to make sure she was healing and doing okay.

"Ahh, come on, Itty-Bitty, don't say that shit. You'll jinx me."

"Stop calling me that! I'm not that damn little."

"Christ woman, your nose is gonna grow with the lies you keep telling. Shit, Executioner almost stepped on you the other day."

She looked at Executioner when Saint told her that. Ex raised an eyebrow and then nodded. He made sure to keep his whole face serious. She scowled, which had all of them howling. Jackie smacked her soon-to-be son-in-law in the arm.

"Stop teasing the poor girl. She's not that short." He gave her an amused look.

"You say that because you're only an inch or so taller than her. Zeus is gonna carry you two off one day." This had Jackie giving him a shitty look. She was tiny, but then all of them were next to him. He was six and a half feet tall.

"I've never had anyone complain about my size before," she snipped. I saw Omen look her up and down. All of us had gotten the clue that he was interested in Jackie. The almost ten years age difference didn't make a difference to him, though he was keeping it on the down low I think until after he patched in. He was a prospect, and she was the mother-in-law to a patched member. However, watch out as soon as he was one. I was positive he'd be after her like one determined man.

That got them squabbling and the rest of us getting our asses in gear. I was taking Luciana for her first ride on my bike. She'd admitted she'd never been on one and she was both excited and scared. Even though we did have to be outside the compound, it was mainly outside of the town limits, and she'd be wearing a helmet and sunglasses. It was highly unlikely anyone who knew her would see her. If they did, we could hopefully draw them out. Brennan was driving one of the trucks. He was taking Zeus and Bear, so they could run around out at Boss' place with his dog and the other animals.

It was about a fifteen-minute drive. As I got her situated on my bike and gave her my instructions one more time, the others got on their bikes. I saw Jackie go to get in the truck with Brennan. Omen stepped up and said something to her. She shook her head and said something back. After a minute, he nodded and went to get on his bike while she got in the truck. I wondered if he had asked her to ride with him. Executioner had watched the whole scene with a faint smile on his face. Omen was his friend, and if anyone would be good enough for Jackie, it might be him.

As we took off, I felt how tense Luciana was. I kept putting a hand on her thigh or over her hands wrapped around my waist, to rub and help her relax. After a couple of miles, she started to relax more and more. The June day was a nice sunny and warm one. It was a great day to be out on the bikes. We pulled up to Boss' house too fast. I wanted to ride longer. Soon, I'd have to get everyone to take a longer ride.

His driveway was filled with bikes and a couple of cars. I recognized Frankie and Blue's cars. We pulled in alongside them and parked. I held on to Luciana's hand as she swung off the bike. Her legs would be a little wobbly after riding. As she stood and got her legs back, I took off her helmet. I gave her a kiss. "How did you like your first ride, *cariño*?"

She smiled and then whispered, "It was great and it turned me on." She blushed as she said it. I moaned softly.

"Don't tell me that. Now all I want to think about is how it was a big vibrator teasing your clit. I want to be the only one to do that to you." She bit her bottom lip, and I saw her squeeze her legs together.

"Behave, or I'll end up making a fool out of myself."

"Okay, I'll be good, but later we're gonna talk about this. I want to hear what it felt like to you." She moaned and then broke away from me. I took her hand and walked around to the back of the house. We could hear talking and laughing. After getting the greetings out of the way, we let the ladies go off inside the house for their time. The guys were heading to the well house. I hoped they had fun. We'd agreed they'd get two hours then we were coming to get them.

Luciana:

I followed the other women into Boss and Jenn's house. She showed us around, for those that hadn't seen it before, like me and Jackie. After the tour, we got drinks and then settled in the living room. I waited to see what we were going to talk about. It was Sara who got the conversation going.

"Okay, ladies, you know why we're here. She needs our help. Not only for just regular stuff, but 'the drive him crazy' things too." I looked around in curiosity, trying to think who she was talking about. My mind instantly went to Lyric. She was getting married to Sin in two weeks. However, they were having her bridal shower next weekend. All eyes turned and looked at me. I froze.

"What? Why're you all staring at me like that?"

"Girl, you need to get with the program. You need clothes and shoes and a whole lot of other stuff," Sara told me with a roll of her eyes.

"I don't need anything more than what I have. You got me things when I left the hospital," I protested. I hated to have people spending their money on me. As soon as the threat from Juan was behind me, I was going to get a job, so I could have my own money.

"Honey, that was just a few things to hold you over until you could get more. Pitbull said you've ignored all his attempts to have you go online and order. Well, we've decided to take care of it. We're gonna do that today as well as send you home with things tonight," Jackie added with a patient tone.

"I have clothes. When this is over with my brother, assuming he didn't get rid of them, I have clothes at the apartment. It's a waste of money to buy more."

"A woman can never have too many clothes or shoes. When was the last time you bought clothes for yourself?" Jenn asked. I squirmed inside. Other than a few cheap things here and there, not in years, but I didn't want to tell them that.

"Exactly, not in ages. Get your ass over here, so we can go on to this killer website we found," Lyric told me. She patted the couch beside her. The others grabbed my hands and pulled me up and then over to her. They clicked on a remote and the television had the internet showing on the screen. This would allow everyone to see it. I tried one last ditch effort.

"I don't have money for this and you're not paying for it."

"It's been taken care of," Skye said. I gave her a puzzled look. She held up a credit card.

"No, I said I'm not letting you pay for it."

"I'm not. This is Pitbull's card. He gave it to me before we left. Said to make sure you got everything you needed and wanted." My mouth fell open. He'd known what they were going to do.

"Well, he's just gonna be disappointed."

"We want you to pick out what you like, but if you don't, we'll do it, and we'll spend a lot more than you want," Paula threatened with a grin. I saw they weren't going to budge. I sighed in defeat.

"Fine, but I'm not spending more than a hundred."

"Bullshit. Your man told me that if this thing didn't come back with at least a grand or more in charges, he's gonna go spend ten thousand on your stuff himself," Sara told me.

"A-a grand, is he nuts? That's more money than I've spent in years on clothes. Sara, he can't charge that much! I'll get a few and then as soon as I get a job, I can buy more." She took my hand. I was upset and she could see it while the others got quiet.

"Luciana, you need to know something about the men in our clubs and that includes your man. They're all alpha males. That can make them bossy and some-times assholes, but they don't only want to take care of their women and kids, they need to do it. There's no way Pitbull would let you pay for your clothes. That's his job as your man. Just like Sin and Executioner won't let those two do it. I bet Boss, Hook, and Chef are the same." All five women nodded in agreement.

"It's not because they think you can't do it. They don't believe you should. It's what makes them happy. Pitbull loves you, even if it's only been a matter of a couple of weeks since you two met. He knows what you've given up and gone without. He wants you to have fun and to get what you need and want. Believe me, he's not gonna go bankrupt over a thousand dollars or two."

"I don't like him charging this. It costs more money. I want to be independent."

"And you can be independent. When you make your own money, you can use it for other things. They do, and he's not paying extra. This is his bank card, not a credit card. The money is in there. He said if we want to buy more than five grand, he'll move around other funds."

I choked on the drink of tea I'd just taken. "Five thousand! Is he insane? No, no way I'll spend that. Okay, if he's gonna insist and you're all gonna side with him, I'll shop for some things, but one thousand is gonna be impossible for me to spend."

With this out of the way, they helped me shop. Over the next hour, I picked out what seemed like a ton of stuff. Every time I tried to go cheaper; they wouldn't let me. After a while, I started to have fun. By the time we were done, I had way more than I'd ever thought I'd find. Things I'd never considered buying though I'd looked at them and dreamed about them in the past, and not all of it was functional jeans and tanks. There were dresses and other pretty clothes, including sexy underwear and bras.

When it was all said and done, there was twelve hundred dollars in the cart. Sara hit the checkout button before I could go back and take a lot of it off. I thought my torture was over when that happened, but I was wrong. Next, they got out bags. They started handing them to me. As I opened them, I saw a lot of very sexy clothes and lingerie, much more so than what I'd just bought. I blushed when I saw most of them.

"Look at her. Honey, we promise if you wear this, Pitbull will forget his damn name, though you might not get out of bed for a few days." Blue hooted. She was holding up a royal blue nightie that was see through and had basically an elastic band as the panties. No way I could wear that. Could I?

By the time they had all commented on the outfits and teased me to death, I was ready to take a nap. We heard the guys' voices coming from the back. They hurried and shoved the clothes back into a few of the bags. "I'll put these in the truck with me," Jackie promised. She sat them over by her purse.

I was in a daze when I went with the other ladies to join the men. As the rest of the afternoon and evening wore on, I couldn't stop thinking about those sexy things in the bags. I needed to talk to Frankie. I wanted to know how long I needed to wait to have sex with Pitbull. She was a doctor. She'd be able to tell me, because it had just become urgent that I do it as soon as possible.

Pitbull: Chapter 9

On the ride back from Boss and Jenn's place, Luciana held on tight but seemed to be much more relaxed than on the ride out to their place. We'd stayed all afternoon and then into the evening. It was now ten, and we were going back to the compound. I knew most of my brothers would be hanging out and partying into the night. No one had to work tomorrow, and they'd want to blow off steam. That would mean the bunnies would be waiting for them.

I had no real desire to hang and watch that. Even though Luciana had told me she was alright with them as long as they weren't there by force, I still didn't want to have her around them if she didn't need to be. This was on my mind as we pulled back into the compound. No doubt, they heard the bikes. The three of them lived in a small apartment-like building behind the clubhouse.

When we parked and got off the bikes, I took her hand. She smiled up at me. She'd been more relaxed today than I'd seen her, and it wasn't due to alcohol. She'd only had a couple of drinks now that she was off the pain meds. I'd stopped drinking like the others several hours prior. No way we'd ride drunk. "Let's go to the house, *bebé*." I saw Sin and Lyric head into the clubhouse. They must be planning to stay for a little bit. The others were at the door, yelling at us to hurry the hell up.

"Let's just go in for a few minutes. I want to see if Boomer can kick Torpedo's butt in darts. They've been bragging about who's the best. Please." She gave me a pleading look. I groaned then nodded.

"Okay, then we're out of here. I want to spend some time, just the two of us." She nodded and smiled. I led her inside. I was happy to see Skye and Ex had come inside as well. Jackie was over talking to Sara. She was studiously not looking at Omen.

The two of them had been tense most of the day. It started when we were at Boss' house and Captain, one of his guys, had come over and was smiling and chatting with Jackie. She'd been laughing with him, and they seemed awfully comfortable with each other. You could see it pissed Omen off.

I had no idea if there was anything going on with Captain and Jackie, though I'd heard her mention him more than once and he came into the flower shop to talk to her. I hoped like hell this wasn't going to become a problem. Our friendship with the Time Served guys was becoming a solid one. A fight over a woman could blow it up. After Omen had seen them talking, he'd been cold to Jackie.

Now, it seemed like she'd decided to ignore him. I sighed. It was their problem. They could figure it out. I grabbed us both drinks and then we went over to watch the dart competition. It was going to be the best two out of three. They were through the first game when the bunnies decided to show up. They were dressed in the skimpiest clothes they could find. I shook my head. Had I really found that attractive? They were decent looking and had nice bodies, but their overdone hair and makeup made them look coarse and desperate.

I saw Luciana glance at them and stare for a moment then she looked away. She might say she understood, but she didn't. Hell, I had to wonder what the fucking attraction to women like that had been all these years. The only explanation was sex, pure and simple. They made their way into the thick of the single brothers. At least they were smart to stay away from me, Ex, and Sin.

Boomer and Torpedo were battling through the second game when I saw movement out of the corner of my eye. It was Jackie. She was quickly darting out the front door. Skye wasn't far behind her. I looked around puzzled to see why, then I saw Barbie hanging on Omen. He didn't look like he was thrilled, but he also didn't tell her to get lost. I saw Ex go over and say something to Barbie. She flounced off with a pout. Omen scowled at the door as Ex whispered furiously at him, then he shook his head and left to go after his woman and her mom.

Omen looked upset. I was wrestling with whether I should go over and say anything to him when he stomped off down the hall. He was probably going out the back to his trailer. Others had seen the scene and were giving each other concerned looks. I'd had enough. "Luciana, are you ready? I think I've had enough for tonight. It's getting shitty in here."

She nodded. "Me too. Let's go. I just need to grab my bags that Jackie put by the front door." As we turned to head that way, we called out our goodnights to the others. They waved and told us the same. We were half-way across the room when Barbie picked up one of the bags. Luciana saw her and picked up her speed. She got to her before she could open it and grabbed it.

"Those are mine."

Barbie tried to tug it out of her hands and succeeded. "Who says? They were just sitting here. I want to see what it is."

"They're stuff I brought back from Jenn's house. The girls got them for me. Please let go, Barbie," Luciana said quietly.

"Oh, Jenn's house was it. So, you're now all tight with the old ladies there too. What in the hell does Pitbull see in you? You're a meek little mouse, who I heard couldn't even keep from getting her ass beat. He needs someone tougher than that, and definitely someone sexier and experienced." She smirked as she said it. I felt my blood pressure rising. I'd had enough of her. She'd done her thing with Luciana that first time, then with Omen, and now she was back to Luciana. I opened my mouth to blast her when Luciana floored me, and I think the whole common room.

"I don't know what your problem is, other than you're a jealous bitch, Barbie, but I'm not going to stand here and listen to your shit. Pitbull is with me. Get over it and get over yourself while you're at it. Take my advice, if you don't want to look fifty when you're thirty, use some sunblock and take care of yourself. And ease up on the bleach, your hair might fall out. I might not have fake tits and all that other shit like you, but at least I'm all natural."

She said it calmly. Barbie's eyes got round and then her face got red. She took a step like she was going to come toward Luciana. "Why you bitch—" I stepped in between them.

"Barbie, you need to shut up and back off. You touch her, and you're gone. She's right. Those are her bags. You don't need to understand why I'm with her, other than to know I am. I won't cheat on her, and she's the woman I love. End of fucking story. Now, put down her stuff," I growled at her.

Luciana came around me. She placed her hand on my chest and looked up at me. She gave me a smile. "Honey, there's no need to defend me, though I love you for it. I can handle her." She turned to glance at Barbie. "Give me my bag, Barbie."

Barbie glared at her and then me. She flung the bag at Luciana and then took off down the hall. The others watched without saying a word. Barbie was getting worse. She was following in Vonnie's footsteps. Tabby Cat and Shy had stayed out of it and just watched from the sidelines. I bent down and picked up her other bags. With another wave to the group, we walked out.

As we made our way to Sin and Lyric's place, I shook the bags. "Can I see what's in here?"

"No, not until we get to the house. Then, if you're good, I might let you see, but first, I need a shower." I didn't speak, I just carried them. I was interested to see what the ladies had bought her. Sara had taken me aside and assured me she'd ordered enough stuff to hold her for a while. I still hoped we'd get some of her stuff back when we could get into her old apartment, if any of it was worth saving. According to Sara, she had admitted to not really buying things for years.

As soon as we got to our room, she insisted, "Cole, take your shower first. That'll give me a chance to look through these, then I'll take mine.

"But you said you really wanted one, why don't you go first?"

"Just humor me, please."

"Okay, I'll be quick. Love you." I gave her a kiss and then went into the bathroom. If we had progressed our relationship to that final stage, then I'd have insisted we could shower together, though I doubted showering would be all we got done. More than once today, I'd gotten hard as hell just looking at her.

As I showered, I let myself think about her. My cock was hard as a steel rod, but I wasn't going to rub one out with her in the next room. I knew she was sexually frustrated and if she had to endure, I would too. I was in and out in ten minutes. As soon as I was done, she took my place. I relaxed back on the bed and turned on the television in the room to watch a racing show while I waited. As she puttered around doing whatever it was she was doing, I flipped through the channels. I lost track of how long she had been in there, but it seemed to have been longer than her usual time. "*Cariño*, are you alright in there?" I yelled.

"I don't know, you tell me," she said softly from the door of the bathroom. I hadn't heard her open it. I glanced over and the air froze in my lungs. She stood there in a sexy nightie. Her hair was fluffed and hanging around her face and curling above her breasts. The nightie was a bright royal blue and see through. I could see her dark nipples through it. I instantly felt my cock grow hard. I ran my eyes down her petite body. The nightie was slit from below her breasts to her belly button in the middle. Glimpses of skin peeked out. Her pussy was covered, barely, by a pair of the tiniest panties I'd ever seen. I could see her lips outlined by the gauzy fabric.

"Fuck! You're gonna kill me dressing like that, woman. Luciana, I can't take this, *bebé*. There's no way I can lie here beside you all night with you in that. Jesus Christ, put on a sweatshirt and sweatpants, something," I begged her. My control was slipping. The only thing keeping me from pouncing was the fact she was still healing and had a wound on her side. She didn't say a word. She merely walked slowly toward the bed. Her hands were knotted in front of her.

When she got to the bed, she stopped. "And if I told you that there's no need to lie here all night, what would you say?"

"What do you mean? We can't. You're not fully healed. I told you, not until a doctor says it's okay," I told her hoarsely. My mouth was dry, and my palms were sweating. As hard as I tried, I couldn't keep from looking her up and down. I could see those nipples even better.

She put one knee up on the mattress. It made the nightie part more, and I groaned, seeing even more of her skin on her stomach. I was clutching the damn bed sheets in my fists to stop myself from touching her. She hopped up on the mattress. Her eyes never left mine as she crawled toward me. She wasn't trying to be sexy; she just was.

"I talked to Frankie. She's a doctor, you know. She said as long as we didn't get crazy or try any crazy positions, I should be fine. If my side starts to hurt too much, then I should stop. Cole, I'm dying, honey. I want to be with you so much. The kissing and touching we've done isn't enough anymore. I think I'll lose my mind if you don't make me yours all the way tonight." Her eyes pleaded with me. "What do you say?"

I lunged across the rest of the mattress and took her mouth with mine. I devoured her lips and fought a war with our tongues, as I lifted her gently in my arms and then rolled her onto her back. I hovered over her as we kissed. Her hands were in my hair and then running down my back to my hips, as I ran mine down the fabric covering her ribs and then up her stomach to her breasts. I could feel her tight nipples pushing out against the fabric. I broke away so I could suck one into my mouth. She cried out. So far, I'd touched them with my fingers and teased them that way, but I hadn't trusted myself to suck on them. Now, I feasted. My teeth bit down on them gently and I tugged them with my teeth. She hissed.

"Shit, is that too hard?"

"No, it just surprised me at how good it feels, Cole. Don't stop." I went back to them, only this time I tugged on the ribbon holding the front of her sexy nightie closed. "Can I undo this?" I whispered. She might not be ready for me to see her bare.

"Yes."

I slowly pulled on it and then parted it until it fell to her sides. Her breasts weren't huge, but they were a nice handful. They were firm and perky. Her light tan nipples were so damn pretty. I cupped them and then went back to teasing her. She moaned and moved restlessly on the bed. I was fighting not to grind my cock into her. I was hard and full, and ready to be inside of her, but she was a virgin. I had to prepare her. I kept telling myself that over and over. Suddenly, her nails bit through the thin fabric of my shorts and into my ass cheeks. I hissed this time. I peered up at her. Her eyes were slumberous.

"Cole, I need you."

"I know, I need you too, *bebé, b*ut you need to be ready. I'm not gonna hurt you more than I have to. Your first time needs to be as pleasurable as I can make it. That means you need to be really slick. You need to get off at least once before we go that far. Can I take these off?" I touched her almost non-existent panties.

She nodded and moaned. "Yes, hurry."

She didn't need to tell me twice. I sat back on my heels and eased them down her hips and legs. I made myself wait until they were off before I looked at her pussy. She had spread her legs and I could see her fully.

CIARA ST JAMES

She had a small, neatly trimmed patch of hair above her clit. Her pussy lips were puffy and red. Her cream was shining in the light. I could smell her scent filling my nose. I didn't waste my time saying anything. I showed her what she was doing to me.

I wedged my shoulders between those creamy thighs and held onto them. I lowered my head and swiped my tongue from her entrance to her clit. She wailed as I did. I wanted to shout. Her taste was exploding on my tongue. It was an instant addiction. I attacked her with my lips and tongue. Her fingers sank into my shoulders, and she thrashed on the bed. I showed her no mercy. I wanted to go slower, but I was too close to losing control. I needed her to come and be prepared for me, because I had to be inside of her soon, or I'd die.

I worked one finger into her tight pussy and then a second one, thrusting in and out. She was tight as hell, and I couldn't wait to feel that around my cock. I could feel the precum leaking from the head of my cock in my shorts. I lapped at her folds, sucked on her hard nub, and fucked her with my fingers. Her legs started to shake and then she clamped down on my fingers and screamed as she came. Her cream increased and I lapped all of it up, using my fingers and mouth to prolong her orgasm. She was coming down when she tensed and cried out again.

I didn't wait for her to come all the way down. I pulled her with me until I could stand at the edge of the bed. She was panting and looking up at me questioningly. I tore off my shorts and fisted my cock. She looked at me and moaned. Her hand reached between her legs to run across the head. I shuddered. "Fuck, don't or I'll come. You're the most beautiful thing I've ever seen in my life, Luciana. I'll try to go slow but tell me if I need to stop. Or if anything hurts too much," I said through gritted teeth.

She nodded frantically and cupped her breasts, tracing her fingers over her nipples. "I will. Cole, please, before I go crazy! Fill me with that beautiful cock."

Hearing her say cock broke the last of my hesitancy. I lifted her ass off the bed with one hand and then lined up my cock with the other. I pressed the head to her opening and pressed inside just an inch. I had to stop and take a deep breath. She was squeezing the hell out of the head, and I fought not to come right then and there. After several deep breaths, I advanced. She was tight and I had to work to get inside her, but she never asked me to stop. She moaned and hissed but that was it. She clenched down on me more than once and I almost cried.

When I finally got to her hymen, I paused, then I kissed her. She kissed me back eagerly and as she got lost in the kiss, I eased back and then pushed through it. She cried out a little, but I kept going until I was all the way inside. I paused again. I lay my forehead on hers. "God, I think I just found heaven, Luciana. You feel so damn incredible, and mine."

I pulled back and then sank back inside of her. She tightened around me, and her breath caught. I watched her face for any sign that it was too painful, but all I saw was pleasure and awe. As we both got more and more lost in the pleasure in our bodies, I thrust faster and a little harder. I made sure not to jar her too hard and to not rub against her incision.

We kissed and I sucked on her nipples. My thumb slid down to rub her clit in circles. I needed her to come with me and I was too damn close to stop it or slow down. I silently promised I'd make it last longer next time. She had her legs wrapped around my hips as I powered in and out of her. The tingling ran up my legs, and I knew I was about to come. I sped up and pushed down on her clit harder. She froze and then screamed as she came. Her pussy clenched down so damn hard; I saw a flash of light. My thrusts stuttered and then I held myself deep and grunted as my cum flowed out of me and into her. She was squeezing my cock and milking it, as I let jet after jet of cum loose.

When I finally stopped coming, she was limp underneath me. I kept slowly gliding in and out of her. I didn't want to leave her body. I kissed her gently. "God, I love you, *amada.* You just slayed me and made me your slave for life. You've just enslaved my heart, soul, mind, and body, Luciana. Don't ever leave me," I pleaded. It might make me sound like a wimp, but I didn't care. She was my peace in this crazy world.

As I slowed and then stopped as my cock softened, she raised up on her elbows and kissed me. "I love you too, *mi alma.* Thank you for loving me. That was beyond anything I ever expected. Thank you." Her calling me *my soul* had my heart galloping. We kissed tenderly until I had to pull out. I flopped down beside her and took her in my arms. I kissed her face and then touched her side.

"Did this hurt?"

"A couple of twinges and that's it. I feel good, Cole. Now, why don't we rest and maybe you can show me that again."

I threw back my head and laughed. "Your wish is my command, my love. But first, stay here so I can get you cleaned up. We'll take a nap and then go for round two." She smiled as I got up and got a washcloth to clean us up with. When I was done, she snuggled into my arms, and we held each other as we drifted off.

Luciana: Chapter 10:

I watched Pitbull as he laughed with his brothers last night. He looked so happy and relaxed. It had been four days since we'd finally had sex for the first time. I was still amazed at how it had made me feel, and how it made me feel every time we were together. I swear it got better every time. He was never far from me even when he was talking to his brothers. He had to be touching me or know where I was. The only thing that intruded on my happiness was when he had to leave and go to work at the bar. I knew he had to be there, but I missed him.

The other thing was I was going stir crazy. I helped to get the last of the wedding things ready for Sin and Lyric's big day and her bachelorette party this coming weekend. Other than that, I had nothing to do to occupy my time. The prospects and bunnies were responsible for cleaning the clubhouse, as well as helping cook a few meals. The ladies were cooking as well, a couple of times a week. I helped as much as I could with those too. I was teaching them how to make several Mexican dishes my mom had taught me.

It usually took no time to help clean the house with Lyric. I tried to do it all, but she wouldn't let me. I even tried to insist since she was working at the school every day. She wasn't having any of it. During the day, I was left alone at the compound with only the prospects. It was lonely but I didn't complain. They were protecting me, and I didn't want to sound ungrateful.

In a fit of boredom, I decided to just go online and see what classes were needed for the local nursing program. I knew Pitbull said I could go to school when this was all over, but I was afraid to believe it and get my hopes up. I was pleased to see they hadn't added any new requirements since the last time I'd looked.

After three days of this, I needed to get outside. I decided to take a walk and take Zeus and Bear with me. Well, Zeus and I walked, his majesty, Bear, expected to be carried. He was the funniest little thing. He thought he was the king, and we were his lowly subjects. That's what Sin liked to say. I think he was right. The three of us made our circuit and were near the gate when the delivery man stopped to make a delivery. I'd been getting my packages from the places where I'd ordered my new clothes. I was excited every time I opened a new one and showed Pitbull what I'd bought. I'd gotten over feeling guilty for spending his money when he had made love to me for the fifth or sixth time after having me model them for him.

I eagerly hurried toward the gate. Dash was on duty right now. He smiled when he saw us coming. He opened the gate only after the delivery man had set the box down and left. He carried it over to me. "Where do you want this, Luciana? At Sin's house or the clubhouse?"

"I can take it. I'll take it to the house. Thanks, Dash. Here, I brought you some water. It's hot." I handed him a bottle of ice water I'd grabbed as we passed the clubhouse. He took it and grinned.

"Thanks, Luci. You sure I can't get one of the guys to carry this for you?"

I was just about to tell him again that I was fine doing it when we heard the roar of an engine. Like what you would hear in a muscle car with a deep V-8 engine. We both turned and looked toward the gate. It was one you could see outside through what looked like glass windows or slits in it. Only they were bulletproof glass according to Pitbull.

An older Ford Mustang screeched to a stop right outside of the gate. The driver and passenger doors opened and out stepped two men. I recognized them immediately. They were two of Juan's main thugs, Miguel and Jesús. They usually went everywhere with him and did a lot of his dirty work. My heart began to pound.

They pulled out semi-automatic guns and fired at the gate. The sound was deafening. As a reflex, I dropped to the ground and screamed, as I threw my hands over my head. Zeus went insane and charged the gate. He was snarling and barking like he wanted to eat them. Bear was barking his little pug bark. Dash was swearing. It became a confusing whirlwind of noise. Terror welled up inside of me. They had found me. I was dead.

I had no idea I was still screaming until arms picked me up and ran with me to the clubhouse. As I started to struggle, I realized it was Blake. Brennan was holding the door open for him and talking on his phone to someone. I looked around for Dash. He was still down by the gate. I wanted to yell at him to get inside.

Blake took me to one of the couches and sat me down. He crouched in front of me. "Luciana, you need to stop. You're safe. They can't shoot through the gate." I took a shuddering breath and tried to stem the tears running down my face. I was shaking like a leaf. I realized I still had Bear clutched in my arms. I sat him down and he went running to his doggy bed. Brennan had run outside to Dash.

I grabbed Blake's hands. "Go make sure they're really alright! What if a bullet got through?" He shook his head.

"They can't, Luciana. It's made to withstand those. Dash and Brennan are fine. You're the one I'm worried about. You have to calm down before Pitbull gets here."

"Oh my God, we need to call them. They could be in danger." I tried to stand up, but he wouldn't let me.

"That's who Brennan was calling. They'll be headed here soon, and they'll keep their heads on a swivel. But if you're fucking this upset when he gets here, Pitbull will lose his shit. Let me get you a drink of water. Stay here." He jumped to his feet and hurried to the fridge under the bar.

I struggled to regulate my breathing and to get my tears under control. It wasn't going to do me any good to cry anyway. Somehow Juan had found out I was alive and that I was here with the Infidels. I'd have to leave for sure. No way would I stay and have these people be killed because of me. If I led Juan away from them, he might forget they helped me. I knew it was a big might, but I'd have to try. The thought of Pitbull or any of the others dying scared me worse than Juan getting his hands on me.

Blake handed me the opened bottle of water. I gulped down some as I started to plan in my head. I knew there was no way Pitbull would help me to leave. I'd have to do it when he wasn't here. It would be tough, but I could do it. No one could watch all of the walls every minute of the day. There was a hidden exit somewhere on the back side of the compound. Pitbull had mentioned it, but where it was or how it was hidden, I didn't know. I'd have to find it.

I lost track of time as I worked on my plan in my head. It wasn't until I heard the roar of more than one bike, that I realized how much time had passed since the shooting. Dash and Brennan had stayed outside. Blake had opened the door and Zeus had come in and was sitting next to me with his head on my knee.

I only had to wait a couple of minutes before the door was torn open and Pitbull raced in with his brothers behind him. He saw me immediately and rushed over to me. As he got to me, Zeus gave him a low growl. He stopped. "Listen, you furry bastard, I know you think she's yours, but she's not. Bite me and Sin will have a fur rug," he threatened. I ran a hand down Zeus' back. He relaxed.

"Behave, Zeus." He laid his head back down. Pitbull sat down beside me and took me in his arms. He squeezed me hard and kissed all over my face then my lips. I kissed him back. When he was done, he looked me in the eyes.

"Jesus, Luciana, what in the hell happened? Brennan and Dash said the delivery guy dropped a package and then left. After you guys brought it inside the fence, a car pulled up and two guys got out and opened fire. Did you recognize them?"

I shivered and nodded. "Yeah, I know them. Juan knows I'm alive and that I'm here, Pitbull. He knows and that means no one is safe. You need to get everyone back here and keep them under guard. I don't know if that'll stop him. He won't stop until he's got me."

"*Bebé*, you need to calm down. We knew he might find you. Not sure how, but this at least brought them out of hiding. Who were the guys? Was either of them him?"

"No, it wasn't Juan. It was Miguel and Jesús, his two lieutenants, I guess you'd call them. They're rarely anywhere without him. They do his dirty work. They don't care who gets hurt as long as they accomplish the job. They'll kill everyone to get to me. They're sadists and love this shit."

"Shh, you're getting more upset again. Tell us about them. Last names, where they live, those kinds of things."

"They're cousins and their last name is Gonzalez. I don't know much about them other than Juan relies heavily on them. They have been his friends for as long as I can remember. They have connections of some kind. He never said what. They're the ones he has do the really dirty or secret stuff. They live in an apartment in

the same building as ours, apartment three-eleven C."
I paused. I didn't want to say the next part, but they
needed to know.

"They're the ones he had strip me and take the
photos. They're the ones who wanted to rape me," I
whispered, so only he could hear me. Pitbull's face red-
dened with anger and then he was standing and swearing. His brothers had been quietly talking nearby, and
they swung around to ask what was wrong.

"It was the two who took the pics. They're Juan
Ramirez's right-hand men. I want to know how the fuck
they found her. Other than that one day on the bike,
which no one could have recognized her, she hasn't left
this place."

"Pitbull, we'll find out. Wrecker and Cuffs just
texted that they're on their way. They had to update
Boss. As soon as they get here, we'll see what we can find
out. Luciana, are you doing okay, babe? You look pretty
shook up," Sin asked kindly. I nodded to him. All their
eyes were on me.

"Sorry, I freaked out. The gunfire was hitting the
gate and all I could think was one of them would come
through it and hit me or Dash. I dropped to the ground
like a ninny. Poor Zeus went nuts."

"Dropping to the ground when you hear gunfire is
smart. Too bad Zeus isn't bulletproof, or we'd let him
loose on them," Sin joked. He looked at Zeus who was
snoring at my feet. His head was lying on top of my feet.
"Damn, Pitbull, you might have to adopt him. He loves
Lyric but he's adopted Luciana. I think he thinks she's

his toy or something."

The guys snickered. I pointed my finger at them. "Don't start with how little I am and that he thinks I'm a chew toy. I mean it," I warned them. I was trying hard not to laugh at their attempts to make me relax.

"Hell, I think he's convinced she's his pup. She could just sit on him and ride him like a horse," Saint teased as he winked at me. I gave him the finger. They kept up the banter for a few more minutes. When they were done, the door was opening and in came the other old ladies and the rest of the brothers. Wrecker and Cuff were with them. They had grim looks on their faces.

Everyone got serious. They took a seat and gestured for me to come over. I did, with Pitbull holding my hand. He squeezed it. Wrecker was the one to break the silence. "Luciana, we're sorry. Someone at the department found out there was no body found, and they got to asking around about where it was. We thought it was covered up, but we were wrong. We think that's how Juan found out. Not sure how he found you here though."

"A fucking cop told them! Are you kidding me? Who? I'm tired of the dirty bastards in that place. Does Boss know what happened?" Pitbull fired back at him.

"Yeah, we told him. He's pissed and on the tear. We need to know the names of those two men. Maybe that can help us find out more about who might have leaked it to them. We'd love to blame Detective Clinton, but who the hell knows. He's not the only one who we think is dirty," Wrecker said with a snarl on his face. I could see it was making him and Cuffs extra pissed. It had to be tough to work with people you couldn't trust, and to not know which ones it was.

"Their names are Miguel and Jesús Gonzalez. They live in the same apartment complex as us in apartment three-eleven C. They go everywhere with Juan most of the time. When he wants something extra nasty done or if he doesn't trust anyone else, they're the guys he has do it. They're the ones who took pictures of me when Juan punished me for helping Lila get away. Well, at least he thought I might have. If he knew I had for sure, he'd probably have sold me that day."

Pitbull looked so angry, I thought he might blow a blood vessel or something. I touched his arm. He glanced at me and tried to smile. "Please, don't get so upset. It's who he's become. They could have done worse. Now that they know I'm here, what does that mean?" I wanted to see if they would suggest sending me away.

"Well, we're not fucking sending you away, that's for sure. It complicates things a little, but we can handle it. You can't go out again with us. Phantom, do we have cameras that look a distance up and down the road? Or are they just at the gate and along the walls?"

"Mainly the walls, but it won't be hard to put up a few more to watch the road and see who or what is coming at us. Should have done it anyway. I'll get on them first thing. And I'll start digging into the two Gonzalez thugs. May take a bit since Gonzalez is such a common surname around here."

"We'll tell the Time Served ladies we're not gonna have the bachelorette party. No use drawing more attention to us," Lyric said.

I protested. "No! I don't want to have this affect your lives any more than it already has! You deserve this, Lyric. Surely, you can go there, and I'll stay here," I told the guys.

"*Bebé*, we'll figure something out," Pitbull said. I knew he was trying to appease me, but I hated that I was ruining something so important for Lyric and Sin. Not only was it supposed to be us ladies doing her bachelorette party, but the guys were going to later patch in Blake and Dash. No way should that get postponed either.

I stood up. "No, I refuse to have it messed up because of me! If it's too dangerous to have anyone leave, then I need to be the one to go. You didn't sign on for this when you helped me. This is becoming too dangerous. I should have left when I had the chance!" I shouted the last part and then took off for the door. I needed to be alone and to think. I'd ruined my chances to sneak off, but I couldn't stand this. Why did everything seem to go to shit around me?

As I rushed out of the clubhouse, I heard Pitbull shout my name and the others protesting. I didn't stop or slow down. I veered away from Sin's house and went toward the back part of the compound. There were a lot of acres back there that I hadn't explored yet. As I ran, I heard the sound of pounding feet behind me. I looked back over my shoulder and there was Pitbull chasing after me. Damn, I knew I couldn't outrun him. His damn legs were too long, but I tried anyway. I wanted to be alone.

I didn't make it far before he grabbed me and clutched me to his chest. The bastard wasn't even breathing hard. I struggled to get loose, but he held me tighter. "Settle down, Luciana. I'm not going to let you go off alone. Knowing you, your ass would be trying to climb the damn wall. You're not leaving me. Do you hear me?" he growled in my ear. I sagged in his arms. All the fight was draining out of me.

"Why not? You could do so much better than me, Cole. Find someone who can bring happiness and not danger to you and your friends. Just let me go," I half-sobbed. The thought of never seeing him again made me want to scream and die at the same time. He swung me around to face him. He lifted my face so he could see my eyes.

His eyes were alive with anger. "I don't ever want to hear you say that again, do you hear me? I fucking love you, Luciana. I plan to spend the rest of my life with you. No way will I let you go. Danger is nothing new to me and my brothers. I'll fight this whole damn town if I have to. Don't even think about leaving, because I guarantee you, I'll find you. And when I do, I'll spank that ass until you can't sit. We knew there was a chance Juan would figure out you were alive and even where you were. We'll handle it."

His mouth came down on mine and he kissed me almost desperately. I kissed him back the same. We couldn't get enough of each other. He lifted and carried me. I didn't know where we were until he pressed my back against a building. We were outside the trailers where the members stayed. His place was here. We weren't staying in it because they were having the bedroom redone. He tugged at my waistband. I gasped as he jerked down my pants and panties. His fingers slid between my legs. I was wet and he could feel it. He groaned.

"Fuck, yeah, I need you now." He kneeled and pulled my pants the rest of the way off. I looked around, worried someone would see us. No one was in sight. He stood back up and kissed me again. I felt his hands on his belt and zipper. I helped him to get them undone and pushed down enough I could free his cock. He was hard and I could feel the precum on the head.

He lifted me in his arms and then slammed me down on his cock. I gave a scream as he stretched me. It didn't hurt but there was a bite to it. He was big and I was small. He moaned and held still. "I'm sorry, did I hurt you, *bebé*?"

"No, it just stings a little. Don't stop. I want you to take me hard," I begged him. I was desperate to have him inside of me, making me forget all the shit happening around us. His fingers bit into my ass as he lifted me and then brought me back down. I wrapped my arms around his neck and my legs as far around his waist as I could. I used my thigh muscles to help lift. It was a hard and fast coupling. Both of us were trying to come fast. I felt almost insane with the need to orgasm and have him fill me.

As I got close, I bit down on his shoulder. He

growled and slammed into me harder and even faster. His teeth and mouth sucked at the skin on my shoulder. "Come for me, *mi alma.* I need to feel you squeezing the life out of me." I tightened my inner muscles, and he groaned. I was coming.

"Oh God, Cole!" I screamed as he thrust and then he came. His cock jerked over and over as he filled me. I couldn't stop milking him. He grunted and gasped as the last jerk came to an end. I was hanging loosely in his arms. I felt boneless and sleepy. He kissed my mouth gently.

"Don't ever take this away from me, Luciana. If you do, I'll die. I can't live without you."

"I want to make you safe, but I think I'd die if I left. God forgive me, I can't do it even if I should," I whispered.

Pitbull: Chapter 11

It had been three days since the attack at the gate of the compound. I still wanted blood. It didn't make me any less blood thirsty when I heard what Phantom had discovered about Miguel and Jesús. Come to find out, they were related to a cop at the department. His name was Anthony Gonzalez, and they were second cousins.

I wanted to go down to the police station and beat the hell out of him. Wrecker and Cuffs had kept me from doing it. They said they didn't have proof he'd been the one to do it; however, he'd been one of three asking questions about the body. One of the others was Detective Clinton and the third one was Officer Hannigan. No surprise there, we knew they all had to be dirty.

As for how they found out she was with us, we think it was a lucky guess. When they were snooping, they saw that Wrecker's name was on the report of the officer who'd filed the false report. They must have concluded we had to be hiding her. It was a good guess and just bad luck she was out where they could see her that day. I couldn't confine her to the damn house or clubhouse. She had to have a little freedom and sunshine.

Phantom had gotten the other cameras installed. Now, if anyone was coming, we'd see them as soon as they rounded the turns in either direction. As if this wasn't enough, the alerts went off in the bunker. Last night, two men were there. They appeared to be alone and weren't carrying or transporting anything obvious, but they had used the bunker and passageways to get to the shack on the other side of the highway. We needed to figure out how to get eyes and ears in that bar. Problem was, none of us could do it. We'd be recognized in a heartbeat. We were going to talk about it with Boss and his guys when they came over later.

Today was the ladies' bachelorette party for Lyric and the guys were going to relax, drink, and have some fun with Sin. Later, we'd all get together and celebrate Dash and Blake's patching in. They had no idea we were going to be doing that. We'd decided not to wait until after the wedding next week.

The guys were assigned to stay at the clubhouse. The ladies were going to be at Sara's house. She and Jackie, with some help from Luciana and Skye, had decorated Sara's house for the party. God knows what they'd done. They were nuts, and I'd heard Luciana on the phone laughing with Paula. If those women were involved, it would be doubly insane. Luckily, we weren't allowing any outsiders, or they would have probably brought in strippers.

The growling of bikes got my attention as Boss and his crew pulled up. Omen let them in the gate. As soon as they cleared it, he shut it. While they entered, we had Dash and Brennan stand there with their guns. We weren't taking any chances. If Juan and his guys were going to try to hit us when we had a bunch coming in, we'd take care of their asses.

I grinned when I saw Pop pulling in on his bike. The man was eighty and as contrary as hell, but he was still riding his damn bike. He was the one who'd helped Boss and all his fellow brothers and even a few sisters build their own bikes when they got out of prison.

My brothers and the ladies came out of the club-house to greet them. There were a lot of half-hugs and back slaps. The women all hugged each other. They were smiling and chatting away. I went over to Luciana and took her hand. "I want to introduce you to someone you haven't met yet." She nodded and came with me. I took her over to where Pop was standing. He saw us coming and his eyes started to twinkle. He got this flirty grin on his face. Damn, maybe I should have thought this through more.

Before I could introduce Luciana, he stepped up to us and took her hand. He raised it and kissed the back of it. "Well, hello, *señorita*. How do you feel about older men? I'm available and a much better catch than these assholes. I'll give you diamonds and orgasms." I heard Boss choke and the others sputter, trying to stop from laughing. Luciana was speechless as she stared at him in shock.

"Pop, I swear to God, you're gonna wish those guys killed you when they shot you," Boss growled.

"You keep hitting on our women and you'll disap-pear old man," Chef told him. The rest of us lost it. Luci-ana was now smiling and shaking her head.

"I don't think I can handle you. You'd be too much for me. I'm just not enough of a woman for you, but it's a pleasure to meet you, Pop," she said as she gave him a kiss on the cheek. Pop beamed and looked at the rest of us.

"See, she knows. Now, since this one seems to be hanging tight to you, you must be Pitbull's woman."

"Yeah, she's mine, Pop. This is Luciana Ramirez. Luciana, this is Bill White. We all call him Pop. He owns the junkyard, and the parts and towing company in town. He's shameless but someone you can trust."

"He's just worried you'll fall in love with me. I'm not shameless. I just know quality and beauty when I see it. I can't figure out how these guys keep finding such women. Must be my good influence." This had the Time Served guys razzing him and telling him how full of shit he was. The other ladies joined us by then and were teasing and hugging Pop. He was in his element. It was good to see him looking healthy again. It had been a few rough months after he was shot and then had a heart attack. He was now back home and out of rehab. Sis and Brea kept a close eye on him. Sis worked for him which made keeping an eye on him easier.

With that out of the way, we were quick to separate and go our separate ways. The ladies walked off laughing as they headed over to Sara's. Sin watched them go. "I think I should be worried. Mom and that bunch could plot world domination."

"Boy, you have no idea. Where's your uncle Harvey?" Pop asked. Harvey was one of his cronies in the old geezer club.

"He's out of town this weekend. He'll be here next

week for the wedding. Come on, let's get this show on the road." We all went inside. We were just gonna drink and relax, maybe play some pool. Nothing crazy, but we'd do that after we talked about what to do with that dive bar, the Liar's Lair. We got Pop settled with the prospects. He got into a deep discussion with Omen almost immediately. The rest of us, along with the Time Served guys went into church. Sin brought the meeting to order.

"We need to figure out what to do about the Liar's Lair bar. You know that Preacher and Phantom saw two guys in the bunker and tunnels run over there last night. We need to find a way to get eyes and ears into that place and soon. Someone that they won't give a second thought to being there."

"Someone that's a bouncer or bartender maybe," Captain suggested.

"That would be ideal, but we have to find someone we can trust. They'll probably be leery around any guys with tats or looking too rough. We could send one of the prospects, but they might be known to be with us. What about the guys who work at some of Pop's places like Soda, Fish, or Chewie?" Saint asked Boss.

"Yeah, they might work, but they've worked for quite a while for Pop, that most people know it. The more I think about it, I don't think that'll work. Shit, we need to find someone who can do it and blend the hell in. I want to know what the hell they're doing over there. Whatever it is, you know it's not good. Why don't we think about it and get back to each other by next weekend?" Sin suggested. All of us voiced our agreement with the plan. We'd love to have someone immediately, but we had to be smart about it. Besides, whoever we put in there, we wanted them to be as safe as possible.

"Any luck on proving Officer Gonzalez or one of the others fed that information on Luciana to Juan?" I asked Boss. He sighed.

"No, but I've set up each of them. I told them different things, or I should say, I let them overhear it. If one of those gets back to me, then I'll know for sure who it was. For now, all we can do is wait, watch, and run down any leads. Keep her here and don't let her go anywhere. It sucks for her, but it's the best way to keep her safe."

"God, can we talk about something else? This is pissing me the hell off. All we seem to do is go over the same shit. Until we get new information or a break, we're beating a dead horse. Let's just put it aside for the moment. I didn't tell you guys this, but later, we're going to be patching in Dash and Blake. They've been with us for over a year," Sin told them. I knew Luciana's situation was weighing almost as much on him as it was me. Anything that threatened the club or his mom and woman made him crazy. Just like it did the rest of us.

"Alright, let's go get this party started. I suggest we go sneak over to Sara's to see what they're up to, because I caught Blue, Paula, Jenn, and Brea all whispering and cackling about something yesterday. They wouldn't tell me what, but I knew it had to do with today. Damn near made me stay home. They can be scary. I hate to say that, but you guys need to sleep with one eye open,"

Stamp told Boss, Hook, and Chef.

"Oh yeah, and what about Frankie? She's just as scary," Bug fired back. Stamp gave them an innocent stare.

"Why would I be afraid of Frankie? I'm not sleeping with her. She's too damn high maintenance for me."

"Bullshit. Come on, you're all in there, we know it," Kitty needled him. No matter how much they teased him, Stamp wouldn't say one way or the other if he was hooking up with Frankie. To divert attention, Stamp turned his attention to Captain.

"What about you and the lovely Jackie? You seem to be awful chummy with her. Is Executioner about to get a stepdaddy-in-law?"

Ex looked at Captain. All Captain did was shake his head. "No, nothing like that. We're just friends and I don't mean friends with benefits. Jackie's great and all, but that's not our relationship." I wasn't sure if he was telling the truth or not. He sure seemed to talk to her a lot, and they had a good time together.

After growing tired of giving them a hard time, we decided to call the meeting quits. I wanted to relax. I hoped Luciana had a good time with the ladies. She was so stressed over the whole thing with her brother that she was having trouble sleeping at night. Not that she would admit that was what kept her up. She needed to learn that she could share her burdens with someone, me.

All of us got up and filed out to the common room.

Pop and Omen were still talking. With everyone secure inside and the cameras set to alert us to anyone coming past the compound, we'd told all the prospects they could join us. They still would be doing gopher work, but they deserved some fun too.

Luciana:

I was staring around at the whole setup for Lyric's bachelorette party. Though I'd helped with some of it, the whole thing together was rather overwhelming. First thing I looked at was all the decorations. They'd found blow-ups and streamers with cocks hanging from them. They were hilarious. They'd made gummies that were various flavors shaped like cocks as well.

I heard them talking about some naughty games they were going to play. Sara had baked and made Lyric a cake. It was shaped like a cock with balls. She didn't seem to be fazed by the fact that all this teasing about cocks was with the woman who was marrying her son. She was thrilled to be welcoming her into her family.

We sat down to play a few of those games. One of my favorites ended up being a dirty version of Pictionary. Lyric's friend, Kerrigan, had replaced the normal cards with ones that said things like *doggy, blow job, bondage* and they got worse from there. The laughing ended up in tears with some of them. After we finished with the games, we moved on to gifts. As you would imagine, there was a lot of sexy lingerie. I got to pay her back for what she did to me when I first came to the compound.

Jackie teased her. "Lyric, if you wear any of these

for Sin, I guarantee you that you'll be pregnant on your honeymoon. Those will drive him insane, though I don't think he has a problem being that way without them. Every time he looks at you, I swear the temperature jumps in the room."

Lyric blushed and laughed. "I have to admit, I can't resist him. His road name is apt. He can make any woman sin. Sorry, Sara, but it's true."

"Honey, I know my son. He's been attracting the ladies since he was a teenager, but none of them hold a candle to you. My son loves you so much. I couldn't ask for more, or a better daughter." She gave Lyric a hug.

We all said "aww" as they did. Along with the lingerie were the sex toys. There were a few vibrators that had me considering seeing if they might be fun to use. Not sure how I would bring that up to Pitbull. I'd be embarrassed to ask him. I was looking at one of them when Blue sidled up to me.

"See anything you like?"

I hesitated. I didn't know her as well as the other ladies. I remember how jealous I'd been when I met her the first time and she'd hugged Pitbull. She was beautiful, and I felt somewhat insecure around her. I think it was because she was one of the single ones in the group and she was very outgoing. I could see how men would flock to her.

"I-I don't think—" She stopped me.

"Hey, you don't need to tell me. I tend to be nosy, but I can say, you can't go wrong with one of these even if you have a man. It can be fun to introduce some things."

"I'm not sure if he'd want to do this or not. I really don't have experience with these," I admitted.

"Luciana don't be embarrassed that you're not experienced. I don't see Pitbull caring and that's what matters. But make sure you communicate with him on what you need or want. He should do the same. If you don't, your relationship will suffer for it. Believe me, I know. In a way, I kind of envy you, your innocence. Mine is long gone. Now, I'm just getting my life back on track and leaving men alone. You ladies seem to be lucking out." She said the last part louder, so the other women could hear her. Sara 'tsked' at her.

"As if you couldn't too. Don't rule out men yet. I think you'll find one when you least expect it. I can't wait to see who you end up with. We'll be planning your wedding soon too."

"Oh, hell no, not this woman! Men find me to be too much work. I'm not needy but I don't want to be someone's second or third priority, which is selfish. Enough about me, we have Skye getting married soon as well. Can't wait for that party and Luciana will be right after that."

"What do you mean, I'll be after her? Pitbull and I aren't getting married," I told her in shock. She gave me a secret smile.

"Babe, I see you getting a ring in the not-too-distant future. He's gone on you. No one will ever stack up, and who knows, Jackie may be before you," she said as she glanced at Jackie.

Jackie's mouth fell open, and she stared at Blue like she was nuts. "What in the world are you talking about, Blue? I'm not seeing anyone."

"What about that delicious Captain? I see him talking to you all the time."

"We're just friends," Jackie explained.

"Oookay, if you say so. Then what about Omen?" When she said Omen's name, Jackie got quiet and pink stained her cheeks. She didn't say anything for a couple of seconds then she hurried to cover herself.

"Omen isn't anyone other than a friend too. I'm not looking for a man and seriously, why would Omen want a woman almost ten years older than him with three kids, one of which is already grown? No, I plan to spend my days being a grandma." She flashed a smile at Skye. Skye was pregnant with her and Executioner's first baby.

Jackie hastily added, "Besides, I'm still married. My husband left ten years ago and never divorced me. I have no idea where he is, so I can't serve him with divorce papers." I gasped. I had no idea she was still married to Skye's dad. I knew that he'd left and they had struggled, but to still be married to him?

"Mom, Ex and the guys are working on it. They'll find him and you can finally be completely free to be with someone if you want," Skye told her. She wrapped her arm around Jackie.

"I know and I appreciate it, but I don't think they'll find him. He's in a hole somewhere and good riddance. I don't need to be divorced. I'm not planning to be seeing a man," Jackie told her firmly. I thought that would be a shame. If anyone deserved a man in her life to help her and love her, it was Jackie.

Sara stepped in at this point and shifted our attention back to the party. "It's time for the Drink If game." A few groaned. Of course, Skye couldn't drink. She'd take shots of cider. As they asked the funny questions and we answered or drank, I felt a warm glow. We were all laughing when Blue stood up.

"I think we should crash the bachelor party at the clubhouse. I wonder what they're doing. We couldn't have strippers, which means they shouldn't have them either. Wanna go peek?"

"We shouldn't," Lyric said, but I saw the excited look on her face.

"Yes, we should. Tell her Sara," Blue insisted.

"I think we should. In fact, I think the poor guys deserve some entertainment. Do any of you girls know how to dance like a stripper?" Everyone stopped talking and looked at her as if she'd lost her mind.

"What? Surely someone other than me knows how to dance? Anyone pole dance?" They were all shaking their heads when I slowly put up my hand. This got all their attention.

"You know how to pole dance? Spill! How in the hell?" Blue practically shrieked.

"I took classes a few years back at the gym. A lady taught them. They're great for keeping fit. She'd been a stripper," I explained. I didn't tell them that I'd been her best student.

"Show us," Lyric said excitedly.

"No, that was a long time ago."

"We don't care. Show us," she insisted. She pulled out her phone and messed with it. She found what she was looking for and smiled at me. "Here's some music. Just show us the moves. I know we don't have a pole."

I blame it on the alcohol for what happened next. As the music started, I closed my eyes and let go of my inhibitions. I swayed, dipped, shook, and shimmied with total abandonment. When the song was over and I opened my eyes, they were all standing around me with their mouths hanging open.

"Oh my God! You have to do that for Pitbull! Even if no one else sees it, you have to for him. He'll be on you so fast, you'll be having a baby next," Paula said.

"No babies for us for a couple of years. We agreed," I told her. She got a satisfied look on her face.

"So, you've talked about kids, have you? Yep, Blue's right. The ring will be coming soon." This got the rest of them talking about me. They were predicting after Skye's August wedding; I'd be up for September. I told them they were nuts.

In the end, we did sneak over to the clubhouse to spy on the guys. I told them I wasn't dancing, and they agreed, but the urge to spy mixed with alcohol had us trying to be quiet as we walked from Sara's house to the clubhouse. We'd have to see how the big bad bikers were partying.

Luciana: Chapter 12

We came into the clubhouse through the back door. Sara was tiptoeing and holding her finger up to her mouth like she was telling us to be quiet. This had us giggling. Why she was worried, I had no idea. I could hear the loud music coming from the common room and the guys talking and laughing. We got to the end of the hall and peeked around the corner. After I did, I wished I hadn't.

They weren't alone after all. Barbie, Shy, and Tabby Cat were there, and they were doing their hardest to get the men's attention. They were grinding on each other and dancing. Their movements were pure enticement. I glanced around to see what the guys were doing. They were mainly over by the pool tables.

I saw several of the single guys watching the bunnies. It looked like Sin, Executioner, Pitbull, Boss, Hook, and Chef were ignoring them. That was a good thing to see until they must have grown tired of the single guys not doing anything and the bunnies stopped dancing. We watched as they slunk over by the taken guys. Barbie was eyeing Pitbull. She'd stayed away since he'd told her off before, but today it looked like she wasn't gonna listen.

She pressed up against his back and ran her hands

up it. He whipped around and took a step back. I saw his mouth moving but I couldn't hear what he said. He frowned and looked at her with a pissed-off expression. She had a pouty look on her face and was batting her lashes at him like an idiot. Anger flashed through my whole body. The alcohol let it come fully to the surface. Before I knew what I was doing, I was across the common room, pulling her away from Pitbull. I saw his surprised look in my peripheral vision, but I didn't acknowledge it. I was tired of her and this shit.

"Are you stupid or just hard-headed? He told you that he was with me, and he's not interested! Have some fucking self-respect and stop chasing someone who doesn't want you. You're making other women look bad," I told her with a bite to my tone.

She gave me a surprised look that almost instantly changed to an upset one. She sneered at me. "He's just playing with you. He may be fucking you now, but these little dalliances never last long. He always comes back to me. I can give him what others can't." Her words cut me to the bone because she was tapping into my deepest fear—that I couldn't be everything he wanted or needed.

"You're full of shit, Barbie! Pitbull doesn't have dalliances. And yeah, he's screwed you, but that's what you're here for, to screw. Don't make it out to be more than it is," Sara said acidly.

"Why are you all so protective of her? She's nothing but a drug dealer along with her brother. She's probably been letting him prostitute her too. She's nothing but trash," Barbie quickly flung back at her. I froze. She knew about me dealing and my brother. How? None of us had talked about it around the bunnies. Had one of the guys told her? She sneered at me with disdain. My stomach rolled.

Even if she was doing it to be a bitch, she had a point. I was the sister of a dealer and I'd been one, even if it was against my will. Plenty of people in town knew me and Juan. They'd always see me like that no matter what I did. No way they'd want me as a nurse, even if I could somehow swing going to school.

I told her quietly, "You're right. My brother is a dealer, and I was one too, but I never did it because I wanted to do it. I had to or suffer the consequences. Ones that would be worse than death to me. I paid the price for not doing as I was told several times, but I never was a whore, nor will I be. Can you say the same? When was the last time you sacrificed to help someone other than yourself? You're a selfish bitch, Barbie. I'm not going to tell you again to stay away from Pitbull," I warned her.

She put her hand on her hip and jutted it out. She looked me up and down since she was taller than me. Her upper lip curled up and she asked, "What're you gonna do about it, if I don't?"

Now, I might be a nice person most of the time, someone who tries to do the right thing. Someone who didn't want to do illegal or unethical things. However, I'd also been living, since the death of my parents, in what essentially was the hood in Tenillo. A girl didn't walk down the street in the daytime without protection.

It had been automatic when I put on my clothes, to slip my knife in my pocket. Some women didn't leave home without their makeup. I didn't leave without my knife. I'd threatened more than one guy with it. They never expected it from a little woman like me. Without a second thought, I pulled it out and flicked it open. It was sharp and somehow survived the beating that night. I'd found it in my jeans pocket. I held it up. Her eyes got round, and the noise dropped to almost nothing. Someone had even turned down the music.

"I'll cut you. That's what people like me do when they get shit from people like you. Don't think because I'm usually nice and quiet that you can fuck with me. You won't like what I can become," I warned her. She stepped back and I saw the color drain from her face. I slowly glanced around at the others. All of them seemed to be stunned. Pitbull was looking at me like he had no idea who I was. Shit, maybe I'd just blown my chances with him, but he had to know the whole me.

"*Bebé*, put away the knife. Barbie, I suggest you shut the hell up. I told you more than once, I'm with Luciana, and I'm staying with her. That means I won't be with other women. Move on. Luciana, why don't we go to the house?"

I shook my head. "Nope, I'm fine right where I am, though I think a few more drinks are in order." I moved around Sara and went to the bar. Brennan was behind it. I ordered a shot of tequila. He looked at Pitbull questioningly first, then must have gotten his permission because he poured me one. I tossed back the first one, as Pitbull slid in next to me. He gave me a once-over.

He reached over and took my knife out of my hand. I'd forgotten I was even holding it. He closed it and then slipped it into his pocket.

"Afraid I'll slice up your friend? Got a good look at what you're getting, didn't you?" I asked him snidely. He frowned.

"Luciana, what's wrong? Why're you acting like this? Is it the alcohol? What do you mean about getting a good look? I know you, *cariño*," he told me softly. I shook my head.

"I'm from the damn Haven, Pitbull. You think the people in this town don't know it. That they won't judge me and you for it? They'll always wonder why you would choose to be with me. The knife I've had for a long time. It's how you stay safe in your own damn neighborhood. I've had it save me more than once."

His face registered his disbelief and anger. He took the next shot out of my hand and he drank it. He slammed down the glass. "Tell me about defending yourself with a knife. Who? When? How many times? And as for people judging you or me, fuck them. They don't know us. I couldn't care less what they think."

"What if it affects the bar because you're with me? People could choose not to go there. That impacts the whole club. You might not have known about me before that night in the Hangout, but a lot of people would have seen or known things. I don't want to drag you down into that. I didn't think of that. All of you have done so much for me. Maybe we should take a step back and rethink this."

It killed me to say that to him, but I wanted what would be best for Pitbull. A tiny voice inside of me said that I wouldn't be the best thing. I loved him enough to let him go, so he could find a happily ever after with someone else. I waited to see how he would react or what he would say. I didn't wait long.

Pitbull:

I was stunned at what Luciana had done. She'd threatened Barbie with a knife then took a shot and started talking about having to defend herself with it more than once and that maybe we should rethink being together. What in the hell had gotten into her? I knew she loved me, even if we'd only known each other for a very short time. Not long enough to be in love, in most people's minds; however, I knew it was possible because I loved her. No way was I going to let her get away. She was my present and future happiness.

The guys and the other ladies stood quietly, observing us. I knew they were just as stunned as I was. I didn't want to do this in front of them. This was between me and Luciana. I stood up then leaned down and swept her off the barstool and into my arms. She tried to struggle out of them. I held her tighter.

"Stay still. I'm not putting you down. We're gonna have a talk." I turned and walked to the door. Boomer was holding the door open. He gave me a sympathetic look. I gave him a chin lift in thanks. Once outside, I wasted no time getting to Sin and Lyric's house. I couldn't wait for my trailer to be finished with the renovations. I wanted us to have space for ourselves, though I was thankful to them for allowing us to stay there ra-

PITBULL'S ENSLAVEMENT: ARES INFIDELS MC #3

ther than in the clubhouse.

I juggled her to get the door open and shut, then took her up the stairs to our room. I sat her down on the edge of the bed. She hadn't said a word. She stared at me with a blank look on her face, which worried me. I kicked off my boots and then kneeled and took off hers. While I was at her feet, I began our conversation.

"Talk to me, Luciana. What happened back there? What set you off so much? You know Barbie was being a bitch to get a rise out of you. You know I want nothing to do with her."

"For how long?"

"For how long, what?"

"For how long will you want nothing to do with her? You said before that we'd be exclusive, but what happens when you get bored with me? Maybe I can't give you what you want sexually. Or if we do have kids and I can't have sex for a while, then what? Will you sneak off to the clubhouse and to one of those bedrooms and fuck her? Will all your brothers know you're cheating on me, but no one tells me because it's against the code?"

I almost sat back on my ass. Where was this coming from? "*Cariño*, why would you say that or even think it? I love you. There's no cheating when you love someone and commit to a relationship. Do you think Sin and Executioner go around cheating on their women? No, they don't, and neither will I. I have no doubt you can more than satisfy me sexually. When we have kids and you can't have sex, we'll find other ways to give each other pleasure. Now, tell me about the knife. When have you had to use it?" Those remarks were driving me crazy. I wanted to know who and when, so I could go kill every one of them.

She looked down at her hands and twisted them together. She avoided my eyes. I wanted to tell her to look at me, but maybe this was the only way she could say it. My stomach was twisting up in knots. "Just like I said, I live in the Haven. If you're a woman out on the street and not a prostitute or willing to be with anyone who comes along, you protect yourself. Being Juan's sister gave me a tiny bit of protection, but not much. I started carrying the knife soon after we moved there when I was sixteen. I was seen as a prime target. I was accosted on the street one day when I was going to the store. It was noon and I thought I'd be safe. I was wrong." She paused and took a deep breath. After she did, she remained silent.

"Keep going. What happened when you were accosted?"

"The man dragged me into the nearby alley and had me up against the wall. He was trying to kiss me and tearing at my clothes. I lucked out. An older man in the neighborhood, who was actually nice and decent, happened along and came to my rescue. He was the one to give me the knife and told me never to be without it. I never was. I got smarter about leaving the house alone, but I had to sometimes. I had a few run-ins after that, but the knife saved me. I think they heard about it because it's been a long time since it's happened."

I wanted to hit something. She'd almost been raped

just because she was walking down the damn street. This only made the need to clean up Tenillo and especially the Haven more necessary.

"Did you know the men who attacked you or threatened you?" She hesitated and then nodded. "Good, I want you to write their names down later for me." She shook her head, and a worried look came over her face. I reached up and took it in my hand and held her still. "You'll do it, and I'll make sure they don't do this to anyone else. Now, what caused you to pull that knife on Barbie? Why didn't you have the knife the night you were at the bar? You could have used it on me."

She sat up straighter with a shocked look on her face. "I wouldn't have used it on you. You were just protecting your bar. I understood it, even if you did scare me to death. You didn't harm me or try anything. I did have the knife. It was in my boot. As for Barbie, she pulled her shit at the wrong time. I don't know why it made me so mad, but I know that if she keeps it up, it'll happen again. Staying here and being around the women you've slept with is going to be hard. If they act like her, then it's impossible."

"*Bebé*, I know it's hard, but I would never sleep with her or anyone else."

"You don't know how hard it is. How would you like it if I had been sexually active with any of the guys here? And we would live here, and I'd be around them every day? Are you telling me that wouldn't bother you?"

I stopped to think over what she said. My mind automatically wanted to reject the idea, and I got this angry feeling. She was right, I wouldn't fucking like it. "You're right. I wouldn't. However, I would trust you not to sleep with them. I can't get rid of the bunnies as much as I might want to. They're here for my single brothers. All I can tell you is if Barbie persists, she's gone. That's the best I can do. One last thing, what is this shit about people judging me for being with you? No one in their right mind would do that. Those that would, don't matter."

She leaned over and placed her hands on either side of my face. She looked at me with such a serious and sad look that I wanted to kiss the look away. "You don't know that. My brother isn't exactly unknown. Not everyone in the Haven is a bad person, Cole. They just can't afford to live anywhere else. Most of them won't even say hi to me if they saw me and I said it first. They turn their backs on me or sneer. I'm trash by association, and I had to deal at the end. Some of them have to know what I was doing. I don't want you to be judged, or for it to hurt you or the club in any way. That's why we need to take a step back and think this through. I won't do that to you. I love you too much."

I couldn't take it anymore. I stood up and tugged her to her feet. As she stood, giving me a puzzled and nervous look, I leaned down and took her mouth. It wasn't a nice kiss. It was one filled with passion, desperation, love, and anger. My hands buried themselves in her hair and I tugged on it, causing her to hiss. I wanted it to sting, so she wouldn't forget this. As I devoured her mouth and nipped her lips with my teeth then thrust my tongue inside her mouth, I ground my cock into her stomach. She shuddered. I was going to show her why she'd never be rid of me. I broke the kiss and whipped off her top then unhooked her bra to fling it across the room. She was breathing hard. "Cole, wait—"

"Shh, it's my turn to talk." I slipped off my colors and laid it on the end of the bed before I tugged off my t-shirt. I gave her another kiss before I finished undressing both of us. When we were naked, I lifted her and laid her in the middle of the bed. I crawled up between her legs after I pulled them apart.

I took in the sight in front of me. Her beautiful pussy was puffy and glistening. I could see her cream had her slick. Any other time, I liked to take my time and give her at least one orgasm with my mouth, but I didn't have the patience to wait today. I needed to be inside of her this instant.

I slid my arms under her legs and hooked them behind her knees, so I could lift them up and spread her more. I then cupped her plump ass and squeezed before lifting it off the bed. I lined up at her entrance. I took time to look her in the eyes, as I slowly sank into her tight pussy. She moaned and shook as I did. I could see the passion on her face.

When I was firmly planted inside of her and could feel her damn cervix, I held still. "Now, you listen to me." I pulled back and then slammed back inside of her. She whimpered and her hands came up to touch her tight nipples. "I. Don't. Care. What. Anyone. Says. I. Love. You. I. Won't. Ever. Stop. Or. Give. You. Up." With each word, I slammed into her to punctuate my words. She thrashed her head back and forth on the mattress. Her breathing became more erratic and labored. She was twisting the hell out of her nipples. I lowered my head and sucked one into my mouth and bit down.

"Oh my God, Cole! Please, I'm about to lose my mind," she pleaded. I could tell she was close to coming. Even though I was too, I stopped moving and then raised up.

"Tell me you won't leave me. Tell me you'll stay and be my wife and the mother of my children for the rest of our lives. Tell me no matter what some people say, you'll always know I love you and couldn't care less. Tell me." I had to grit my teeth to keep from bringing both of us the relief we were desperate for, but I had to have this first. If she left me, it would be the end of me.

She looked at me with pleading eyes. "I love you too, Cole. So much it hurts. I hate the idea of me causing you pain. It could happen. I'd love to be your wife one day and have your children. I'll stay but only if you're one hundred percent certain you want me and won't ever let anyone come between us, because if that happened, it would kill me."

That was all I needed to hear. I pulled back and then pounded back inside. As I lost control and fucked her like this might be the last time, her whole body shook. She was back to playing with her breasts. "Pull them harder. Knead them like I would. I wanna see you really love them," I panted. My hands were busy kneading her ass. She did as I asked.

As she wound tighter, I slipped my finger down to tease her clit and get it slick with her cream. She was soaked. She cried out and pushed into my thrusts. Her face and chest were flushed. Her breath was ragged. I felt her tightening and I knew she was about to go off. Just as she tightened to an almost painful level, I slid my wet finger down and breached her asshole with it. I only put in the tip, but it had her screaming.

Her startled eyes met mine, I waited to see if she would tell me to stop. If she did, I would. She finally nodded and I sped up. She whimpered and I pushed my finger deeper. She was tight like I knew she would be. I wiggled my finger and teased it in and out as I kept up the pounding. She suddenly tensed and clamped down on me as she screamed out her pleasure and she came. She came hard and long, milking my cock as I shouted her name and shot my load of cum deep. I came over and over. It felt like it was coming from somewhere deep inside of me. I knew if she hadn't been on birth control, I'd have gotten her pregnant with that release. A tiny piece of me was disappointed she was.

When we were both done. I eased my finger out of her then my softening cock. I dropped down beside her and tugged her into my arms. I kissed her mouth softly. She teased my lips with her tongue. She eventually broke the kiss.

"I love you, Cole. I'm sorry I went crazy and ruined the party! They were going to give Blake and Dash their colors. Damn."

"They'll forgive us. This was important too. What did you think of that?"

"What?"

"The finger in your ass. Did you like that?" I wanted

to know for future reference. If she liked it, then I'd explore it further with her. If she didn't, I wouldn't do it again.

She gave me a shy look then nodded. "I did like it. At first it shocked me, and it burned, but after I got used to it, it felt really good. I never thought that would feel good. It made me get off harder, I think," she confessed.

"Good. If you don't like anything I do, tell me to stop, and we'll never do it again. But if you like that, there's more we can try."

"You mean toys and—"

"I mean toys and if you want, then one day my cock."

"Does that feel good for you? I'd think it would hurt too much for the woman."

"It does burn and hurt some for you, but if I do my job right, it quickly turns to nothing but pleasure for you. And yes, it does feel good to me, but only if it's good for my partner. Think about it. I don't expect an answer right now. However, since I need a bit of recovery time before round two, let's get you cleaned up." She smiled as I got off the bed and held out my hand. She was staying and that was all that mattered to me.

Pitbull: Chapter 13:

We spent the remainder of the night in bed. I sent a text to Sin to tell him we wouldn't be back and that everything was fine. I also asked him to tell Dash and Blake I was sorry. I'd make it up to them. He told me not to worry about it and to take care of Luciana.

I made love to her three more times by noon the next day. When we finally got up to seek food, I was feeling drained but more satisfied than I'd ever felt. We got ready then headed over to the clubhouse. Everyone would be there. I'd sent a group text asking them to be there if possible. I needed to do something and to apologize to Dash and Blake in person. I had something for both of them.

When I opened the door, I was pleased to see it looked like everyone was here. I smelled food. It must be the old ladies' day to cook. On Sundays, whoever did, made us lunch since most were recovering from the night before. It was served at one o'clock. Everyone shouted out greetings when we came in. I could feel Luciana shrinking back as if she expected them to be mad. I tugged her tighter into my side and led her over to one of the tables where most of the other ladies were sitting. I pulled out a chair and had her sit down. I gave her a kiss.

"*Bebé*, I'll be right back." She smiled and nodded. As I walked away, Lyric had her engaged in conversation about the bachelorette party. I was curious to know what they had done before crashing Sin's party. In the kitchen, I grabbed two plates and began to load them with food. I was looking over the selections when Barbie came in. I held my breath. Would she try her shit today, after what happened last night? I stiffened and waited, though I acted like I didn't see her. I didn't have to wait long. She came over to stand next to me. I looked at her with a bored expression on my face. She looked pissed.

"I don't appreciate your whatever, pulling a knife on me, Pitbull! She's dangerous and shouldn't be allowed to stay here. You know she's nothing but a lowlife drug dealer. Hell, she was probably a prostitute too. You don't want or need a woman like that. Tell her she should leave. I'll take care of you." She practically purred the last. I set down the plates and crossed my arms. I made sure to give her my best pissed look. She shrank back a little. I'd never hurt her unless she seriously threatened the club in some way.

"Barbie, you need to shut your mouth right now. One more thing comes out of it against Luciana or if you try one more stupid move like you did last night and right now, and you're gone, out on your ass like Vonnie. Why can't you get it through your head? I love Luciana. I'm going to marry her and have babies with her. I won't ever want you or anyone else. Period. Stick to the single guys who want you and leave me and the other married guys alone. Luciana was forced to sell drugs. You have no idea how terrible her life was, and I can promise you, she was never a prostitute. I know that for a fact." I smirked on that last part.

Barbie had her mouth hanging open. She blinked then said softly, "Marry her? Have babies? You're serious, aren't you? Oh my God, why is this happening? Why can't you guys be happy with us?" She turned and hurried out of the kitchen. That's when I saw the doorway was full of my brothers and the ladies. I met Lucina's gaze. She looked stunned. I picked up our plates and went over to her.

"Let's eat, then I have to do a few things." She didn't say a word, just followed me. After getting her seated, we dug into our food. Everyone else did the same. It was quiet except for the scraping of silverware on plates and the occasional soft moan of pleasure. By the time I was done, I was full. Luciana had eaten only a portion of hers.

"Did you get enough, *cariño*? There's a lot left on your plate."

"You made me one the size of yours. It's way too much. Believe me, I had more than enough. I need to take a walk to burn some of this off," she said with a smile as she rubbed her stomach.

"Okay, just wanted to be sure. I know we burned off a lot of calories last night and this morning," I teased her. She blushed and gave me a stern look. I laughed. A few of the guys did as well. When I was finished teasing her, I turned my attention to Dash and Blake.

"Sorry we missed your big moment last night." They both had on their colors. Blake's now had his road name, *Phalanx* on it. On Dash's was the name, *Bullet*.

Both names went back to their military days. Phalanx was an actual weapon system on Navy ships and Blake had been an electronics technician or fire controlman as they call them in the Navy. He'd worked and fired those guns, hence his road name. Dash had been in the infantry in the Marine Corps, so he had fired a lot of shots.

"No biggie, Pitbull. We understand," Bullet said. I felt Luciana squirm next to me. She'd told me this morning how embarrassed she was to have missed it because of her outburst. I'd reassured her it was fine, but she was still worried the guys would be angry at her. I gave Boomer a chin lift, and he nodded. He pulled out a box he had under the table and laid it on the table. Everyone smiled. They knew what it was, or at least the patched members minus Bullet and Phalanx did. I usually did this in private but thought this would be a good apology as well as a welcome to the brotherhood. I took the box and opened it.

I took out the first one and handed it to Bullet, then gave the second one to Phalanx. Both of them looked at what I handed them and then to me with puzzled looks on their faces. "This is your welcome gift. I usually do this in private. I like to give new members something to celebrate joining the brotherhood. Welcome."

Their eyes widened and they gave each other shocked looks. Each of them held a Glock 19 handgun. Nothing fancy, but it was a great gun and what most of us carried daily. What was unique was the grip. I had a guy who made custom ones and he made the ones I gave to new members. It's leather with the club's emblem and the name Ares Infidels burned into the leather.

"Man, this is too much. We know you guys all have one, but we thought it was something you bought after you got patched," Phalanx protested.

"He's right," Bullet added as he caressed the grip.

"No, it's not. I've gotten each of my brothers one. I have the means and want to do it, so take it and enjoy it. Welcome, brothers," I told them. They both came around the table to shake my hand and give me a half-hug and back slap. They thanked me. After they settled down to admire their guns, I held out my hand to Luciana. She took it and let me help her stand up from her chair.

"I need to give you something as well. You know I love you and we're gonna be together for the rest of our lives. You're my old lady, Luciana. I want everyone to know it, but especially you. Please say you'll wear this." I gestured and Phantom handed me a box he had under the table. She slowly opened it and took out the leather inside. It was her property rag. Besides saying *Property of Pitbull* on the back, it had her nickname. I'd gone with what I called her the most, *Bebé*. Maybe not your typical road name, but it fit her.

She slipped her arms in the holes and put it on. It fit her perfectly. It outlined her body and made me want to take her again, even though we'd gone all night long. I tugged her to me by the side of her new rag and kissed her. She eagerly returned it. We got lost in kissing each other until the others got loud with their teasing. When we parted, she told me with a blinding smile, "I love it, I love you, and I'd be proud to wear it."

The guys and ladies all cheered. I felt a weight leave my chest. I'd been worried she might say no. I'd gotten Phantom to order it as soon as I brought her here from the hospital. I knew even then she was going to be mine. As secretary for the club, he did things like this.

We were all celebrating and having fun when both Wrecker and Cuffs got calls to come down to the station. It had to be big if they called both of them in on a Sunday. They told us goodbye and went to get dressed in proper work clothes. For them, it was still civilian clothes. They were out the door in fifteen minutes. All of us wondered what had happened.

A couple hours later, we found out. Most of us were still at the clubhouse. The ladies were talking about last-minute wedding things. The wedding was only six days away. The door of the clubhouse opened and in came Wrecker, Cuffs, and to our surprise, Boss with his whole club. All of them wore grim expressions on their faces. The common room got quiet. Boss was the one to speak first.

"Sin, we need to talk. Can you call church? I think all of you need to hear this." His serious expression and the growl in his voice put me on edge. What in the hell had happened now? Sin nodded and we all got to our feet. Sin sent a text to the few who weren't in the common room. They were around somewhere.

I gave Luciana a kiss. "I'll be back. Keep your planning going. After we're done, maybe you and I can take a walk or something, so we can be alone."

"That sounds nice. Go find out what happened."

I noticed that Sin and Ex were kissing and speaking to their women too. It was still a little amazing to me that I had a woman of my own. That she and I had fallen so fast for each other, but I wasn't about to complain. She was the best thing to ever happen to me in my whole life.

Once we were all in our meeting room behind closed doors, Boss got down to explaining, with help from Wrecker and Cuffs, what the hell was going on. "Sorry for interrupting the weekend, but this couldn't wait. Sometime last night, a man was killed. His throat was slashed, and he bled out. No one as far as we know saw or heard anything. We're still talking to all the employees. The body wasn't found until this afternoon, when they came in to open for the day and went into the alley behind the place to take out the trash."

"Okay, not sure why this had to be discussed today. I mean, I feel bad that someone died, don' t get me wrong, and I hate that this happened in our town, but what is the deal, Boss?" Sin asked him.

Wrecker finally spoke up. "It's a big deal because the man was found behind the Hangout, Sin." All of us grunted in surprise. Wrecker continued, "But that's not all. He died because of his slashed throat, however, that wasn't the only thing we found." He nodded to Cuffs, who took out his cell phone. He tapped it for a couple of seconds then handed the phone to Sin. When he looked at it, we all heard the hiss leave his body.

"What's wrong?" Saint asked.

Sin handed him the phone. From there it made its

way to me. I looked at it curiously then swore. "Are you fucking kidding me? Are they crazy? No way that's ever going to happen. Over my fucking dead body, will it happen," I practically yelled.

"Calm down, we know that. It's just their sick way of doing shit," Wrecker said to calm me down. Only there was no calming me down. As the other guys looked at it, I closed my eyes to regain my control. The image from the phone was seared to the back of my eyes.

It had been a photo of the dead body behind the bar, but that wasn't what had gotten to me. I'd seen plenty of dead bodies. It was what else was there that pissed me off. I was ready to go on a damn hunt and exterminate some fuckers. The man's throat was slashed, and his shirt cut open. Carved into his chest with what I assume had been the knife that cut his throat was a message. It said in bloody letters, *Give Luciana back or else.* I'd wipe out the whole damn bunch of them, even if I had to use Chef to cook me up some special poison or Boomer to make me one of his specialty bombs. I opened my eyes once I could control myself. All the guys were staring at me with concern.

"I'm fine other than wanting to go wipe their fucking asses out right this second. No way he gets her back. He has to be crazy or desperate. First, the attempt to get in the gate, and now this. Why is he trying so hard to get her back? It can't be just because he's pissed that she lived. There has to be more to it than that."

"I agree. We need to see what we can get from our few confidential informants out there. Someone surely knows what he's up to these days. He appears to be unraveling, which makes him an even more dangerous man. Keep her here no matter what. We'll work on finding out what his angle is. Just don't go off half-cocked, Pitbull," Boss warned me.

"I won't unless there's no other choice. If they make a move to take her again, I'll be leaving bodies where they fall. Make no mistake, I'll kill them without a second thought," I warned them. Everyone nodded.

"I know and I don't blame you. There's one other thing. I hate to add to your plate, but I think we need to place that person in the Liar's Lair ASAP. We all said we'd think about who it could be. I had a thought and it's not what I prefer, but this is the only person I think has a chance to stay under the radar."

"Who?" Captain, his VP, asked. Obviously, Boss hadn't talked to his guys yet about who he'd thought of. I thought that was interesting.

He shrugged and then said quietly, "Blue could do it."

A roar broke out, not only from his guys, but ours as well. However, none of us were as loud as Preacher. He scowled, looking pissed. "Are you fucking joking? You can't send her in there! They'll be all over her in a second. She won't be able to get anything done, because she'll be fighting off a bunch of drunken, doped-up perverts. There has to be someone else, a guy who we can find."

"I thought through everyone. They're all known to be associated with us or the Infidels, Preacher! Blue has only been back a few weeks and working at the Hang-out. No one knows she's friends with Brea. She can hold her own. Blue is one tough woman with street and prison smarts. Besides, she wouldn't be totally alone." This quieted everyone down.

"You and Phantom could come up with some kind of listening device that would allow her to talk to us and hear us back. Plus, give her a camera she could wear that would allow us to see what she does. If it looks like she is getting in over her head, we can move in and help her or extract her."

"Boss, I agree none of the men we know can do it, but how do we even know she'd agree. She just started working for Pitbull. That leaves him shorthanded," Santa said quietly. He didn't look happy. Blue was his sister. I expected he wouldn't like the idea.

Boss stood up and walked around the room. "Because I already talked to her about doing it. Other than finding a replacement for her at the Hangout, she's good to go. Well, she will be as soon as her left hand heals a little from that fight she had the other night at the Hangout. I still can't believe what the hell went down. Four men all going after a woman. Fuckers got what they deserved. Blue can obviously take care of herself. She proved that. We already have the cover story ready. She'll be suspended or fired from the Hangout for that fight. She can have time to get prepared. They might not think anything about her leaving us. She did ask that if it's possible, she'd like to come back to work for you guys when she's no longer needed over there, but if you can't swing it, she understands. She wants to catch these guys as much as we do. She has the skills to protect herself. I don't see any other option. If you do, tell me. Otherwise, it's her and we need to get her in place and set up ASAP."

We spent over twenty minutes debating other choices and then discarding them. In the end, we all agreed, Blue was the only choice. None of us were happy about it, but Preacher seemed the most unhappy. I wasn't sure why. He tended not to like women, so it might simply be because she was a woman in his club, however, we didn't have the luxury of being picky. We needed to find out what was being run through those bunkers and tunnels. The best way was to have someone in place who would hear and see almost everything happening in that dive bar across the interstate. It was with less than relief, that we tied up the meeting.

Boss, Wrecker, and Cuffs would finish investigating the man's death. They hoped someone might have heard or seen something, but they didn't think they had. I'd keep Luciana on lockdown and work to find a temporary replacement for Blue at the bar. Preacher and Phantom would work on the equipment for her while they tried to find out why Juan was acting so desperate to get his sister back. Needless to say, we had our plates pretty full, as usual. It was a relief to come out and see her smiling face. I went straight to her. I needed a kiss.

Luciana: Chapter 14

I looked at the parking lot of the clubhouse which was filled with more bikes and a few cars. I hadn't realized, in addition to the Time Served guys and ladies coming to the wedding, there would be others. Lyric had her best friend, Kerrigan, as her bridesmaid. Saint stood up as Sin's best man. Judge McAllister was the one who officiated the ceremony. I didn't know him personally, but I'd heard his name. My brother's loser friends had been brought before him on more than one occasion.

I didn't know many of the others who came who worked for the club at their various businesses. I hadn't been in the nicer areas of town that much over the last five years. It was kind of making me nervous. I wanted to make a good impression on these people. They were important to the club. I prayed none of them knew me or who my brother was.

In addition to them, there was a group of older men who were hanging with Pop. After the ceremony was over, Pitbull walked me over to the table where they were all sitting, chatting away. They got quiet when they saw us, though big grins broke out across all their faces. Pop sprang up and took my hand. He pulled me in for a hug. As he did, I heard Pitbull sigh.

"Really, could you not look like that when you're holding on to my damn woman, Pop? It's practically indecent. If you were a younger man, I'd kick your ass."

"Boy, I'm still young enough to take you on. If you're feeling froggy, jump." The other guys laughed. I gave Pop a pat on the chest as I drew back.

"Behave, or he won't let me dance with you later. Or are you gonna tell me you don't dance?"

"Darlin', I'm like Fred Astaire. You save that dance no matter what old growly says," Pop said with a twinkle in his eye. I shook my head at him. Pitbull tugged me away from Pop and turned me to face the other men.

"Luciana, let me introduce you to these reprobates. This is Harvey Korbyn, he's Sin's uncle and runs Harvey's Garage in town. To his left is Hal Markham. Hal owns the hardware store. On Hal's left is Tom Dolby. Tom owns the donut place, Hole in One. Lastly, this is Jack Bentley. Jack owns the real estate office. Gentlemen, this Luciana Ramirez, my old lady." He said the last part with a look of pride on his face. It still amazed me he felt that way about me. I was working to get used to being referred to as an old lady without feeling insulted.

"Hello, it's nice to meet all of you," I told them softly.

"Sweetness, the pleasure is all ours. How Pitbull caught a prize like you, we'll never know. You make sure you save us each a dance too," Harvey said as he winked at me and then Pitbull. My man just rolled his eyes.

"Okay, enough flirting. She's too young for you, and I don't want you to scare her off. Though, Pop, I do want to talk to you. Would you have time for me to stop by tomorrow?"

"Sure. Can you give me an idea of what you want to talk about or is it a secret?"

Pitbull glanced at me then back to Pop. "Not a secret, I just didn't want to take you away from the festivities. I'd like to have you look at your construction crews' schedules and let me know when you could start working on a house for me and Luciana. I know they're still working on Skye and Ex's house as well as Jackie's. I'm not sure what else you have going on in town."

I stared at him in shock. Had he really said what I thought he had? He smiled at me. "I want to get us into a house. She's gonna need to have a quiet place to study. She's gonna start the nursing program soon, we hope. My trailer is okay, but I'd like something farther away from the clubhouse."

"Honey, I haven't even asked about school yet. I don't need you to build us a house. I can live just fine in your trailer. You said it would be done within a week," I protested.

"Well, I need it. I want you where we can have total privacy and you can concentrate. We're going to need a house eventually when we start to have kids. We can't raise them in a two-bedroom trailer."

"Kids are a few years off. It can wait," I argued. Pop cut off our argument.

"It would be better to start sooner rather than later, because I anticipate there's going to be a lot more building happening around here. We're building a few more houses on my place for more people to use when they get out, but that shouldn't affect other jobs. Let me check but I think we can start for sure in October. That gives you a few months to find the floor plan you like and then I can get the blueprints."

"Sounds like a plan. Thanks a million. You have anyone getting out soon who's going to be moving in on your place?"

"Maybe one or two, if they get out on time."

I had no idea who they were referring to, but I was content to stand there with Pitbull's arm around my shoulders. It was while I was listening that I caught sight of another man staring at us. He was younger, probably in his thirties. He seemed to be staring at me in particular. An uncomfortable feeling went through me. I was about to say something to Pitbull when he came marching up to us. He stood there staring at me hard. Pitbull and Pop stopped talking.

"Jon, what the hell are you doing?" Jack snapped.

"Do you know who she is?" he asked harshly.

"She's Pitbull's lady. Stop embarrassing me and apologize. Luciana, I'm sorry, this is my son, Jonathan," he said angrily. Jonathan narrowed his eyes.

"Pitbull's woman? Do you know who her brother is? She's a drug dealer's sister. How in the hell did you get caught by her? I'd get clear if I were you," he told Pitbull spitefully. As my stomach sank, I had the presence of mind to grip Pitbull's arm tighter. I felt his whole body stiffen and I could feel the tension vibrating through him. He was about to take a swing at Jonathan.

"Don't," I whispered.

Jack got an outraged look on his face along with the other old men. He got in his son's face. "Boy, you're not too old to have me beat your ass all over this yard. You don't talk to a lady like that!"

Jonathan snorted and rolled his eyes. I was glad that Sin and Lyric weren't close by to witness this. I didn't want to spoil their special day with a scene. I tugged harder on Pitbull's arm. "Let's go."

Pitbull pulled away from me and got right in Jonathan's face. I saw him pale, and he looked like he wanted to run. "What's your fucking problem, Jon? This is my woman and you not only insulted me but her. I might be able to overlook the insult to me, but not to her. However, your asinine remark raises a question. How in the hell do you know who her brother is?"

"I-I, well, I've seen him around," he stuttered.

"And you know he's a drug dealer, how?"

"People talk. What difference does it make? She's like him. I always heard the Infidels don't mess with stuff like that. Guess I was wrong." Pitbull moved toward him. In the end, he didn't hit him, because his dad, Jack, beat Pitbull to it. He hauled off and punched Jonathan in the mouth.

"I'd better never hear you talk like that again. The Infidels and the Time Served are all here protecting our town from shit like that. Luciana's brother isn't her. I suggest you get your ass home." Jonathan gave his dad an angry look, then he turned on his heel and stomped off without saying another word. I was mortified. I had caused this to happen.

"I'm so sorry, I—" Jack cut me off.

"You have absolutely nothing to be sorry about. I'm the one who's sorry. I have no idea where I went wrong with him. I thought he'd change with him and Ben running the business. I think I might have made a mistake. I don't care who your brother is. We can't pick our family, sweetheart. Don't let people like my son make you feel bad about yourself."

I couldn't keep from looking away. My enjoyment of the day was washed away in a matter of a few minutes. Jonathan might have been an asshole, but he wasn't wrong. People would judge me based on Juan, not on me, and I hadn't been innocent in the whole thing. I'd sold drugs, even if it was against my will. I tried to swallow the lump in my throat and keep the tears in my eyes from falling. I pulled away from Pitbull.

"If you'll excuse me," I told them hurriedly, and then I turned and almost ran toward Pitbull's trailer. I heard Pitbull and the men with him yelling my name, but I kept going. I needed to have this breakdown alone. I tore around the clubhouse and into the trailer. After I slammed the front door shut, I ran to the bathroom and locked the door. I sat down on the rim of the tub and let the tears and sobs free. Would I ever be free to have a happy life and not be judged for the things I had no control over? Would Pitbull someday grow to resent or even hate me because of it?

Pitbull:

I didn't know what to do. My woman had run off in tears. I knew she was back to feeling like she was a terrible person who would forever be judged for her brother's deeds. My fucking heart hurt. She had no idea how beautiful she was on the inside and out. Anyone who spent more than five minutes with her could see it.

I was also fighting the urge to go after Jon Bentley and beat the hell out of him. Who the hell was he to say anything to her? His lame explanation on how he knew who Juan was didn't ring true. I swiveled around to go after her. A hand on my arm stopped me. It was Jack. His face was creased with worry and anger.

"I'm so damn sorry, Pitbull. He had no right to say that to her. Please, get her to come back. We need to show her that what he said is bullshit. Anyone can see she's not like that. Let me know if we can do anything." I saw the other old geezers nodding solemnly.

"Thanks, Jack. it's just he voiced what she was already afraid would happen from the beginning—that she'd be judged because of her brother. She did sell drugs." They all looked startled. "But only because if she didn't, he was going to sell her or force her into prostitution. She took the lesser evil. She can't seem to forgive herself for not letting him do the other. She's tried to leave more than once. I'll tell you now, if Jon's dumb remarks make her run, I'll kill your son. You can tell him that. He's got an ass beating coming as it is." He only shook his head in disgust. I nodded to them and then went after my lady.

As soon as I entered the trailer, I could hear the muffled sobs coming from the bathroom. I walked up and tried the handle. It was locked. I couldn't say I was surprised. I knocked on the door softly. The sobs lessened.

"Luciana, *bebé*, please open the door," I pleaded with her.

"Please, leave me alone, Cole. I can't talk right now. Go back and join the party." I could hear the huskiness in her voice from crying. She sounded so defeated and hurt. I laid my head against the door.

"I can't, *amada*. I can't leave you in here hurting like this. Nothing Jon said is the truth. Jack and the guys all said to tell you that they want you to come back outside. Jon is a dumbass."

"They don't know what I did. They'd change their mind if they did," she said with a hiccup at the end. She was sniffling and trying to stop the tears.

"I told them. They don't care. They know it wasn't your fault."

"You told them? Oh God, why? Now, I really can't show my face out there again. It'll be all over the place in a few minutes. There's nothing people love more than to gossip and tear down other people. I've just ruined Sin and Lyric's wedding reception! I should have stayed inside," she wailed. I rattled the handle.

"Open the door, Luciana, now! I'm not going to ask again. If you need to cry, then you can do it out here in my arms, not behind closed doors," I told her sternly. I was about to say the hell with it and kick the damn door in. I'd have to have it fixed, but I couldn't care less about it. Getting to her was worth the cost of a new door.

"No, just leave. Please," she whispered. I didn't argue. I stood back and raised my foot until it was level with the door handle, then I kicked out with the flat of my foot, using my steel-toed boots. The door splintered as it swung in half off its hinges. She screamed. I strolled inside and straight over to her. She was sitting on the rim of the tub with her hand over her mouth.

Her eyes were huge and round. She looked shocked. Her eyes were red and swollen from the tears. I didn't say a word. I crouched down and picked her up. I took her out of the bathroom and into our bedroom. I laid her down on the bed. She was staring at me speechless. Good, it would give me a chance to say what I had to say. I toed off my boots and then crawled onto the bed with her. I rolled her onto her back and straddled her waist. I took her wrists and raised them over her head and held them there with one of my hands.

"Rule number one, no locked doors between us, ever. If you're pissed, then tell me. We'll work it out. Two, no going to bed mad. Three, if you're hurting or sad, no crying alone. I get to hold you. Four, you won't ever be expected to be around people who treat you like shit. If any of those people out there do, they can fucking leave just like Jon did. Not a single one of my brothers or their women would expect anything less. Five, I love you and that's not going to change. I'm not going to let you leave me, Luciana. I'll find you even if I have to search the ends of the earth to find you." She opened her mouth, but I didn't give her a chance to reply. I took her mouth with mine. I took it hard. My lips and tongue, along with my teeth, ravished her mouth as I made love to it, like I wanted to do to the rest of her. How I was planning to do to the rest of her as soon as she realized I meant every word I'd just said.

She moaned and kissed me back. I couldn't get enough of her taste or feel. My cock was instantly hard and begging to be released so he could sink into her pussy. I let go of her hands and slid mine down to knead her breasts and tease her nipples through her bra. Not getting what I wanted, I growled and sat up. She was panting as hard as I was.

"Take off your dress and underclothes." She hesitated for a second then sat up. I got off her and tore at my own clothes as I watched her get undressed. As she revealed that lush, sexy body of hers, I groaned. She looked at me and then her eyes got round, seeing me standing there naked and fisting my cock. I was pumping up and down, smearing the precum down my length. She licked her lips, and I shuddered. I got closer to the edge of the bed. We should probably finish talking about this, but I couldn't wait. I had to be with her.

"I need that sexy mouth on me, *bebé*." She slid over and then lay on her back. It put her at the perfect height —with her head hanging over the edge—to take my cock in her mouth. "Yeah, that's perfect. Suck my cock. I need that hot little mouth on me," I told her hoarsely. Her hand ran up the inside of my thighs then she grasped me at the base. I watched as her mouth opened and she licked her bottom lip before she sucked my cock inside slowly. I jerked. Her mouth was scalding hot and so damn wet. She slid up and down my length, taking more of me inside each time. As she did, she had her hands teasing my balls and scraping her nails down my inner thighs. Fuck!

I leaned over the top of her. She gagged and then relaxed as it forced more of my cock down her throat. I pushed her thighs apart and looked at her dripping wet pussy. Her scent hit my nose and I inhaled deeply. Groaning, I lowered my head and swiped my tongue from her clit to her entrance. She whimpered and jerked.

As I pumped my cock in and out of her mouth, I devoured her pussy. I licked and sucked all over, paying attention to tease her clit with a fluttering of my tongue. As she moaned and pushed up into my mouth, I grinned. Oh yeah, my woman liked to have her pussy eaten. It had never been my favorite thing to do, even though I did it. I wanted whoever I was with to enjoy sex as much as I did. But with Luciana, I craved the taste of her pussy, the smell of it on my face, the feel of it on my fingers.

I lifted my head and groaned as she sucked me deeper and then swallowed, making my cock slip down her throat more. She was squeezing the head of my cock. I swore. She giggled and then lashed me with her tongue as she pulled back. I looked down between us and saw her eyes were closed. She had a look of bliss on her face. I wanted to see even more pleasure on it.

"*Bebé,* this pussy tastes so damn good. Do you like how my cock tastes?" I whispered. I wanted her to talk to me, to tell me what she liked and what she loved. I wanted to talk dirty to her until she lost control.

"Oh God, yes, I love the taste of you, Cole." She moaned. Her hands worked my base and balls faster.

"Do you want me to come in your pretty little mouth, in your pussy, or maybe that tight little ass?" I asked. We'd talked about anal and over the last week, we'd played more and more down there. She'd been able to take more fingers and even toys. I wondered if she was ready to take my cock. The thought of being buried in her ass made more cum ooze out of the tip of my cock. She moaned as she sucked it off, then her mouth left me. I wanted to protest.

"Cole, I-I" she stammered. I lifted away from her. I sat down beside her head on the bed and ran my fingers down her cheek.

"You don't need to say yes if you're not ready. You don't ever have to do that if you don't want to. I know you've enjoyed the other playing we've done. I can wait or even take it off the board. I don't ever want you to do anything you don't want just to please me." I kissed her gently on the mouth. As I did, her hand grasped my cock at the root again and she pumped up and down. I threw back my head and groaned. I needed to be inside her soon, or I'd lose my mind. I tore myself away from her and stood up. Before I could tell her to move, she did it herself. She rolled over and got up on her hands and knees. She laid her cheek on the mattress and looked at me over her shoulder. Her ass was in the air. Her hands came back, and she spread her ass cheeks. Her pussy glistened with her juices. I growled and crawled up behind her.

I rubbed the head of my cock up and down her slit then slid into her pussy in one hard push. She cried out and shook. I couldn't help but swear. "Fuck." She was tight and swollen. I pumped in and out of her a few times, going deeper and harder each time. I wasn't going to last long, but I'd make it up to her.

I'd pulled back and was about to slide back deep when she pulled away, letting my cock slip out of her. I glanced up at her in concern. Had I hurt her? She was flushed and her eyes were bright. She was panting. "Did I hurt you, *bebé*?"

"No, Cole. I want you in my ass. I want to find out how that feels," she whispered. I hesitated. Was she just saying this to please me?

"Luciana, we don't have to do that. It was just a question. Believe me, being in you like this is perfect." I leaned forward and started to push back into her pussy. Before I could do more than touch her entrance, she wiggled her ass and my cock slid up and into the star-shaped entrance to her ass. She took a deep breath and then pressed back into me. The head of my cock barely breached her back door. She moaned. I froze. I knew what I wanted to do. I wanted to sink into that ass and fuck her like a beast, to mark her forever as mine in every damn hole in her body. I wanted my cum to bathe her insides, but did she really want it?

"Fuck me, Cole. Fuck my ass and show me what I've been missing. Show me how much better your cock can feel than your fingers or those toys. Though, if it does, I just might die from pleasure," she moaned. Her words took the decision out of my hands. I grasped her hips and pressed inside more.

"Relax and breathe. You know what to do. Tell me if it's too much," I gritted out between clenched teeth. I had just the head in her ass, and it was already heaven. As I slowly worked my cock into her ass, she wiggled and pressed back into me, taking me deeper.

"Not so fast, we have time," I told her. Though if the raging in my balls were any indication, I was getting close to erupting. I was halfway there and dying. She didn't say a word. She lifted up on her elbows and looked over her shoulder at me. Holding my eyes, she took a deep breath and then shocked the hell out of me. She thrust back on my cock. That movement drove it into her ass to the root. She screamed and I swore. I started to pull back. God, had she hurt herself? Her words froze me.

"Don't you dare pull out or I'll kill you! You were trying to kill me with your waiting. It burns and hurts but not that bad. I know what you want to do. You want to pound my ass, don't you? To fuck it like a crazed beast and then fill it with your cum?" Her sultry tone and the look made me groan.

"Yeah, I do wanna take you like a caveman, but not if it hurts you."

"You won't. I've found that a little pain only makes

it better when I come. Do it. Show me how you want to take me." She slipped her hand down between her legs and I felt her fingers brush against my thighs. She was fingering her clit and then I felt her fingers enter her pussy. It made the tightness around my cock tighten just a fraction more. It was too much. I broke.

I gripped her hips and pulled back then slammed back into her. She shrieked and her fingers sped up, thrusting in and out of her pussy, as I fucked her ass. I fucked her hard and deep. I knew she'd be sore, but I wanted her to feel me long after I was done. She was all mine. No man had ever had her mouth, her pussy or her ass and I wanted to announce it to the fucking world. Only my cock and cum would ever be inside of her.

As I rode her hard, she thrust back, riding my cock and her fingers. She was whimpering, and the juices flowed down our thighs. The slap of our flesh coming together and the smell of sex filled the room. I was getting so damn close.

She tightened just a fraction and then she was whispering, "I'm so close, honey. Tell me you are too. Get there, Cole. Fuck me harder. Come with me." Her fingers sped up even more. I thrust harder and faster. I was panting like I'd run a marathon. My chest was burning, and my cock was on fire. I could feel the cum ready to burst out of me. As the tingling raced up my legs, I reached under her and pinched her clit. She screamed and slammed back on me and froze. Her ass clamped down like a damn vise and she came.

Her inner ass muscles milked my cock like a machine, and I got two more strokes, then I detonated. I roared, "Jesus Christ!" as I jerked over and over, filling her with my cum. I came so long and hard with her doing the same, that when we were done, my cum was leaking out around my cock and she'd collapsed flat on the bed. I was propped over top of her trying to breathe and clear my vision.

When I finally did, I slowly pulled my softening cock out of that glorious ass of hers. She shuddered and then curled up on her side. I got worried. Had I hurt her too much? I hugged up behind her and kissed her neck. "*Bebé*, did I hurt you too much? I'm sorry. Let me see." She shook her head vigorously.

She rolled over to face me. "No, it didn't hurt too much. It was so damn good, I wanted to die. I think I might have lost a few brain cells on that one. You literally fucked me stupid, Cole." I burst out laughing. The bed shook with our combined laughter.

"Well, I've never been told I fucked someone stupid. Luciana, when I'm with you, it's always love I feel, not just fucking. You're incredible. I don't even know what to say to the gift you just gave me." I kissed her tenderly.

"I can. You can soak with me in the tub, then we can do that again and again. I want it all, Cole." I could tell she was serious.

"I can do that, but only if you promise me one thing." She raised her eyebrows at me in question. "Don't let whatever idiots say make you doubt yourself or me. I love you, Luciana Ramirez. Nothing will ever change that. Stand tall and spit in their eyes. If you promise to do that, I can promise to give you more pleasure and love than you could ever imagine in one lifetime."

She didn't answer me other than to take my mouth and kiss me until I felt faint. When she was done, she whispered, "Okay, I will." I got her up and in my arms. It was time to soak with my woman and then we could go rejoin the party or maybe stay in bed and see how many items we could ravish each other before morning. Either way, I'd be a happy man.

Luciana: Chapter 15

It had been almost a week since the wedding. After that intense session of lovemaking, we'd eventually rejoined the others. I was a little self-conscious, but no one made a big deal of us disappearing. They teased us about not being able to wait. Jack and the other old geezers, as Pitbull called them, had found us later. Jack once again apologized for his son and then went on to tell me that whatever I did to keep myself safe was the right thing. If anyone thought differently, they could come talk to him. I had to give him a hug after he said that. He'd winked at Pitbull and said, "See the ladies can't resist me." Pitbull had rolled his eyes.

Sin and Lyric had gone off for their honeymoon and would be back next week. Saint was running things while he was gone. We were all hanging around the clubhouse tonight. It was Friday night. The music was loud, and I was sitting with Jackie, Skye, Sara, and Kerrigan. Kerrigan was telling us funny stories about her students. I couldn't believe some of the things she was saying.

Pitbull was playing a game of pool with Wrecker. Zeus and Bear were sleeping on their bed in the common room. I had no idea how they could sleep with all the noise, but they did. When Kerrigan was done with her stories, the conversation took a more serious turn.

She asked me about what had happened at the wedding reception. I knew the women had been wanting to ask. I think Pitbull had warned them not to, or at least warned their men.

"Okay, we've been as patient as we can. Tell us what went on at the reception last weekend? Why did Jon Bentley storm off and his dad and the other old geezers look so pissed? We all saw you leave upset and Pitbull go after you. Spill," Sara demanded. She had her serious mom look on her face.

I sighed. "Because he made remarks about knowing who my brother was and that he was a drug dealer."

"So? Who cares if he is?" Jackie asked, puzzled.

"He said that I was like him and that Pitbull should get rid of me. I guess I'm tainted by association, even if Pitbull thinks otherwise."

They all became outraged. "No, he didn't! That asshole. I can't stand him. He's the one who made his brother, Ben, fire me. Said he didn't need me doing their books, but I think something is hinky over there," Skye said as she gnawed on her bottom lip.

"What do you mean by hinky? And what an asshole," Kerrigan growled.

"Jon handles the books for the real estate business as well as the rental property side. When I looked at it, they have a whole lot of rental properties—both homes and land. When I mentioned it to Ben, he seemed not to know about them. He told me that Jack had never had much to do with it because being a landlord was too much work and a pain. I got curious and one day took a ride out to see some of those places. A lot of them are outside of town in the same area. When I did, that's when things got weirder."

"Weirder, how?" I asked.

"The ones with houses looked abandoned—long grass and no yard work. The ones for large tracts of land that you'd grow stuff on or raise cattle were all overgrown too. All of them are bringing in rent every month, but I don't know why."

"Did you tell Ex and the guys about it?" Sara asked her as she frowned.

"I told Ex and he talked to the guys. They're looking into it, but my gut is telling me something hinky is going on. What if they're using them for illegal stuff? I don't want that around here. I don't want our baby to be raised in a place that's not safe and we have to worry about them every second to just be outside in our own yard," Skye said sadly. I wrapped my arm around her shoulders.

"It won't. I don't see the Infidels or the Time Served guys allowing that to happen. We have to trust they can handle it. I agree it does sound awfully suspicious, especially since Jon fired you right after he found out you were doing their books. I wouldn't cry if they found the asshole was doing something they could bust him for. He's always been a little shit," Sara growled. You could see her dislike of him written all over her face.

"Do you think Ben or Jack would be involved?" I asked her. She shook her head emphatically.

CIARA ST JAMES

"Not in a million years would I think either of them would. Jon, I don't trust him as far as I can throw him. He's always been a little off and creepy."

We were interrupted from saying more because the door to the clubhouse opened and in came Barbie. She was the last person I wanted to see. I hadn't seen her since the incident with me pulling my knife on her two weeks ago. She wasn't her usual primped to the nines' self. Her hair was messed up and her face looked like someone had punched her. She had mascara running down her cheeks from the tears she'd obviously shed. I stiffened. I didn't like her, but I didn't want to see any woman hit. She shocked me when she kept walking until she was standing next to the table where I sat with the other women.

Someone turned off the music. The guys stood watching us. I saw out of the corner of my eye, Pitbull laid down his pool cue and was coming toward us. Barbie glared at me then pointed her finger at me. "It's all your fault!" she shouted at me.

"What's my fault?" I asked her, confused and shocked.

"This. My face is because of you. If you'd never come here, then none of this would have happened!" she yelled louder. By this time, Pitbull had made it to the table, along with most of his brothers.

"I have no idea what you're talking about, Barbie."

"Sure you don't. Your drug dealer brother did this. That's how it's your fault."

"What does her brother have to do with this or her?" Pitbull asked her. She turned to him, and I saw the change. She got all teary-eyed and looked at him pathetically. God, she was a piece of work.

"Pitbull, you have to make her leave. She can't stay here. If she does, no one will be safe. He told me we wouldn't. All he wants is her back, then he'll leave the rest of us in peace."

"He, who? Her brother?"

"Yes, he and a couple of his men caught me in town. They took me out of town and roughed me up. They told me to tell you that next time it won't be this nice. That it'll be one of the old ladies or even me again. No one person is worth this. Please, you have to send her back to him. He's crazy. He's not going to stop until he gets her back. He said he'd burn us out if he had to," she sobbed. She tried to throw her arms around his neck, but he side-stepped her.

"Calm down and tell us exactly what they did and every word they said," Saint growled. He pulled out a chair, and she slowly sank down on it. She twisted her fingers and looked at the floor.

"I was walking down the street and suddenly a car pulled up and two men jumped out. They grabbed me and dragged me into the car. I thought they were going to rape or kill me," she said with a sob. I couldn't see her face, but something about her answer seemed like an act. Like she wasn't as afraid as she pretended to be.

"Who were they? Where did they take you?"

Wrecker asked. It made sense he would. He was, after all, a cop. Cuffs was on duty tonight.

"It was outside of town. It was dark and they put a bag over my head. I didn't know the guys' voices," she hurried to tell him. Funny, she didn't say they covered her head until they asked about who the men were. If that were the case, how did she know my brother was involved? How did they get her in the car and off the street without her seeing them? I watched Saint and Wrecker exchange a silent communication. I wasn't sure if they believed her or not. Barbie must have felt the same way because she started to cry harder.

"You don't believe me! I swear, it's true. When they got me out into the country, they stopped and pulled me out of the car. A man was standing there when they took off the hood. He told me who he was and what he would do to the rest of us if we didn't give her back." She pointed to me.

"Describe the man who talked to you," Wrecker told her.

"He was five foot nine or ten, kind of built, but not like you guys. His hair was dark brown, and he had brown eyes. It looked like he was Mexican. His skin was tan. He had a tattoo of a cross on the back of his left hand." Her description could be my brother. It was hard to tell. The tattoo was right, but I knew several guys with those on their hands.

"What about the men who took you?" Saint asked her as he watched her every move.

"I didn't see them. After they got me out of the car,

they stayed behind me and in the shadows. What does it matter? They were after her. I don't want anyone else to get hurt because of her. He meant business. He said we have until Monday to return her, or they're not going to be responsible for what happens next. They'll let you know where."

"How do they plan to contact us?" Wrecker asked her.

"I don't know. They didn't say. Maybe they have our phone numbers or something. It's all so hazy. I was scared and just wanted to get out of there alive. Before they brought me back, the leader told his guys to make an example out of me. That's when they hit me."

"Did they only hit your face or are you hurt somewhere else?" Pitbull finally asked. She smiled at him.

"I have a few bruises. I can show them to you."

"No, if they hurt enough, tell us and we'll take you to the hospital. What time did this happen?" he asked her, ignoring her offer to let him look at her body. I bet she'd have to strip to do it.

"How did you get back here?" Boomer asked.

"They took me back to town and dropped me off at my car. I was too afraid to wait and call someone to come get me, so I drove. I think I need to lie down and get my nerves under control. Will someone stay with me?"

I watched as Boomer sighed in exasperation. "We'll get Shy or Tabby Cat to sit with you."

"Oh, I was hoping it would be one of you. I'd feel so much safer if it was." Her flirting was starting to come out stronger and making me grit my teeth in annoyance.

Boomer stood up. "Come on, I'll walk you to your place and call over one of the girls. You'll be fine, and besides, we need to talk about this as a group."

She looked around and saw that no one was going to side with her. She harrumphed and then flounced to her feet. "I'll go by myself. I guess only old ladies are important around here now." She stormed back out like she'd stormed in. I glanced at the others.

"Do you think she's telling the truth?" I asked them.

"Someone beat her ass, just not sure if it was Juan or someone else. I think she might have gotten mouthy with the wrong person and got her ass handed to her," Talon said wryly. The others were all nodding in agreement.

"But we owe it to her to be sure it wasn't someone we should take care of. If it was women getting into a cat fight, that's between them. But if a man did that, even if it wasn't Luciana's brother and his bunch, we can't let it go. People need to know there are consequences for messing with any of our people," Saint added with a frown of concentration on his face.

"Agreed. Now, how do we go about proving it one way or the other? I wouldn't necessarily put it past Barbie to have gotten into a fight with some lady, most likely because she was flirting or worse with that woman's man. However, it could have been what she said or another guy," Pitbull said as he paced. Any mention of my brother made him upset.

"You know that my brother and his men wouldn't hesitate to beat a woman, you all saw me, but why Barbie? Is it well known around town who the bunnies for the club are? And if it is, why her and not Tabby Cat or Shy? All of them leave the compound alone. And why now? They could have grabbed one of them anytime in the last few weeks since they figured out I was here. I think those are all questions you need to figure out. It might help answer if it was Juan and probably Miguel and Jesús, since he almost never is without them."

The guys all got quiet and looked at me. I shrank back. Had I said something wrong? I saw a darting movement out of the corner of my eye, and I reacted without thinking. I ducked my head and threw up my arms to cover my face. The room got deadly quiet. I knew immediately I'd overreacted. I slowly lowered my arms and looked around me. All of them stared at me with degrees of worry and anger on their faces. The women looked sad. I hurried to break the awkward silence.

"Sorry, I didn't mean to do that, an old habit. Where were we?"

Pitbull came to sit beside me. He hauled me off my chair and onto his lap. His strong arms enveloped me, and he kissed me gently. When he was done, he said quietly, but loud enough for everyone to hear, "You don't ever have to worry about anyone here hitting you or touching you the wrong way, *bebé*. I'd cut off my own fucking arm before I'd ever do that, and so would my brothers. I know you have a lot to unlearn from those years with your brother. It kills me to see you react that way, even though I know it's involuntary."

"I know, it's just a reaction. Anyone coming at me fast was almost always followed by pain. I'll work on it. Let's get back to the topic at hand. Anyone have any ideas on what I asked?" I wanted them to stop staring at me. It took them a second or two and then they got back into the discussion.

"Luciana is right. We do need to find out those answers. It's not broadcasted who our bunnies are, but then again, it's not a secret. Some people would know. I can't answer why Barbie and not the other two, but maybe it's purely the amount of time spent away from here. We don't police them leaving. I suggest we talk to the other two and find out how much they've been off the compound. After Barbie calms down, we can ask her where exactly in town she was taken from and returned. And why now, I have no clue. Unless they thought the firing at the gate and then the body would be enough to get us to send you packing," Saint mused.

"If it is my brother, I'm afraid of what else he might do if I don't go back. None of the women can go out unescorted and what about you guys? Are you going in pairs at least? They wouldn't hesitate to try and take one of you on, maybe even kill you," I exclaimed. The idea of any of them being killed over this was making me sick to my stomach.

Pitbull gave me a comforting squeeze. "We'll be careful, I promise. If possible, we'll go in pairs. None of the women, including the bunnies, can leave without an escort. It's too dangerous. We need to figure out if it was Juan. The description was vague enough; it could have been a bunch of Hispanic males in town. I'll question her more in a little bit," Wrecker volunteered.

"You do that. We'll talk to Tabby Cat and Shy about if they've had any run-ins and the new escort rule. Same goes for all of you—no leaving without one of us or a prospect. It might be a pain, but it's necessary." All of us nodded our agreement to Saint.

Everyone was just settling down and trying to get back into a better mood when the doors opened again and in came a grim-looking Cuffs. I knew immediately something terrible had happened. He went straight to Saint and whispered in his ear. When he was done, Saint looked around at the guys. Now he looked grim. "I need everyone in church, now." Executioner and Pitbull gave Skye and me a kiss, then they filed out.

I tried to slow my breathing. I just knew whatever put that look on Cuffs' face, it had to be terrible and something to do with my brother. Why was he so damn determined to get me back? Was it because he wanted to punish me more or kill me? I'd lost the socializing bug. I stood up. "I'll see you all later. I need to go lie down. I have a headache." They protested and even said one of them would come with me, but I waved them off. I had to be alone.

Pitbull: Chapter 16

I didn't like the look on Saint and Cuffs' faces. They were grim and that could only mean one thing, shit was about to get worse for the club, and that most likely meant it had something to do with Luciana. We all quietly took our seats and waited for Saint to start the meeting since Sin was still on his honeymoon. He slammed down the hammer.

"Ok, listen up. I filled Cuffs in on what Barbie told us. You need to listen to what he has to say. No interrupting. Let him finish, then we'll talk about it and decide what to do. Understood?" He glanced around the table at all of us, though his eyes lingered the longest on me. Yep, it was about Luciana. The tension in my neck got tighter. When would it stop? She needed to be safe and able to lead a normal life with me.

"Cuffs, you have the floor." Cuffs sat forward and rested his elbows on the table. He looked like he'd been awake for days. I recalled he'd picked up an extra shift today for one of the other detectives who called in sick.

"Let me start at the beginning. We got a call to go out to Bubble's Strip Club on Cloud Court. It was right before the club was due to open at five tonight. One of the bartenders had gone out back to take out some trash that hadn't been thrown out last night. He found a woman's body next to the dumpster. She was a young woman, in her early twenties. She was tiny and had dark hair. She was Hispanic." I stiffened when he said that.

He darted a glance at me then continued, "She had been badly beaten and raped. We ran her prints, and it came back that she was a local prostitute. Not a surprise in that line of business, unfortunately. On any other day, we'd chalk it up to a boyfriend or pimp doing it, only that wasn't the only thing we found." He paused to take a deep breath.

"She had been cut. On her chest in ragged letters was one word..." He paused again and looked at me. "It read *Luciana*." I let out a roar and came bounding to my feet. I knew Saint said to let him finish, but I had to do something, or my head was going to explode. I walked over to the wall and drove my fist into it. Luckily, since we tended to do shit like this at times, Sin had installed mats on the walls, so we'd stop fucking up our hands.

Cuffs kept talking. He was talking faster now. "Of course, we figured it had to be her brother Juan. Hearing from Saint what Barbie alleges happened, it fits, but that's not all. Pitbull, I need you to stay calm," he warned me. I swung around to glare at him. How much worse could it get?

"Just say it," I said through gritted teeth.

"I had a confidential informant call me tonight. He wanted to meet. Said he had some information. So, after the body was taken away, I met him. He told me that there is a rumor going around town. It's a reward to bring Luciana to her brother, unharmed. However, my CI is good at his job. He found out more, but I need Phantom to confirm it. Apparently, according to him, Luciana has been sold and her owner is chomping at the bit to have her delivered to him ASAP."

I lost it as soon as he stopped talking. I flipped over the chairs closest to me and then pounded my fists into the wall harder and harder as an animalistic roar came out of me. All I could think of was killing and making it as messy, painful, and long as possible. I was snapped out of my rage by several of my brothers dragging me back to my chair. They pushed me down and then held me there.

"Calm down, Pitbull. I know you want to go out and kill someone or several someones, but we have to confirm it. I promise you, we'll find her brother and end him. If she's been sold, then the buyer will end the same way. We can't have you going out and getting yourself killed. Luciana needs you," Executioner said softly. He leaned closer to me. "I promise, I'll fucking help you tear their hearts out when we catch them. No one fucks with our women and gets to live. Period." His words, as ugly as they were, did calm me down. He knew what it was like to have a woman you loved and needed to protect. I took several deep breaths. I sat for a good five minutes before I was calm enough to speak.

"Phantom, do you have an idea where to look to see if she is for sale? Would it be on the internet?" I asked him. He already had his phone out.

"It might. I have to go into the dark web and look. I want to ask Preacher to help check. He's got even more contacts than I do. If it's there, we'll find it. Of course, if they privately messaged about it, then that won't show it. I've been searching for his phone to be in use, so I can break into it and trace his calls and messages, but he must be using a burner phone. Same with Miguel and Jesús, his two cronies. We need to see if we can get into their old apartment. I might be able to link through their hardline or Wi-Fi and find him that way. Plus, I need to ask Luciana if there are any other people in his gang he might communicate with and what their phone numbers are. He has to be talking to them, and I don't think he'd do it all on that burner. He's too arrogant."

"I'll ask Luciana, but we can't tell her about this woman. If we do, she's gonna lose it and go back," I growled.

"Surely, she wouldn't give herself back to them to sell!" Talon exclaimed.

"Yes, she would if she thought she'd save lives. This is two people killed because of her brother. She'll say it's because of her. My woman has a soft heart for other people. It's what's going to make her one helluva nurse."

"So, she's gonna do the nursing thing?" Boomer asked with interest. I nodded.

"If I have anything to say about it, she will. I'm gonna have her get into the program as soon as she can. She's got too much talent to waste, but we're getting off topic. We need to make sure to keep this under wraps. Saint, can we go later tonight and search their old apartment? The sooner we do it, the better."

"We can. I'd say it's more likely the bottom feeders

are out during the night. I'd go right before dawn when they're all starting to settle in to sleep or are too high to care. We'll go in as a small team—all black, no identifying markings. You know the drill. Phantom make sure to take anything you think you could possibly need. If you want, have Preacher come too. It's time we flush out the fucker and this buyer. I hope to hell he's the one behind the missing women in town and the surrounding area. Time to take out the trash."

"Are we gonna tell Sin or wait until he's back?" Wrecker asked.

"I promised Sin if anything major went down, I'd tell him. I told him to wait, but he insisted. I'll wait until after the run tonight, so I can only call him once. They'll be back next Friday. We'll get as much of this done as we can. I'd love it if we could have it all wrapped up by then, but we'll have to see. Before we leave tonight, Wrecker, I want you to go question Barbie and take Cuffs. She needs to be aware we're taking this seriously. Get out of her every detail you can."

"The first victim was outside our bar and this time the strip club, which thankfully isn't ours. Do you think we should have more security at the businesses at night? The ones that are open late anyway," Rampage suggested.

"Good idea. We'll call and get more people at the Hangout and Infidels' Ink. I'd also like to have them at Tenillo Cycles and Infidels' Armory. Both those have a lot of high-end things they could destroy or steal. I don't want them to get their hands on more guns," Saint added.

"Should we warn any other businesses to take their security more seriously because of Bubble's?" Rampage asked.

"Shit, we should. Call Pop and get him on it. He can talk to the old geezers and have them reach out to the various business owners. Just tell them we're concerned with the deaths and don't want to have anyone else have issues. No need to tell everyone it relates to Luciana. Pop will know what to do," Saint agreed.

With that figured out, I asked him the next obvious question. "If we can't locate Juan this way, how can we get him out in the open?"

Saint gave me a hard look then he sighed. "I don't want to do it or say it, but we might have to set it up to look like she's out of our control and left. If they think that happened, we can nab them when they make a move."

"Goddamn it, Saint. I'm not putting her out there to be caught! No fucking way!" I half-yelled. He held up his hand.

"I know that. I'm not suggesting we do it, only make it look like we did. We just have to find a way to do it."

"I might have a way," Cuffs said quietly. He'd been whispering to Wrecker. Saint waved at him to continue.

"We have a female officer who's in her early to mid-twenties. She's close to Luciana's height and shape. If we dress her right and cover anything that might be different, we could use her as the decoy. She's done undercover stuff before."

"Is she one that can be trusted? There seems to be a lot of them there who can't," Bullet asked. He was right. A lot of the police department was thought to be dirty. It was taking time for Boss and Wrecker to prove it, though they had an idea of who was and who wasn't.

"I've seen nothing to indicate she's on the take. Boss agrees, so I'm as positive as I can be when it's not one of our own. She came here not long ago from somewhere else in Texas. I agree with Cuffs, she's our best bet. We don't want to use a civilian and certainly not Luciana," Wrecker chimed in.

"Okay, then it's settled. After tonight, we'll see if we can get a bead on Juan. If not, we get that female officer onboard for a sting operation. Now, I know we're all tired and stressed, but let's try and relax before we turn in. The women will want to know what's going on. No one says a word about the body or the buyer. Tell them we had news about more missing women, and that Boss wanted us to put our heads together again. Alright?" All of us nodded in agreement with Saint's plan. With that out of the way, he rapped the hammer and we stood up to leave. I'd have to work hard not to give away my anxiety to Luciana. I hated to lie or omit things, but it was for her own good. I had an idea how I could do that. Back in the common room, I looked around but didn't see Luciana anywhere. I walked over to the ladies. They all looked upset.

"Where's Luciana? Did she go to the bathroom?"

Sara shook her head. "No, she went to the trailer as soon as you guys went into your meeting. She said she had a headache and wanted to be alone. We tried to get her to let one of us go with her, but she insisted she had to be alone. I'm sorry, Pitbull, she was upset. She's positive whatever you guys were talking about involved her brother and her. Did it?" The other guys had come over to stand behind me.

"Nah, it didn't involve that. Another woman was taken, and Boss wanted Cuffs to talk to us and see if we'd come up with any ideas on where we needed to search to find them. The number keeps climbing and we need to find the source," I lied. She was watching me as if to catch me in a lie, but I'd perfected my ability to lie when it was necessary. It came in handy over the years.

"Well, good. Not that I'm happy another woman went missing, but it's good that it has nothing to do with our Luciana. You should go talk to her and let her know. It might help her headache," she said with a smile. I gave her a kiss on the cheek.

"I'm going right this minute. Thanks, Sara. Ladies, I'll see you all later. Have a good night." They all called out goodnights along with my brothers as I left. I knew Saint would text the details on when we were going into Juan's apartment later. In the meantime, I had a woman to cheer up. I quietly went up the steps to our trailer. I didn't want to wake her if she was asleep. However, that wasn't necessary. As soon as I opened the door, I heard raised voices, and I recognized both. It was Luciana and Barbie's. What the fuck was she doing here? I slowly crept through the door and found them standing in the kitchen.

Luciana was pissed and Barbie was shrieking at her.

"Why don't you just leave? You're not what he needs. You just took advantage and came up with some sob story about how your brother beat you. I say bullshit. I bet it was one of the guys you were screwing or leading on. You saw Pitbull and thought you'd found a meal ticket. He'll figure it out soon, then you'll be out on your ass and I'll be back in his bed where I belong." I wanted to interrupt and tell her she was full of shit, but Luciana caught my eyes and gave a tiny head shake. She was facing me. Barbie couldn't see me standing behind her.

"Barbie, I told you to leave. I'm not going to stand in our home and listen to this. Pitbull is with me. I'm sorry if that hurts you, but it's true. You're a bunny and I know that means you're here with whoever wants to have sex with you. You weren't in an exclusive relationship with him, and he didn't want one with you, otherwise he'd be with you. I didn't lie about my brother to trick Pitbull into protecting me. It's true, he did beat me and leave me for dead. I want you to leave."

Barbie took a step closer to Luciana. I saw she was watching Luciana's hands and kept a distance between them. She had to be remembering the time Luciana pulled her knife on her. "Your home? What a joke? You think this is your home?"

"Well, our temporary one until Pop's crew can get our house built. He said they can start in October and maybe by the end of January, it'll be done. I can't wait. A two-bedroom trailer is fine, but we'll need more room to raise our kids," she said with a note of spite in her voice. I almost laughed out loud. She was turning the knife. My woman could be a little mean when you pissed her off.

Barbie shrieked, "He's not building you a house!"

"Oh, but he is. He wants it built, then while I'm going to nursing school, we can make it what we want for when the kids come."

"Your brother will make sure that never happens."

"Oh yeah, the brother you say you met and who beat you. I doubt very much he did. You probably pissed off some woman by messing with her man and she whipped your ass, Luciana taunted back.

"You bitch, I did not! It was Juan. I recognized him and his guys, Miguel and Jesús. They're not stopping until they get their hands on you. I figure it shouldn't take much more for the Infidels to send you packing. You're bringing too much heat to their door. When that happens, Pitbull will see I'm the best one for him. I'll be living in that house, having his babies, not you," she said with a smile on her face. Damn, she was delusional.

"Where did they take you to have this conversation and beatdown? Back to their place? Maybe you partied with them and their buddies, and you were the entertainment. After all, don't you spread your legs for everyone?"

Barbie screamed and launched herself at Luciana. I raced to grab her, but I didn't need to worry. Luciana was ready for her and decked her as soon as she got within arm's reach. Barbie dropped like a stone and clutched her mouth. She was now bawling and yelling. "You'll pay for that. When they get you, I'll laugh my ass off. And for your information, I didn't party with them, they took me out to one of the houses outside of town. One of those out in the country on the north end of town. I bet when they get you, they'll make you the entertainment."

I'd heard enough. I walked over so Barbie could see me. Her eyes got huge, and she looked pale. I tugged Luciana into my arms and kissed her. When I released her mouth, I looked at Barbie. She was still on the floor holding her mouth. "Get your ass up. This is the last straw, Barbie. Your ass is out of here. I'll call for the vote, but I doubt anyone will object. Cuffs and Wrecker want to talk to you. Get your ass to the clubhouse. Don't go anywhere else or I'll know. I'll let you know the outcome of the vote. I'd start packing if I were you."

"But Pitbull, you don't understand—"

"I heard the shit you were shouting. Just so you know, there's no way you'd be moving into my house, having my kids, or even warming my bed ever again, if Luciana left. She's my old lady and soon she'll be my wife and then the mother of my children. Get over it. You need to leave. Now," I told her a little harshly. She stood up and was sobbing as she ran out of the trailer.

"I kind of feel sorry for her. She obviously has feelings for you, Cole," Luciana said sadly.

"Then they're her feelings and she has to get over it. I love you. I'll always love you." I was walking her down the short hall to our room. I made sure to stop and lock the front door as we passed it. Once I had her in the room, I sat her down on the edge of the bed and I crouched down in front of her.

"Well, you sure made her feel sick, telling her you were going to marry me. I thought she was going to puke." Luciana laughed. I kissed her knuckles.

"I wasn't lying, *bebé*. I do plan to marry you. No waiting until other people think we've known each other long enough. We never have a guarantee that tomorrow will come for any of us. I know it's fast and crazy, but we love each other, and I know we're meant to be together. Do you want to be my wife?"

She didn't say anything for a couple of seconds, which made my heart pound. What if she said no? "Of course, I want to be your wife! I love you and even if it is crazy and a short time since we met, I too think it's meant to be. Yes, Cole Landis, I'll marry you one day." I took her mouth in a passionate kiss. I devoured her and when I had to surface to give us air, I reached into the inner pocket of my cut. I pulled out the small box I had been carrying in there for the last week and a half. Her eyes got huge, and her mouth formed an "O" when she saw what I held. I opened the lid.

Inside was the engagement ring I'd bought for her. It was a one-carat cushion-cut diamond set in platinum. It was wrapped in petal-like shapes lined with more sparkling diamonds and the detailing was an intricate milgrain, according to the woman at the jewelry store. I had no idea what that meant, but it was beautiful and reminded me of Luciana. It was a little vintage. I took it out of the box and lifted her left hand. I held it at the tip of her ring finger. "Can I?"

She nodded her head and whispered, "Please." It slid

on without a problem. She looked down at it then back up at me. I opened my mouth to ask her if she liked it. I didn't get the words out because she launched herself at me and took me to the floor. She was lying on top of me, kissing me as she sobbed. I let her do it because I was busy running my hands all over her body and getting hard. It looked like I had a fiancée, and I planned to initiate our new status with a night of lovemaking.

Luciana: Chapter 17

I was still overwhelmed that Pitbull had given me an engagement ring after only knowing each other for a month. It sounded insane when I thought about it, but for us, it worked. After I'd said yes that night, we'd made love for hours. Right before I'd fallen off into a deep sleep, he'd told me he had to go do some work for the club, but not to worry. He'd be back in a few hours. Something about doing a security check on their businesses.

That was three days ago. Since then, I saw the guys in small groups whispering a lot. Not sure if it had to do with that or something else. I hated the thought it was about my brother. Tonight, they were in their regular weekly church meeting. I was sitting with the other old ladies. We couldn't wait to see Lyric when she got back in four days. I wanted to show her my ring.

I looked down at the glittering diamond on my finger. I still wanted to pinch myself to be sure it was real. The next day after I said yes, we'd told the club we were getting married. Everyone had been so happy, and the ladies were clamoring to see my ring. The high from that still hadn't faded. In fact, it got bigger because Pitbull wanted me to set a wedding date. He was giving me a deadline of October thirty-first, just three days after his thirty-second birthday. He swore he couldn't wait longer than that.

Lucky for him, I didn't want to wait. Besides, I didn't have anyone to really invite. It would be his friends and family. All I needed was help in planning it once I came up with a theme. That was what the ladies were doing tonight, helping me with the theme. I had an idea; it was one I'd had for years. I just didn't think it would go over with the groom. A bunch of bikers weren't going to embrace what I had in mind.

We'd been talking for about fifteen minutes when Jackie huffed. "Spit it out, Luciana. You have something on your mind. I can tell you're not excited about the ideas so far. What do you want for your wedding? Please say it's something I can sink my teeth into."

I shyly glanced around at them. Seeing they were all waiting for me to tell them, I threw caution to the wind. "Okay, it's crazy though. It's an idea I had for years. I don't think Pitbull or the guys will go for it. You know I'm part Mexican. Well, it kind of comes from that. You've heard of the Day of the Dead." They all nodded. "Well, it's a looser interpretation of that combined with the books I used to read. I've always had this idea that doing a gothic wedding would be cool. Not your typical light and airy, but dark and dramatic colors like black, silver, and red, maybe a little white." I bit my lip as I waited to see their responses. I didn't have to wait more than a second or two.

Skye squealed, Sara laughed, and Jackie clapped and smiled. "Oh my God, I love it! Do you have any pictures or anything?" Skye asked. I was stunned that they thought it was a good idea.

"Sure, but the guys won't go for it."

"Honey, they'll go for whatever you want. They may grumble, but it's all in fun. They'll bend over backward to make this wedding perfect for you. Pitbull even more. If they have to dress up for one day, they can live," Sara told me as she rolled her eyes.

"I do have pictures. I created this Pinterest board for it. Wanna see?" They all eagerly gathered around the laptop that Skye had brought with her. I pulled up my board. They all gasped when they saw the pics of the dress, cake, décor, and groom's clothes.

"Oh my God, Luciana, you have to do it, or I swear, I'll kill you! It's perfect and so beautiful. Tell us the date and we'll get to work on it," Jackie exclaimed.

"You're working on Skye and Executioner's wedding," I protested.

"That's easy and most of it is already done. This will take a little more time but so worth it. What date? Does Pitbull have a preferred date other than October thirty-first as a deadline?"

"He told me he didn't have a preference, but I do. I want to get married on his birthday. It's October twenty-eighth. Think he'll like that?"

"He'll love it. Perfect. That gives us just over fifteen weeks. First thing we need to do is find this dress and get you fitted, and it ordered. Then we'll get the décor, cake and music set," Sara said as she jotted down notes on a notepad she had.

"We can do the flowers, of course," Jackie added.

"I bet Paula can help us find some of the décor and even jewelry. She does all that crafting stuff. Do you mind if we ask them to help?" Skye asked.

"No, I don't mind as long as they have time. Aren't some of them getting married too?"

"Yeah, but they have time. Plus with all of us helping, it'll be easier. You don't stress about it. We'll handle it and you handle the other thing," Sara admonished. I gave her a questioning look.

"What other thing?"

"Getting signed up for classes so you can start your nursing program. Are you on the list yet? If not, you need to be. It can take time to get in I heard."

"Actually, I've kept my name on a list for the last three years. I knew it was unlikely I'd ever get to go, but I hoped I might get away from Juan or he'd let me go since it might help him and his thug friends. Each time my name came up, I had to defer. They're due soon to ask again. I'm not sure if I'm on the chosen list again for the new program or not," I admitted with butterflies in my stomach.

"Well, call their asses tomorrow and ask! Pitbull won't let that go. He wants you to do it. He knows how much it means to you and therefore, it's important to him. Besides, sometimes their dumbasses come in here needing to be stitched up too. We can't expect Paula and Frankie to always take care of them. Stupid men need to learn to duck or run faster," Sara muttered. That made all of us laugh.

We were laughing and talking when the guys got out of their meeting. I lowered the lid to the laptop. I preferred to show him at home just in case he hated the idea. He and Executioner came right over to us. A few of the guys went to the bar and the rest to tables nearby. Pitbull kissed me and asked, "What have you been working on, *amada?*"

"Our wedding," I told him with a smile.

He perked up. "Really! When is it? What did you decide?"

"I want to have it on your birthday, honey. I do have an idea, but we can talk about it later. I'll show you some pictures."

"My birthday? You want it on my birthday?" he asked me softly. I nodded. He groaned then kissed me. It wasn't one of those quick touch of the lips; it was a full-on kiss until your toes curl kind of kiss. When he let go, I was panting, and we had a smiling and laughing audience. "I love that you want to do it then. Why wait, show me the pictures, unless you don't have them here."

I slowly opened the laptop and brought up the screens. I watched his face as I clicked through them as I bit my lip. I was trying to gauge if he hated them or not. His face gave nothing away. My heart started to sink. He hated it and didn't want to tell me. "It doesn't have to be this. It was just a silly idea. You tell me what you want." I went to close the laptop again. He grabbed my hand.

"Don't. I love these, Luciana. It's so different and

beautiful. I never thought of doing something like this. What do you consider this to be?"

"It's mostly gothic. The ladies think we can get the Time Served ladies to help. The dress will be the big thing then the attire for you guys. We won't go too crazy. I hate that you have to end up paying for it. It should be my parents or my *los padrinos*, my godparents, but they're gone. We sure won't get Juan to pay," I said a little angrily. I had no family to stand with me on my big day.

"*Bebé*, I'm sorry you don't have them, but you don't need to worry about the cost. I can cover it."

"Honey, we have the house being built. Until I can start working, I can't help with it. We should go simpler, concentrate on building the house. As soon as Juan is taken care of, I can get a job. I don't have experience, but there are lots of jobs that require no experience. I can work a couple of those full-time." He gave me an incredulous look. I saw the others staring at me with their mouths hanging open. "What?" I asked them.

"You're getting your ass into a nursing program, not working two fucking jobs to pay the mortgage on our house. I have the money for the house and this wedding. We're not going to skimp on it," Pitbull told me with a bite to his tone.

"I'm not going to expect you to do everything while I sit on my ass!"

"You won't be sitting on your ass! You'll be going to school and taking care of me and eventually our kids. I take a lot of work, *bebé*. I have to pay you to put up with me." He growled as he gave me a heated look. This time it was a sexual one.

"Get your mind out of the gutter, Pitbull. You're practically undressing her with your eyes," Rampage joked. Pitbull didn't say a word. He stood up and pulled me with him. He swung me up and over his shoulder. I yelled in surprise. He slapped my ass.

"Be quiet, we need to go figure this out, naked. I think best when I'm naked and I've been inside of you." I gasped at him saying that out loud. My face flamed. The guys and ladies all laughed as he walked out of the common room. I vowed to get him back for that.

Pitbull:

My woman had a lot to learn about her man. One of those things was that I expected to be the one to take care of our family. That didn't mean she couldn't work or have her own money. I just wanted to be the main provider. She could use hers for other things but not the big household stuff like the house or the wedding. I know she was used to taking care of herself. It was time she learned what it meant to be cherished and taken care of.

I carried her all the way to our trailer. She had stopped trying to get down and wasn't saying anything. I couldn't see her face to tell if she was pissed at me or not. If she was, I'd have to soothe it away. Orgasms would help in that department. My woman was very sexual and held onto her tensions. She needed to decompress often, which I had no problem with. When we got in the trailer, I sat her down to take off my boots. She had her back turned toward me, standing in the center of the living room.

"Luciana, look at me. Are you pissed that I did that?" She shook her head no but didn't look at me. I set aside my boots and walked up behind her. I gently turned her around. That's when I saw her face. She had tears running down her cheeks. I sucked in a breath and held it for a couple of seconds.

"God, *bebé*, I'm sorry. I didn't mean to embarrass you or hurt you. I just wanted to get you alone so we could talk about this. Come here." I took her hand and led her to the couch. I sat down and pulled her down to sit beside me. I wanted her on my lap but thought she probably wouldn't like that. "Luciana, talk to me," I pleaded.

She raised her head and looked me in the eyes then erupted. Tears ran down her face as she laughed. "I can't believe you said you think better when you're naked and have been inside of me! Jesus, how do you make decisions at the Hangout? Do you strip down in the office and pace around naked? And you'd better not tell me you would have some woman come in to help you with the other part," she warned me through narrowed eyes. I held up my hands in surrender.

"Only with you does that work, I swear. And no, I have to keep my clothes on at work. Though now that I think about it, when I have a tough decision from now on, I'll call you to come visit. How does that sound?" She grinned and slid up close to me. Her arms went around me, and her hands grabbed both of my ass cheeks then she squeezed.

"Well, why don't we get naked and into each other so I can think. You may be on to something." I didn't have to be told twice. I tugged off her top as she tackled the belt and zipper to my jeans. It was a flurry of clothes for several seconds. When we were finally naked, I ran my eyes up and down her body. No matter how many times I looked at her, she got sexier and more beautiful. Some stupid men would be turned off by her lush curves, but I wasn't. I loved them. I could see them getting even lusher after she had my babies.

Her hands were running all over my chest and stomach. She was tracing my tats. I hoisted her up in my arms. Just that little touch had me hard. She wrapped her arms and legs around me. I shifted her so she was right above my throbbing cock. I teased her slit with the head. She shivered. I kissed her, my mouth consuming hers. I wanted the taste of her on my tongue. Suddenly, she moved and dropped down on me, her pussy slid down my cock, taking me inside of her heat. I groaned. "Fuck, Luciana. That's a bad idea. I can't take much right now. I want to make this last, *bebé*," I pleaded.

"We can make it last next round. Right now, I need to come with you deep inside me. I've been thinking about this for hours." She panted as she rode up and down my length. I was helping her by using her hips as handles. She was making sure to slam hard when she came back down. It was making my balls tingle and draw up closer to my body.

I took a couple of steps and pressed her back to the wall going down the hall. "Then hold on, it's gonna be a hard, fast ride," I growled. Her arms and legs tightened along with her pussy. Using the wall for leverage, I pounded in and out. I was determined to get as deep as I could. I hit her cervix and she hissed. I didn't stop. As I sped up, our panting and moans did as well.

Each time my pelvis hit her clit, she'd moan and shudder. I could tell she was getting close. I knew that I was. I slammed into her faster. I nipped her earlobe and growled, "Wring me dry, *mi alma.* Take my seed. God, if we weren't waiting until you're done with school, I'd be giving you that baby right now."

That thought, along with her cry and the tightening of her pussy walls, pushed me closer to the edge. "Give it to me, Cole. Give it to me and we'll wish the birth control doesn't work." That was it, I couldn't stop. I thrust three more times. As I felt my balls tighten in preparation to come, she clenched down on me and made me see stars as she screamed and came. I stroked in and out twice then gave her the cum she wanted. It was a long stream that wouldn't stop. By the time I was done, she was hanging on to me exhausted. I stood there until I was sure I could walk, then I carried her to our bed. I laid her down and gently pulled out. She whimpered.

I leaned down and kissed her. She bit my bottom lip and sucked on it. When she let go, I kissed down her neck and chest, then across her stomach. As I got to her mound, she raised her head and asked me, "What are you doing, Cole? I need to go clean up."

"I am cleaning you up." I lowered my head and swiped my tongue up and down her slit. My cum had started to leak out, and I got it on my tongue along with her juices. I had never gone down on a woman like this, probably because I always wore a condom. Thinking about it, I didn't think I'd have wanted to do it. But with Luciana, I wanted to taste what we tasted like together. It was saltier and a little musky mixed with her taste. It wasn't unpleasant. I sucked hard to clean her up, making sure not to take more than what ran out. I was secretly hoping it would get her pregnant despite the birth control. A bad idea I knew, with her wanting to go to school and her age.

She was moaning and squirming on the bed. She was getting slicker. Hell, this was turning her on. I kneeled and got to work eating her pussy and teasing her clit. My hands were caressing and tweaking those perfect breasts of hers. The nipples were rock hard. She was panting. "Cole, I'm gonna come. Oh God, I'm gonna come again." I increased my efforts. In a matter of a few minutes, she grabbed my head and screamed. Her thighs clamped around my head, and I was nose and mouth deep in her pussy. I was smothering and loved it.

When she calmed enough to realize what she was doing, she let go. "I'm sorry, honey. I didn't realize what I was doing. Jesus, you're trying to kill me," she panted. I licked a few times to get her juices that had spilled out along with more of my cum. When I was done, I stood up.

Her eyes got round as she saw my cock. I stroked up and down it. Eating her pussy and tasting my cum had gotten me hard. I was ready to go again. "Get on your hands and knees and scoot to the edge of the bed," I growled.

As she did, I opened the drawer beside the bed. She turned her head. "Close those eyes." She did as I asked, but I could see the question in them before she did. Once she did, I pulled out what I wanted. I'd gotten a tube of lube, a blindfold, and soft cuffs. I was in the mood to see how adventurous she was.

"*Bebé*, do you trust me?"

"Of course, I trust you, Cole. Why?"

"I want to try something. I need to cover your eyes. Is that okay?"

She barely hesitated. "Yes, that's okay." I wrapped the blindfold around her eyes and secured it.

"Still trust me that I'll never hurt you or take it too far?"

"Yes."

"If you don't like something or it hurts, tell me. I'll stop. Now, put those pillows by your head under your chest and then put your arms behind you." She fumbled to get them in place and do as I asked. It was sexy as hell to see her do it. As soon as her hands were behind her back, I slid the first fur-lined leather cuff around her left wrist. She jumped when she felt it tighten, but she didn't tell me to stop. I quickly secured the other. Then I stood back and admired the view.

She was kneeling with her arms behind her back, her chest to the bed and her ass in the air. She was at my mercy, and it made me fucking hot. I opened the lube and laid it beside her legs. I got up behind her and teased the head of my cock in her entrance. She tried to thrust back, but I pulled away. After doing this a few times, the next time I did it, I slammed into her. This had my cock pushing through those swollen muscles. It caused her to scream as she reluctantly opened to me. I could only groan in ecstasy.

When I was all the way in, I pressed on her lower back and began to pound in and out of her. She was going to come again before I got to the real action. Her pussy was tight, wet and so damn hot, that I had to fight not to finish in her right away. I gritted my teeth and kept going.

Sweat was breaking out on my forehead when she clamped down and came sobbing and jerking. I held onto my wits and kept from coming through pure determination. As she slowly calmed, I covered my finger in lube and stuck it in her ass. She whimpered. "Cole, what're you doing? Oh God, you didn't come."

"No, I didn't. But I will." I slowly pulled out and notched my cock at the entrance to her ass. She moaned. I pushed inside slowly. She hissed but the wiggling she was doing told me she was okay for me to continue. It didn't take long for me to be fully inside of that ass. I took a deep breath then began to work in and out. I needed to come and badly. I rode her deep and hard, my pelvis slapping off her ass. Every couple of thrusts, I slapped her ass, making it turn red.

She took no time to start slamming back into my thrusts. She was panting, moaning, and sobbing as she chanted, "Harder, go deeper, smack me harder. Fuck me, Cole." All that made me lose control. I don't know what happened over the next few minutes. All I know is when I came, I felt like my soul was leaving my body. I was swearing and shouting her name. She was screaming and begging me not to stop.

At the end, we fell into a heap. Tangled limbs were everywhere. I could hardly catch my breath. My cock was softening but still jerking. She was having tiny quakes. I took a deep breath and then pulled out. She cried out but didn't move. I kissed her neck. "Are you alright? Did I hurt you?"

"No, I just can't move or think. If this is what you need to think, we're gonna have to rest afterward until my brain regenerates. Otherwise, you're out of luck." I burst out laughing. She was right, I couldn't think at the moment either. We'd have to discuss working and paying for the wedding later. I removed the blindfold and cuffs then curled around her.

Pitbull: Chapter 18

I was able to convince Luciana not to worry about paying for the wedding. It took another session in bed, but in the end, I think I wore her out and she just couldn't argue. The other thing I got my way on was she called the college about the nursing program. She was happy to see she was still on the waiting list and that she would be one of the ones they would be asking about starting classes September first. It didn't leave her long to get her paperwork entered, but she was working on it. I could tell how excited she was. She was insisting on filing for financial aid. I let her but knew when the time came, I'd be paying off her student loans. No need for her to have that hanging over her, but I'd wait to tell her that until after she was done.

I was surprised to find that with her taking some classes in high school, she had her general courses done. It would be two intense years, but then she'd be done. I loved seeing the excitement on her face. That goodness had to be balanced against the bad.

Sin and Lyric had come back from their honeymoon yesterday, which was good. We were having church again to get him up to speed on everything. Saint had told him some, but not all since we wanted him to enjoy his honeymoon. From the looks of them, they did. We teased the hell out of him as we welcomed them back and again as we took our seats in church. All he did was grin. Once we were all seated, we got down to business. Saint was the one to start since he was the VP and had been in charge while Sin was gone.

"Let's go over what you know. You know about the woman found outside Bubbles with Luciana's name carved in her chest. We upped security at our businesses that have people there at night. So far, things have been good and no more killings, or at least not like those. We didn't tell Luciana about her. She'd only get more upset, and Pitbull doesn't want that. It's bad enough we had Barbie come in here beat up and blaming it on her. She said Juan and his guys did it."

"Did we ever prove that to be true?" Sin asked.

"No, but she seemed adamant it was him. She went as far as to get into it with Luciana. Pitbull put an end to it. and we had a meeting. The club voted her out as I told you. She had until Monday to go, but she left yesterday. She was still ranting and raving about Luciana and how she was all at fault and ruining the club. That we'd be sorry we kept Luciana and didn't give her up." Sin just shook his head and rolled his eyes.

"The worst is we found out from a confidential informant of Cuffs that Juan sold Luciana to someone. Phantom has been trying to see what he can find out on who the buyer is and when it's supposed to go down. No surprise, we haven't told that to Luciana either. Though we did decide we're most likely going to have to draw out Juan using a decoy. There's an officer at the police station they believe is trustworthy and looks enough like her to be believed at a distance."

"Do we have a time and place set for this decoy sting to go down?" Sin asked as he looked at Wrecker and Cuffs.

"Not yet, but I did quietly vet her to see if she'd do an undercover sting and she's ready. Boss agreed with using her. We only have to decide when and where. It will be best to do it after dark, since it'll be harder for someone to recognize it's not Luciana. We talked and wanted to ask what you think of outside of the Hangout? We own it. She's with us and most likely would be at one of our places," Wrecker told us.

"But wouldn't that make them leery? They would expect us to be there," Talon remarked.

"There's that chance, but where else could she go that wouldn't be one of our places of business? Unless we send her out with the other old ladies, but that could get hairy because we'd have to watch all of them, not just the decoy," Cuffs mused.

"I don't want to risk the others. It will have to be one of our businesses or someplace only she has to go to," Sin said adamantly.

"She's going to the college next week to have orientation for classes starting in September. Why not have our decoy go sooner and get snatched? They shouldn't be that busy and we know they have to have eyes on the compound in the hopes she does leave. What do you think of that?" I volunteered and asked.

"Congrats! She's doing the schooling, awesome. I

think you're right. It would be a good time to do it. We'll get some of Pop's guys to help. They'd be less noticeable than us. They'd expect a few of us to go with her. Not sure how they'll get their hands on her, but we'll make sure they don't," Sin said with satisfaction.

"We'll hash those details out. Do you think this officer can do it on Monday? The sooner the better," I said. I was anxious to have this over with.

"I don't see why not. I'll pull her at the last minute, so no one finds out what we're doing," Wrecker assured us.

"Is everything set up with Blue moving over to the Liar's Lair? What about a replacement bartender for her at the Hangout?" Sin fired off.

"We found a bartender—some guy who's new to town. He's not looking for it to be long term, which will work for us. His name is Lon, and his background checks out. Blue will start over there as soon as they're ready for her," I told them. I hated to lose her even for a short while, but it was needed.

"Preacher and I have the audio and voice worked out. She'll wear a tiny earpiece that no one will even be able to see. We'll be able to hear her and talk to her. She'll be able to do the same with us. Also, he's found or made the tiniest camera I've ever seen. Tiny enough to be put into something and look like a jewel, like a diamond earring or some shit. She'll wear it and we can see whatever it's pointed at," Phantom told us. You could hear the excitement in his voice.

"Damn, that's kind of scary when you think about

it. You could be watched and never know it. I hope like hell Blue doesn't have to work there long. That place is a hellhole. The scum who comes in there makes me sick," Boomer growled. You could see the distaste written all over his face.

"I don't think any of us want her there, but at least she can take care of herself. I have a feeling it won't be long before she sniffs something out. She may have to hurt a few guys first, but knowing Blue, she'll have fun with that part," Rampage joked. We all laughed. Blue was a badass.

"Anything else we need to talk about?" Sin asked. I nodded. He indicated for me to talk.

"I didn't say anything at the time, but Luciana had a run-in with Jon Bentley at your wedding reception. Something about it didn't sit right. He somehow recognized her as Juan's sister and made a big deal out of it. He insisted she was like him, and we should get rid of her."

"What the fuck? Did you knock him on his ass?" Saint growled.

"I didn't get the chance to. His dad, Jack, popped him in the mouth and told him to go home. She was upset, and it took a while to settle her down. He stirred up her fear that others would think the same."

"He still needs to have his ass beat for it. I can go pay him a visit," Executioner volunteered. He was our enforcer and had no problem bringing pain when it was warranted.

"Thanks, Ex, but he'll have his day. His remarks made me wonder, how does he know Juan? I mean, I guess he's known to a lot of people, but I'd think most of those would be those who get their drugs from him or his people. Do you think Jon has a drug problem? I can't think of any other reason why he'd know him and be able to recognize Luciana."

"He could. There's something off about him. He lost Skye the Bentley's account because he was upset that Ben hired her. The rental properties they have don't appear to be occupied, and he manages those, not his brother, Ben. Skye said she saw monthly income coming in for them and we drove by several and they looked all overgrown and deserted. Do you think he's laundering money from his family's company?" Executioner asked.

"Maybe he's using it for something else. We should look into Jon Bentley, if for no other reason than to see if he is on drugs. If he is and Jack doesn't know, he should. He gave over the running of the company to his boys. I'd hate to see it run into the ground because of Jon having a drug problem. It won't be long before the money needed to pay for his habit grows. You know that happens to most people who get hooked. Maybe that's how he knew Luciana. After we find out what's happening, then Pitbull can bust his head for doing that to her. Luciana has had enough crap in her life. She doesn't need more. Speaking of your girl, congrats on the engagement. Any idea when she's gonna make an honest man out of you?" Sin asked with a smirk on his face.

"Yeah. Sorry I did it when you two were gone, but the timing was right. She's gonna marry me on my

CIARA ST JAMES

birthday, October twenty-eighth. She and the ladies are already planning it. They have the theme and she's excited about it. So be sure all of you have no plans to be out of town if you can help it. She won't have anyone from her side, so I want all of us, the Time Served crew and our other friends to be there. Maybe she'll have a couple new friends from school by then she can invite."

"That's fantastic, man. We'll be there. The house will be done hopefully after the New Year. You're moving fast. Just like those two," Saint replied as he grinned and pointed at Sin and Executioner. The two of them just shrugged and gave him a big smile.

"You wait, it'll happen. I thought it wouldn't and Brea warned me it would and sooner than I expected. That woman might be a little psychic," I joked.

"If anyone is psychic, it's our man, Omen. He's freaky with shit. He told me the other day that my bike needed new tires. I told him they weren't that old. The next day, the front one went flat. Had a big nail in it. I know he's a prospect, but we might want to get him involved in the planning of shit sometimes, in case he has any of those 'feelings' of his," Talon said. He wasn't joking either.

"Omen has his mojo, that's for sure. It was right almost ninety-nine percent of the time. Those who knew him in the Corps listened to what he said. When we didn't, we paid the price. It's all his Cajun mother's fault. According to him, that side of the family all has the sight, even though his dad was Cajun too," Ex told us. I didn't know if I believed in that or not, but it wouldn't hurt to listen when he told us shit.

The others all murmured over what Ex said. They were cut short by Sin. "Be sure you're all here at seven. Want to go over one more thing. In the meantime, get out of here. Relax. I'm having dinner brought in tonight so no one has to cook. Start off the weekend right." I wondered what he had to discuss and why he wasn't doing it now. But having a night that the ladies didn't have to cook was a good thing. We all got up and moseyed out after he hit the hammer on the table.

Luciana:

The guys seemed to be in church longer than usual. Not sure if that was true or if I was just nervous. I'd been having this feeling all day that something would go wrong. I had no idea why. All I had to worry about was Juan and his guys, and according to Pitbull, they were still in hiding. Maybe it was because I didn't know where they were that this feeling was growing.

I tried to ignore it and listen to Lyric tell us about their honeymoon. She looked so happy as she talked. I'd never seen her look this happy. Being married was good for her. Sin had returned looking like he couldn't be happier either. I loved seeing two people that much in love. It was like what I saw when I looked at Executioner and Skye. He constantly watched her and had a hand on her if he could. The way Pitbull was with me now that I thought about it.

"Tell Lyric your idea for the wedding," Skye said excitedly. I'd already told Lyric our good news.

"Here, let me show you. All the other ladies think it's great. Tell me the truth, even if you think I won't like it. Is this too weird for my wedding theme?" I asked as I pulled the pics I had on my phone up for her to look at. She went through them all before she looked up.

"I think that is one of the greatest ideas for a wedding I've ever seen! God, I'm jealous. Those bridesmaid dresses are to die for and your dress. Oh my God!" she gushed. "When are you getting the dress? Where?"

"It's hard with this whole hide from Juan thing, even though he knows I'm here. I found a lady online. We took a bunch of measurements and sent it to her. She's making the dress and then I have to go for a fitting once it's ready. She lives in McKinney. I couldn't believe she was that close. I'm praying that by the time it's ready, this craziness with my brother is done."

"If I know the guys, they'll have it figured out soon," Lyric assured me. I gave her hand a squeeze.

"I hate to break this up, but we need to figure out what's on the menu tonight for dinner," Jackie interjected. It was almost five o'clock.

"Wait, don't fix anything. Sin said he was ordering food. He didn't want anyone to have to cook tonight. Damn, I forgot to tell you," Lyric said hurriedly.

"Awesome! I won't say no. I don't care what it is. I'm just hungry," Skye told us as she rubbed her stomach. You could barely see anything there to indicate she was pregnant.

"Lord, don't let the preggo go hungry. They need to hurry up with that meeting so we can feed you," I teased her. She stuck out her tongue at me. The guys must have heard me because they came streaming into the common room a couple of seconds later. I got up and went over to Pitbull. He held out his arm, and I stepped into his side and planted a kiss on his mouth. We enjoyed a few moments kissing before whistles had us parting and laughing.

"You need to get Sin to order the food. Skye is hungry," I told him.

"He said it's already taken care of, though I'm not sure when it's supposed to get here. I'll find out. Can I get you anything?"

"No, I'm fine. I'm talking about the wedding and stuff with the girls, filling Lyric in on what she missed. Did you guys have a good meeting?" I asked innocently. I knew that he wouldn't tell me anything. It was considered club business. He shrugged.

"The usual. I'll be right back. Why don't you go back to the ladies?" He gently pushed me in that direction. I did as he suggested and saw him go over to Sin. When he came to the table a while later, he had a drink and another water for me. He sat down. Sin and Executioner had joined us, and the others were scattered around the room. I laughed watching Zeus and Bear compete for Lyric and Sin's attention. While they were gone, Saint had been looking after the two of them. Bear was the one who cracked me up the most.

He stared at Sin like he thought he could back him down. When Sin bared his teeth at him, I swear Bear sniffed and turned his back on him. He sauntered over to Lyric. She picked him up and she snuggled with him. As she did, Bear looked around at Sin and I thought I saw a doggie smile on his face, as if to say, *I'm the one she really loves*. Sin must have thought the same thing.

"Lyric, I swear that little shit is asking for it. He's giving me that look of his. I'm the alpha dog in this family," he growled. Lyric broke out laughing.

"I swear, Sin, he's not doing that. Bear loves you."

"Like hell! He tried to push me out of bed last night when we got home. I put him out with Zeus, and he snuck in. I have no idea how he got on the bed. When I took him back to his bed, he sneered at me."

That had everyone laughing and teasing Sin. He flipped several of them the bird, and I heard him grumble, "Goddamn dog is going to need an ass whooping."

It was while we were laughing that Omen came inside. He had a huge box in his arms. "There's more food down by the gate." Talon, Phantom and Boomer all jumped to go get it. This must be our dinner.

When they got back and everything was unpacked, we saw it was Italian. There was lasagna, Alfredo, chicken parmesan, salad, breadsticks, and even cannoli. When we were done eating a half hour later, I felt like I was going to burst. I'd eaten way more than I usually did, but I had been starving. The guys were all groaning, and the ladies were looking like they wanted a nap like me. The prospects had cleaned up the mess along with help from Shy and Tabby Cat. They had been called to the clubhouse to have food. They tended not to spend a lot of time with the whole bunch of us, but they needed to eat. I felt bad for them. They had such a weird place here. I was glad Barbie was gone. She would have probably caused a fight.

Before everyone broke up and went their ways, Sin whistled to get our attention. I was sitting on Pitbull's lap as he teased me about being in a food coma. "Can I have your attention? I told the guys there was one more thing we had to discuss after the food got here. I want to do it now. We're going to be getting a new member of the Infidels joining us in the not-too-distant future."

This caused all the guys to look at each other in astonishment. They must not have known. But didn't they vote on stuff like that? Sin continued after the murmuring died down. "This new member is going to take a lot of time and will need to be introduced slowly."

"Why? What the hell? Sin, you've never brought in someone without us talking about him and taking a vote on it," Saint told him. "Why didn't we talk about this in church?"

"There are unique circumstances for this member. I wanted to talk to everyone together about this one, not just my brothers." Sin looked around at all of us. I saw several looking a little upset and others just puzzled. Omen seemed to have a smile on his face for some reason. Lyric, lightly punched Sin in the ribs.

"Stop toying with them, Sin. Tell them." He smiled at her and gave her a kiss. When he was done, he raised his head and announced, "Lyric and I got news while we were on our honeymoon. It's great news, but not what we expected. We're going to be having a baby. A second Infidel baby will be joining Ex and Skye's little one."

This wasn't a complete surprise. Even in the short time I'd known the two of them, I knew they both wanted to have kids right away. Lyric loved kids. That's why she was a schoolteacher. Her love for her students is how she found the Infidels. We all gave them hugs and congratulations as we all chatted at once.

I was truly happy for them. They would make great parents who would love and protect their children, but a tiny hollow piece of me felt let down. I knew we needed to wait to have kids. I was young and needed to get my schooling done first. However, it didn't completely take away my urge to have one in my arms. I was going to miss out on my niece or nephew because of Juan. It would have been nice to have some other blood relative around to love.

When they got to the point where they were chatting to others, I slipped out of the common room and went outside for some air. I didn't want to bring down the celebratory vibe. I'd barely made it around the clubhouse and sat down on one of the picnic tables when Omen came out of the darkness. He walked straight up to me and sat down. "Wanna talk about it?" he asked.

"About what? It's just hot in there. I needed some air."

"Luciana, I know this is hard for you, to see so much family and then have to think about your brother, but the Ares Infidels and the Time Served are your family and friends. We will fill that void you feel. I promise in the not-too-distant future, you'll have more family than you know what to do with. Your schooling will be behind you and your dream of being a nurse will become a reality. You'll have a family with Pitbull, and you'll get to see your niece or nephew grow up."

He sounded so positive. I shook my head. "How can you be so sure, Omen?"

"Some of it is just a feeling I get. Sometimes, I get a flash of what you or the others will experience. I have no idea the exact time, but it won't be easy. You need to stay alert and able to protect yourself. I know my brother, Pitbull, thinks he can keep you safe. Maybe he can, but never be without your own weapons either. Do you carry that knife all the time, Luciana?"

"I did. Here in the compound, I sometimes forget. Why?"

"Wear it even here. Please. I don't know why it's so important, but I know it is. Will you do that for me?"

I took his hand. "Omen, I hear things about you. That you know things and that there are seers in your family. I was raised not to discount things like that. Who knows, it could be your ancestors speaking to you from the other side. I promise I'll always keep it with me, even here. Will you tell me if you discover something for sure? Even if it might not be a good thing?"

He sighed. "I'll keep my brothers in the loop. It's what I have to do. I don't always see everything. The closer I am to the person, the hazier it can be. But I'd never keep anything that could put you in danger a secret. I know you have to be worried about the woman's body they found outside Bubble's strip club. That's the second one left as a warning. Your name on her had to mess with your head. Don't let it make you do something rash. It's not your fault. It's Juan's and his gang."

I scrambled to my feet. Omen frowned at me then understanding came over his face. He swore. "Fuck, you didn't know. Damn it, I'm sorry, Luciana. I didn't know they hadn't told you. You knew about the first one, so I assumed you did the other. Jesus, Pitbull and the guys are going to kill me." He gave me a hug. I clung to him as what he said whirled around in my brain.

Pitbull: Chapter 19

It took me a few minutes to realize Luciana was no longer in the common room. I'd gone over to talk to Wrecker about the decoy we were setting up next week. I wanted this done, so we could get on with our lives. Finding out Sin was having a baby, only made me want it more for myself. I'd wait until Luciana was done with school, then we'd get serious about starting a family. Something I knew she wanted desperately. She felt like she hadn't had one since her parents died.

Thinking of them, I then went over to Phantom. I wanted to ask him to do something, and I didn't want Luciana to know. "Hey, brother, you got a minute?" I asked him. He nodded and sat down his Shiners beer on the bar. We were at the back corner.

"Sure. What can I do for you, Pit?"

"When you get a chance, would you dig into the death of Luciana's parents? It was five years ago. She said she was told it was a home invasion. Thankfully, she wasn't at home that night. My gut feels like something is off. The whole thing of Juan getting custody when he was such a fuckup makes me even more sure that nothing kosher went on. Don't mention it to her. I don't want to stir up memories if we don't have to. It's more for my knowledge," I explained. I knew I wasn't doing a good job of it, but I couldn't shake the feeling it was important.

"I can do it. Shouldn't be hard. Wrecker or Cuffs can get us the official police report and then I'll go from there. Give me a couple of days, since we have this other crap happening."

"No rush, the other stuff takes precedence. Thanks, Phantom. I appreciate it." I gave him a man hug. We chatted for another minute or two, then I went to find Luciana. That's when I found she wasn't inside. I quickly searched the kitchen and rooms, but nothing. I hurried out the backdoor to the barbeque area. I came to an abrupt halt when I saw her sitting with Omen and he had his arms around her. I was instantly pissed. What the hell was going on here? I stomped over to them.

He raised his head from murmuring in her ear and saw me just as I got within a couple of feet of them. I lashed out. "What the fuck is going on here? Why is my woman in the arms of a prospect in the dark? You need to tell me something?" I growled. I knew I was being an asshole, but why were they back here like this?

Luciana looked up and I saw she had tears on her cheeks. As I took a step closer to her, she launched herself off the picnic table at me. It wasn't to hug or kiss me. It was to attack me. She shoved me. As tiny as she was, it didn't rock me, but it got my attention. She swore and then shoved again. I stood still. I grabbed her wrists.

"What the fuck are you doing, *bebé*? You're all up in Omen's arms one second and now you're pushing me."

"I'm pushing you because you're a jackass! Omen

was comforting me. We were just talking, and he was giving me some sound advice. Imagine my shock when he mentioned a woman was killed outside Bubble's with my name on her. Why didn't you tell me, Pitbull? Why?" she shouted.

I gave Omen a pissed look. Why had he told her?

"Listen, Pit, it was an accident. I had no idea she didn't know. That you were keeping it a secret. She knew about the first one, so I assumed she knew about the second one. I was advising her to always keep her knife with her for protection, even here. You can never be too careful."

"It's my job to take care of her. If she has worries or issues, she comes to me, not you. You're here to do what we tell you, not what you want. Stay away from Luciana, Omen," I warned him.

She stepped back and put distance between us. It pulled her arms straight and taut. She jerked on them. "Let go of me, Pitbull, or I swear, everyone in this place will hear me scream. And when they do, you won't like what I do next. I'm not a goddamn prisoner. I'm not your child to be told what to do and to be kept in the dark. If you think that's your job, we need to rethink this engagement. I'm not going to trade one prison for another or be lied to and kept in the dark." Her words stunned me. I let go of her wrists. She rubbed them. I was instantly worried I'd hurt her.

"*Bebé*, let me see. Did I hurt you?" I reached to take her hand. She clamped them to her chest. I felt a presence behind me. I looked over my shoulder, and there stood Executioner, Sin, and Saint. They were giving all of us worried looks.

"I'm fine. Since I have most of the main officers here, I want to know why I wasn't told about the woman with my name on her. Was she cut up or was it a note?"

"Luciana, we didn't want you to be worried. You have enough stress as it is. You know Juan is after you. Pit asked us to keep it to ourselves. How did you find out?" Sin asked. Omen stepped up.

"From me. I'm sorry. I had no idea she wasn't told. I messed up. Pit is pissed at me and thinks I'm after Luciana. I'm not. I was just giving her advice. She's like a little sister," he insisted.

"Do you hug and hold your sister like that?" I hissed.

"Yeah, if I still had them. Since I don't, I've been fortunate to start to get some here and from Boss' club." I could see sadness on his face. I knew he'd been investigated before he became a prospect. Only Phantom and the officers usually knew all the background. Something in the way he said those things about his sisters made me think something terrible had happened.

"Omen, you said if you still had them. Where are they? What happened?" I asked him.

"Omen, you don't need to tell him if you're not ready. Though, I told you it's something you'll eventually need to share," Sin cautioned him. Omen took a deep breath and then his shoulder sagged.

"I had two younger sisters, Traci and Tori. They were twins and eight years younger than me. When I was overseas in the Marine Corps, they went out one night. My *maman* tried to tell them that something didn't feel right. She begged them to stay home, but they were young and wanted to have fun. They told her she was letting her mojo mess with her head. That was the last time she ever saw them alive. They didn't come home and three days later, their bodies were found in the bayou. The gators had gotten to them, but it was determined they had been raped and strangled."

Luciana gasped and then began to cry. She ignored me and went to Omen. She wrapped her arms around him. I didn't get upset. I could see the anguish on his face. "Did they catch whoever did it?" she whispered.

"No. But there have been more women since. They have serial killers attacking women. They seem to do two killings at a time, then go dormant for months before it happens again. One day, there'll be a slipup and when it happens, I'll be there to make sure my sisters get justice. That's what I think about when I look at Skye, Luciana, and Lyric. They're my sisters and I'll do everything I can to protect them."

"Brother, we've got your back. We typically don't have prospects in church, and no one told you to keep quiet. It's understandable you let it slip. I think we need to have you come into church next time. Your gut might come in handy. We'll be here to help when you find whoever killed your sisters," Sin promised. Omen shook the hand he held out. The rest did the same. This time, Luciana came to me when I tugged on her.

"I'm sorry I jumped to conclusions. I saw you together and acted like a jealous asshole. I appreciate you wanting to keep her safe. Does your gut tell you anything about her and the situation?" I asked.

"Only that the danger seems to be getting darker and closer. It'll soon present itself. I think really soon. I have no clear vision how. It's harder to see when you're close to the people, like I am all of you. I told her to be armed at all times, even on the compound."

I looked at Sin, Ex, and Saint. *Should we tell them both about the decoy who was going to hopefully smoke out Juan?* Sin nodded. "You two need to come with us. We have something we need to tell you." Instead of going back to the clubhouse, I took them to our trailer. We all took a seat in the living room. With five big men in it, the place felt tiny. I couldn't wait for our house to be done. That was half a year away.

"The second woman did have your name on her. Juan wants you. He's desperate to get you. Phantom and others were able to discover why. There's a rumor out there that your brother..." I paused. I hated to tell her this.

She interrupted me. "He sold me, didn't he? He carried out his threat. He's sold me and now needs to deliver the merchandise, me. Has he said when he wants me?" She seemed to be awfully calm when she said it. I thought it had to be shock.

"Yes, he sold you. No deadline, but he seems to be pressing for as soon as possible."

"When do you want me to go outside so he can make his move?"

"You're not! No way will I risk you, Luciana. None of us are willing to put you in that kind of danger. We found another way. Someone who is used to and trained for this."

"A cop? A female undercover cop? Am I right? Can you trust her? I know some guys are in Juan's pocket. They'll tell him the plan," she warned. Again, she was very calm and matter of fact.

"This one, Boss, Wrecker, and Cuffs assure me is a good cop. She's done undercover work before. She's trained and we'll have lots of surveillance on her at all times. We're debating a plan to have her to be seen outside the Hangout. Darkness will help. She's about your height and build with the same hair. As long as he or his guys don't get right up to her, they won't know it isn't you, Luciana. If not, then we'll have her go to the college one day."

She stood there never taking her eyes off mine. I was worried about what this was doing to her mind. "Say something, *bebé*. You're too damn quiet and calm."

"Who did he sell me to?"

"Why does it matter?"

"Because if it's who he threatened me with, then he has more backup than you can imagine. If it's Hector De León, forget it. He's got too many connections to stop him." After she said it, I saw fear briefly show on her face.

"Who is Hector De León? You've never mentioned him."

"He's a guy Juan got involved with a year ago, when he started doing things outside of just drugs. It had something to do with women. I never knew all the details, but he was helping Hector. One night, he had him and his guys over to the house. He made me come out and cook for them. Hector was very touchy and kept telling my brother he'd love a slave like me. He made my skin crawl."

"What did Juan say? Was that the only incident?" I wanted to punch something, listening to her talk about someone wanting to use her like a slave. What the fuck was wrong with these people?

"He tried to laugh it off. Told him I was too valuable to him. Hector didn't stop though, because he's been to the apartment a few more times after that and pushed more. I'm positive if Juan sold me, it's to Hector. Not only would he pay him well, but he'd also get favoritism, in his mind. He'd climb the ladder in their business." A sob broke this time. I hugged her tight and rocked her. She didn't cry for long before she raised her head.

"I don't think he'll fall for the decoy. Just be prepared. He's evil and there's no telling what he'll do. When is this supposed to happen?"

"We're doing it on Monday. We want this done and hopefully over with. We'll get Phantom and maybe Preacher started on finding out everything on Hector De León. Is there anyone else you can think of that is part of the drug and trafficking businesses?"

"I told you the names of his main guys. He surrounds himself with what I call foot soldiers. They do the work and have no clue what the real deals are. Outside of that, he refers to someone called 'H' when he has to get drugs. He sends Jesús and Miguel to get them most of the time. They come back with bricks of cocaine, heroin and even meth."

"How often and do you know where they meet?"

"Monthly unless he sells out early. They meet in the daytime sometimes. I don't know where, but they always come back laughing. I wish I knew more, but it was safer if I didn't."

"*Bebé*, there's no need to apologize. This helps. If you think of anything else, tell me. I think you've had enough. Why don't we call it a night? We have a lot to do before Monday. I'll get with you tomorrow, Sin. Omen, sorry again and thank you," I told them.

All of them agreed and said a quick goodbye before they left. I was now alone with Luciana. I needed to hold her and show her how much I needed and wanted her. I didn't say a word. I swept her up in my arms and carried her to our bedroom. It was time to love the woman who'd made me her slave. Tomorrow, I'd run through all the variables with my brothers and the Time Served guys. We had to catch Juan and get the threat of Hector eliminated. Hopefully we'd stem more of the drugs and disappearances around Tenillo and its surrounding areas.

Luciana: Chapter 20

I was a bundle of nerves. All weekend it had been stressful as the guys had meeting after meeting. I knew it had to do with the sting operation they were running today. Pitbull did tell me enough that I knew the bare facts and what was expected of me. I was to stay inside the compound and let the guys left behind guard me, in case Juan didn't fall for it. They did let Omen into those meetings which had the other prospect, Brennan, looking at Omen with envy in his eyes. I hoped it wouldn't cause tension between them.

Lyric, Skye, Sara, and Jackie worked during the day as usual. I was kind of glad. Though having them here to talk to would have been good, I didn't want them to be asking me more than I was willing to say about Juan. It made my body tense, and I felt sick thinking of what he'd become.

It was now dark, and they were getting set to leave. They decided to go the Hangout route versus the college. The female officer would arrive around ten o'clock. Some of the guys had left hours ago. I knew that Boss and his men would be there too. I prayed that no one would get hurt. Right before they went out the door, Pitbull came up to me. He held me close and kissed me until I was breathless and seeing stars. He stared into my eyes. "Try to stay calm. Don't worry. We've got this. We have men all over the place. Stay inside and do what Brennan, Bullet, Phalanx, Talon, or Boomer tell you. They're here for all of you ladies. I'll be back as soon as I can. I love you, Luciana."

"I love you too, Cole. I'll try my best not to go crazy. Be careful and don't underestimate him. Please." We kissed one more time, then he left. Skye came over to me first.

"Do you want to hang out with us or be alone?"

"If you don't mind, I want to be alone. I think I'll go clean the kitchen here in the clubhouse. Give me something to use up this energy. Give me a little time then we can talk," I told her. She nodded and patted my arm. I hurried to the kitchen. Everyone worked to keep it clean, but sometimes you just had to do a deep clean. I felt in the mood to do that. The fridge was my target. I was going to strip it out, scrub it, and then arrange everything to be put back. After that, the pantry could use some organization, and the stovetop needed an extra shine.

I got lost in the work and let my mind concentrate on it. When intrusive thoughts about what was happening popped up, I'd beat them back down. I kept telling myself this would soon be over. I hoped someone upstairs was listening. I don't know how long I was working when I felt a presence behind me. I turned to greet whichever lady had broken down and came to check on me. I froze when I saw it was Barbie. She looked like hell. Her hair was ratty and dry looking. Her skin was sallow and dry. Her eyes were red rimmed. She seemed to be antsy, and her eyes were darting all over the kitchen. I knew that look. She was high. How in the hell did she get in the compound? What did she want? I shifted slightly, so I presented my side to her. It was a smaller target.

"What are you doing here, Barbie? You were told not to come back. Did you forget something? Who let you in? You should have called, and we'd have packed whatever you needed." I quickly threw all those questions at her. She was too high to comprehend them quickly and it would make her more off balance. I was debating if yelling for help would be the best thing. Was she alone?

She sneered at me and wavered on her feet. Her hand reached out to grab the counter so she wouldn't fall. "I came to get what's mine. Pitbull belongs to me. No drug dealer is taking him away from me. Juan is gonna pay me a lot when I bring you to him. You won't be in my hair anymore because he's got Hector ready to take you to South America. I hope you enjoy being some sadist's sex slave. I wonder how long you'll last?" She laughed. My blood ran cold. She knew his actual plans. How?

"How do you know what Juan has planned, Barbie? Didn't you say you didn't know him then told me you did? Which is it?" I sneered.

"I know Juan. He's been supplying me for months. No one had any idea. When I wasn't here and visiting friends, I was really meeting Juan at a motel outside of town. I've helped him a time or two when he's had problems with things. Imagine my surprise when I found out the bitch the club had brought to the compound, the one they were so adamant needed protection, was Juan's sister. The one he thought he'd killed. You should have seen his face when I told him where you were."

"You're why his goons came here that day, firing their guns. What if someone had gotten hurt?"

"I don't care as long as it's not me or the Infidels. Everything was wonderful until they started this bullshit of settling down. If they wanted to do that, why not settle with me, Vonnie, Shy, or Tabby Cat? They slept with us, but we're not good enough to marry! I hate you. With you gone, he'll have no other choice but to turn to me. I can comfort him in ways no one else can. He may have given you that ring, but he won't honor it. I'd be surprised if he even goes through with the wedding."

"The date is set. He's excited about it. Barbie, you made your life when you chose to be a bunny. How can you think any of these guys would pick you? Why don't you go somewhere and start over where they don't know you? Then you can find someone to settle down with and raise a family if you want."

"I'm not leaving! I want Pitbull. If he wants a brat, I'll give him one. You, on the other hand, need to come with me. Miguel and Jesús are waiting down the road. I told them I could get in here. Don't make a sound or I'll kill you and anyone who tries to help." As she said that, she pulled a gun out from under her shirt. Though she was high, the gun seemed steady.

"Head for the door to the pantry. Go to the back wall. There's another door to the outside. Makes it easier to bring in lots of things to be stored. Go!" She waved the gun. I slowly passed her and walked into the darkened pantry. Faint light shone from a lamp. I weaved through the shelves. I knew if she got me outside and off the compound, it was all over. As we got closer to the door, I had to find a way to disarm her. She knew where Juan was. I knew it by the way she was talking. If she was sleeping with him, she'd go wherever he was.

I came around one of the shelves. It put me out of her sight for a second or two. I slipped the knife Omen had told me to always carry with me out of the sheath I had it in. It fit perfectly inside the waist of my shorts. I glanced at the shelf and saw a twenty-five-pound bag of flour. It was heavy and would help to distract her. I hoped.

I quickly slashed the bag, as she came around the corner. "Why're you standing there? Stay where I can see you. Move!" I stood still. Her face got red.

"I said to move your ass, bitch!" she yelled. I grabbed the bag of flour and tugged. It fell to the floor and flour burst up into a cloud—a cloud that went straight for her face. She coughed and waved her hand in front of her face to clear it. I made my move. I screamed, "Help, in the pantry," as loud as I could, then I charged her. We crashed together. I sliced at her wrist that held the gun. She shouted as she dropped her gun. I didn't bother to bend down to pick it up. I kicked it so it slid under the shelving. She wouldn't be able to easily get it. As we fought, I swept my leg behind hers and she fell on her ass. I hurried to pin her to the ground. She tried to throw me off of her, but when I held my knife to her throat, she got really quiet.

"You're gonna tell me where my brother is and everything else you know about his business."

"Why the fuck would I do that?" she snapped. She was glaring at me, but I let her see I was serious. I flicked the knife enough to have it nick her skin. She gasped.

"Because if you don't, I'm gonna cut it out of you." Before she could say more, the lights flared on, and the room was filled with the guys left behind. The other women weren't with them. "Where are the ladies?" I asked them worriedly.

"We sent them to the safe room. What the hell happened?" Talon growled. He had out his gun just like the other guys.

"Her gun is under that shelf. Make sure you get it. She came in the back way through here and cornered me in the kitchen. She was going to take me to my brother. His two thugs are waiting down the road," I hastily told them.

"How did you end up on the floor, on top of her, and covered in flour? You look like a ghost," Bullet said with a smile on his face.

"Pure fucking luck, I guess. I felt the need to let my badass out. She happened to be here and got the brunt of it. You interrupted us. Do you mind if I finish?"

They gave me startled looks as Boomer said, "Carry on." I saw Talon and Phalanx were texting furiously on their phones. Shit, they were calling back the others. I pressed my knees harder into her chest. She was struggling to breathe.

"Barbie, I warned you before not to mess with me. You didn't listen. Be smart this time. Tell me where Juan is. Who does he get his drugs from? How are women funneled out of the area to be sold?" She jerked when I said the last part. I knew she had information on everything, but she wasn't going to give it up without a fight. One I was looking forward to. I looked up at Boomer.

"She needs to go to the place you all take people to who need to tell you stuff."

He stiffened. "I don't know what you're talking about, Luciana. Pitbull is on his way back. The sting was a bust. We'll wait and see what he and the others want to do."

"Don't play games with me, Boomer. I know you all aren't angels. You've talked to people before, right? Where did you do it? I want to go and have a little girl-to-girl chat with her." I smirked at Barbie and pressed the tip of the knife into her skin a tad more. A tiny, steady stream of blood flowed.

"Luciana, get off her. We'll take it from here. Give me the knife," Talon said as he stopped and held out his hand. I shook my head.

"I'm not giving her a chance to run. You guys get suckered by pretty faces, I don't. But if you want to wait, we'll wait. Exactly as we are." I bounced on her chest, and she wheezed.

No matter how much they demanded, argued, and cajoled, I didn't let her up. It was almost a half hour before the roar of bikes was heard. A couple of minutes later, in came the guys. Pitbull was first through the door. He stopped and stared. The others behind him peeked over his shoulder to see what was going on.

"Hi, honey, welcome home. Look what I got. She's a little messy, but I caught my very own informant. She knows Juan really well. She even gets her cocaine from him and gives him other comforts. She knows where the hell he's hiding. Did you see anyone along the road?"

"*Bebé*, get off her and put away that knife. She's not going anywhere. We didn't see anyone along the road. We looked. They must have fled when she didn't come back."

"I want her taken to your torture room. Boomer and the others said no."

"*Mi alma*, we don't—"

"Don't blow smoke up my ass, Pitbull. I know you guys do. If not here, somewhere. I understand you don't usually share this, but we need to ask her questions. We can do it there in relative privacy, or here on the damn kitchen floor. I don't care. I want my life back! I can't get that or have one with you as long as all this is hanging over me!" I shouted. I was tired of being on the edge of a razor every second of the day. I hated to get ugly, but this was me or my brother and his friends. I planned for it to be me.

Pitbull stared at me as if he was in shock. "Luciana, let me and the guys take care of it. We'll get the answers." I shook my head.

"No, I will. She's a woman and though you'll do

what needs to be done, it'll bother you. All of you have had a relationship with Barbie. One that wasn't bad. Mine has been the opposite. She's been a bitch from day one to me. I won't hesitate. You guys are all trained, I know, but I don't care. She's gonna tell me what she knows. You can watch if you want. Or better yet, let me and the other ladies 'talk' to her." Sin and Ex exchanged worried looks. I knew Sara would be all for this. The others, maybe not as much.

"There won't be any other ladies talking to her. You need to let us handle this," Sin told me sternly. I nodded.

"Okay, if you want to handle it that way." I got up, turned, and began to walk to the door. Pitbull stopped me.

"Where're you going, Luciana?"

"To pack my shit and get the hell out of here. I'm done."

"*Bebé*, no! Settle down. You're upset."

I ignored him and turned to Wrecker. "You uphold the law right, when it comes to innocent people?" He slowly nodded. "Then I want to be escorted out of here. I don't want to be here." His face registered shock. I heard all the guys draw in their breaths with a hiss.

Pitbull growled, "Luciana, stop it. You're not leaving. Wrecker won't take you out of here. What the hell?"

I held up the knife I'd held on Barbie. She was sitting there smirking, the bitch. She was going to enjoy this. I was too tired to care anymore. They thought I didn't have it in me to be tough. That I needed them to fight every battle. Pitbull was acting like he made all the decisions in my life. It was time I was in control. I laid the knife to my own throat. All of them made sounds of protest.

"So, this is what I have to look forward to, a life of still being in someone else's control? Forget it. I'm dead if Juan and Hector get me. I'm dead, at least emotionally, if I stay here. You think you're protecting me, but you're not. You're doing the same thing as my brother. Why don't I make it easy for everyone and end it all right here? Barbie can come back. Hell, she might even clean up the mess. I know she'll be there to comfort you tonight." Pitbull's eyes got round, and he took a step toward me. I pressed the knife to my neck, and I felt a tiny sting. He froze.

"God, *bebé*, please drop the knife. We can talk. There's no need to do this. I love you. I don't want to control you. I want to protect you. I don't understand where this is coming from?" he pleaded. The others were frozen as well.

"I can't live like this, caged. I won't bring a baby into this either. I'm tired. I want to rest. From where I'm standing, there's no happy ending for me. Either Juan kills me, Hector does eventually after he's done raping and abusing me, or I die here being treated as a toy, never really allowed to be a partner with you. This is about me, and you won't let me be involved. I'll take option four." I tightened my hand on the blade. Pitbull yelled my name. The guys all shouted. I closed my eyes. A hard-hitting sensation came over me and then darkness.

Pitbull: Chapter 21

I sat beside the bed watching Luciana. She was still out. I couldn't shake the fear that had come over me when she held that fucking knife to her own throat and threatened to end her own life! It made me sick. I was pissed at myself that I hadn't seen how close to the edge all of this had pushed her. She was so good at projecting she was better than she was. Movement had me lifting my head.

Sin, Saint, Boss, Jenn, Paula, plus Omen and a few others stood in the doorway. We'd called in Boss and the others after she blacked out. I didn't know what to do. I stood and went to Omen. I grabbed him and gave him a man hug. "Thank you. Thank you for saving her. I can never repay you," I told him. He'd snuck in during the argument with Luciana and gotten behind her. He'd jumped her and got the knife away from her throat. She'd passed out when he did.

"You don't have to thank me. I knew something was coming. I didn't know it was this. I'm not totally sure this is all of it. I saw an opportunity, and I took it. I'm glad it worked. I know she's your woman, Pitbull, but she needs more care than she likes to admit or show. Some of that is being in control of her life to a big extent. Barbie was just the final straw that broke her."

I swallowed back the tears. He was right. She did need to have more control. I thought I was helping and showing her how much I loved her. I had no idea I was making it worse. I looked at Sin and Boss. Paula had gone to the bed and was assessing Luciana.

"What the hell do I do? She's gonna wake up and then what? She still may want to leave or worse, kill herself. I want to protect her, not smother her, but letting her possibly torture Barbie... What kind of man does that make me to allow that? What will it do to her mentally if she does?"

The answer came but not from where I expected. It came from Jenn. "You let her do it. You guys think you're the only ones who have a need for justice. The only ones who can handle the ugly side of life. You're not. Women can be just as mean or meaner. We can handle it. Luciana needs to do this. She'll be fine. I know she will because all of you and all of us at Time Served will be here for her. You have no idea what it feels like to know you're able to protect yourself and your loved ones as a woman. Most of the world sees us as the weaker sex. We're not."

"She's right, Pitbull. Jenn and I, along with Blue and Brea, handled shit. It doesn't keep us up at night. Do you know why? Because it was justified. I doubt Luciana will need to do much to Barbie to get her to talk. But you'll have to decide if her punishment goes beyond that. And if it does, who does it? Don't shut Luciana out. She's young, but she's tough. Help her know she is," Paula added. She laid down her stethoscope.

"Is she okay?" I asked since I had no response yet to what they both had just said. It went against the grain to not protect women.

"I can't find anything wrong. I think her mind just needed a break from the stress."

"Do you think she'll try to kill herself again? Does she need mental help?" I hated the thought of her needing to be hospitalized for this, but I couldn't let her walk around suicidal.

"I need to talk to her when she wakes up, but I doubt she's truly suicidal. She just hit a wall and reacted with the only control she had. Let her sleep. When she wakes up, let her be the one to direct the conversation. I wouldn't do anything with Barbie yet. That's one thing Luciana won't deal with well, if you take it on yourself to do it while she's out. You want her to be your wife. That means letting her in and treating her as your partner. Now, she could be out for a while or wake up in a minute. I think you need to talk to the guys. Why don't you go do that and me and the other ladies will stay here? If she wakes up, we'll come get you right away," Paula said as she took a seat beside the bed. The other ladies and Jenn all gathered around the bed with her. I didn't want her to wake up without me, but Paula was right. I needed to talk to the guys.

"Thanks, Paula and the rest of you. I'll be back. Come get me if she wakes up." They nodded, and I left the room with my brothers and the Time Served guys on my heels. I didn't waste time. I headed to church. I looked back. "Omen, I want you with us." He gave me a chin lift and filed into the room. We all took seats. Sin stayed quiet. I knew he was giving me the room.

"I don't even know what to fucking think. What just happened blew my mind. I had no damn idea," I started out. Boss and his guys nodded. One of my brothers had filled them in when they called.

"None of us did. But now we have to decide. Do we do what she wants and let her take the lead in finding out what Barbie knows? Which sounds like it could be a lot. The damn sting was a bust. They either weren't watching or knew about it somehow," Sin stated as he rubbed his hand over his bald head in frustration.

"I agree. We need a new plan. The shock of Luciana interrogating her might be what gets Barbie to talk faster than if one of us did it. We can torture her for you since you have a relationship of sorts, but I don't think that would be best for your woman," Boss added.

"It goes against the grain to allow it, but I agree. We need to let her have some kind of involvement. Have we learned anything new?" I asked. Phantom knocked his knuckles on the table.

"I did. Not about where Juan or this Hector is, but I looked into what you asked me to do the other day. Wrecker got me the police report on Luciana's parents' death. I looked at it and then had Preacher read it. It's a clusterfuck. The whole damn thing smells like a dirty coverup. The police didn't even do a half-assed investigation before ruling it a home invasion. They had Luciana's statement, which wasn't much since she wasn't there that night. They didn't even talk to Juan.

The report on their deaths was gruesome along with the coroner's report and pics. The report just mentioned the house was wrecked and the electronics and some jewelry were gone. That's it."

"He's right. Cuffs and I read it. They didn't do shit. I hate to say this, but they either didn't give a shit, or they knew who did it and they're in their pocket. Guess who the investigating officer was?" Wrecker growled.

"That asshole, Clinton?" Sin hissed. Wrecker nodded. We all swore. He was dirty as hell. How in the hell could we prove it? He needed to go down and disappear; however, we had to have proof.

"Isn't that enough to get him brought under official investigation or something?" I asked Boss. He sighed.

"I can open an official one, but right now, it is his word against the old chief, who signed off on the investigation. I hate Clinton and think he's crooked, but he could have been just a patsy doing whatever the old chief of police told him to do. He could have felt it was the only way to keep his job. Though if he was a man, he'd have told him to go to hell. I'll need to bring in someone from outside the department we can trust. Because if this goes the way I think it will, we don't want anyone to know it when he disappears," Boss said as he gave an evil grin. I was totally on board with the idea, though I had no idea where he'd find someone like that.

All the others nodded their heads. "Who would you get? Do you know someone like that?" I asked.

Boss grinned. "It so happens I do. We have more than the brothers and sisters you've seen so far in the

Time Served MC. They live all over the world. One of them, Denny Gray, is a PI. We call him Hammer. I know we could get him to come and work on this. Preacher and Phantom have enough on their plates right now and for the foreseeable future with all the shit going on in Tenillo. They can't do it, and it's more in his wheelhouse anyway. I could have him here within a month or two at the most. Depends on what he's working on."

"Great, I say we do it. Everyone in agreement?" Sin asked the table. All hands went up.

"Okay, back to the home invasion. I hate to ask it, but do you think it's just because he no longer lived with them that the police never questioned Juan? Or is it more than that?" I hated where my mind was going. Surely, he hadn't had anything to do with the deaths of his own parents. Then I thought of what he had done to Luciana and had planned. Yeah, the fucker would have done it in a heartbeat. The thought made me want to kill him even more.

"You're thinking what I am, Pitbull? I think the bastard was in on it. He might not have been there when they did it, but he knew about it and most likely set it up. Other than getting them out of the way, was there anything else to gain by killing them?" Saint mused.

"There was. When I was checking, I found they had a life insurance policy. One that left their kids equal shares in one hundred thousand dollars. Since Luciana was underage, Juan would be the one to oversee her half until she came of age. They must have forgotten to change it after he started doing drugs and running with those friends of his. From what I can find, he blew all of it. They moved into that apartment and the house was sold. He got all the money from that too. Luciana was robbed of seventy-five thousand dollars. More than enough to pay for her schooling and to live while she got her degree as long as she was frugal," Phantom said quietly. I saw the disgust and anger on his face.

"You have to be kidding me! Jesus, will it ever end? She's gonna be devastated if she finds out he might have had something to do with their deaths. To know he spent her inheritance too, I don't know if she can handle it," I told them. She had already broken down. What would this do to her?

"You tell her and then we support her. Don't keep it from her, Pitbull. If you do, you'll regret it. She might never forgive you. This is on Juan. Tell her soon what we suspect. And when or if we find proof, then tell her that." This came from Santa. I glanced at the others. They all looked pissed but were nodding their heads. I sighed. He was right. I'd have to tell her. Just not tonight. I'd wait a couple of days.

"I will. I need to get back to her," I told them.

Talon interrupted, "What do we do with Barbie? She's out in the Gallows right now. She's claiming it was all a lie and Luciana attacked her. That she came back to get a few things she left. I don't believe it. Do we leave her there until we decide if Luciana is helping? Or do we let her out to stay in a room under guard?"

"Screw her, she stays there. She knows shit. She was going to take my woman. Just because she's a woman, we don't treat her any differently than a man. She can stay there. Hopefully, it scares the shit out of her, and she'll spill her guts," I growled. I wasn't feeling charitable toward Barbie.

"I agree, just wanted to put it out there in case someone felt differently. She can stay there and think about what we're going to do to her."

All my brothers and Boss' were grumbling out their agreement. I looked at Sin. "If that's all, I'm going back."

"That's it for now. We can talk a bit more, but you go back to Luciana. I'll fill you in on anything you miss. Take care of her," Sin ordered. I stood and hurried out of the room. I needed to have my eyes on her. It was worrying me that she hadn't woken yet.

Luciana:

The pounding in my head was annoying. I didn't want to open my eyes in case it made it worse, but I knew that I needed to do it. Only why the urgency, I had no clue. I cautiously opened one eye. Seeing that the room was dimly lit, I opened the other. That's when I saw Pitbull. He was sitting beside the bed rather than in it with me. His eyes were closed.

I glanced around and then the memories started to pour back into my confused, aching head. I'd almost been kidnapped by Barbie. The guys had come and wanted to take her somewhere. I'd argued with Pitbull that I wanted to question her. She possibly knew where Juan was. He'd told me to let them handle it.

As I thought of what had happened next and how mad it had made me, I cringed. Not that I felt bad that I'd demanded what I did. I hated the fact that I had to resort to something that wrong to get them to see I was serious. Had I been mistaken in believing he and I could have a life together? One where we shared things and were partners. I knew there were things he couldn't tell me, but this wasn't one of those things. The exhaustion of hiding and always being worried had caught up.

I must have made a sound or something, because Pitbull's eyes flew open, and he was off the chair and kneeling beside the bed in an instant. He grabbed a hold of my right hand. "God, I thought you'd never wake up, *mi alma*. You've been out for over two hours!" he said with an urgent and worried tone in his voice.

"I need a drink," I croaked. My throat felt as dry as the desert. He got up and went into the bathroom. I heard the water run. Though I wanted to go back to sleep, we needed to talk and get this settled now. If he wasn't going to let me be me, then I needed to leave today. He was back a few seconds later with a glass of water. I pushed up on my elbows. He didn't hand me the glass. He held it to my mouth, so I could take a drink. I drained it. "Thank you."

"Do you need me to get more?"

"No, that's enough. I need to get up anyway." I rolled to the edge of the bed and sat up. The room spun a little, and I wavered. He slid his arm behind my back.

"Lie back down. You shouldn't be up and moving. I want Paula to come back and check you out again."

"I don't need to be checked out. I'm fine. We need to talk about what happened before I blacked out. First, what happened? I remember something hitting me, then nothing." He didn't answer. I sighed. So, this was the way it was going to be. I pushed him away, sat up, then stood. When I thought I could walk, I started for the door. He got between me and it.

"Where are you going, Luciana?"

"Away from here. It's obvious we're not on the same page. If Wrecker or Cuffs won't help me leave, I'll find someone else. Move out of the way, Pitbull."

"I'm not letting you leave. We need to talk. And what's with this Pitbull, shit?"

"It's your club name, right? That's what people call you."

"Yeah, but not you. Not when we're alone. It's Cole. I thought you wanted to talk."

"You won't even answer a simple question on what hit me. That tells me that the harder stuff will go unanswered, or you'll ignore it. I've had enough of that to last me two lifetimes. I don't belong here." I reached him and tried to squeeze between him and the door. I knew I couldn't move him. Next thing I knew, I was pinned to the door. He was holding me tightly and looking down into my eyes. I could see so many emotions on his face. Anger, pain, and worry were the main ones.

"Luciana, *bebé,* don't be like this."

"Like what? A thinking woman who wants and needs to have a say in her own damn life! Don't be like that? Just sit down and be quiet and do as I'm told. I think you got the wrong impression. Just because I had to let Juan treat me like that for the past five years, doesn't mean I don't have a backbone. Or that I need a keeper. I thank you and the club for what you've done. You can deal with Juan as you see fit. I'm going to do what I should have done as soon as I got out of the hospital—get the hell out of Tenillo."

"Come on, sit down and we'll talk." He pulled me away from the door and toward the bed. I struggled but couldn't break his hold.

"No, you'll talk and make all these excuses for why I can't be the one to talk to that bitch, Barbie. She tried to kidnap me. She wants me gone. Well, lucky for her, she's gonna get her wish. Now, let me out of this goddamn room!" I screamed the last part. I was quickly losing what little cool I had left. Leaving was killing me. I loved him and we had no future. Would I ever have one? Or was I doomed to be alone forever?

The bedroom door swung open and there stood Sara. She walked in without asking if she could. She touched his arm. "Let me talk to her." He looked at her for several seconds, then sighed and let go. He slowly went to the door. When he got to it, he looked back.

"I'll be outside, waiting to talk. I love you, Luciana."

"In this case, I'm afraid love isn't enough," I told him softly. His eyes widened, and he hurried out the door, slamming it behind him. I sank down on the bed. My legs were suddenly weak. Sara sat down on the chair he'd been in when I woke up.

"Talk to me. Tell me what's going through your head. I heard what you did. I want to know what made you so desperate, that you'd do that."

"Are you supposed to soften me up, Sara? Make me see my place. Well, it's not happening. I went off because Pitbull is trying to make all the decisions and have all the control in this relationship. I want a partner. If I wanted to be told what to do like a mindless drone, I'd have gone back to Juan. They won't let me question Barbie. Is it because they don't think I can handle it? Or is it because they're gonna let her get a pass? Either way, I'm not going to stay around for that life."

"Honey, Pitbull doesn't want you to have no say. He's a man and they like to think with the alpha brain. The 'I'm a man and it's my job to protect my women and family' gene. Not because you're weak, but because he has to show he's worthy of your love."

"So where does that stop, and my wishes come into play? I need to show that I'm strong and can take care of myself. I've been acting weak and pathetic long enough. I'm taking back my life. I wanted it to be with him, but not if this is what I have to look forward to. It's another version of being someone's servant. I won't be like that again. If I can get out of Tenillo without being seen, I can get to where Lila is. We can raise her baby together, so he or she has a family. One that isn't a drug gang."

"When the boys take care of Juan and whoever is helping him, she can come back and raise that baby where you can be part of their lives and part of ours. We love you and want you to stay. Please, just talk to him and listen. If you leave, I don't know what he'll do."

"He'll survive. He has for this many years. He'll eventually find the kind of woman he wants." I'd barely gotten the words out before the door slammed open and Pitbull came charging into the room. He looked like he was going to explode. It scared me a little. I flinched and shrank back. He saw it.

"Sara, leave please. I need to set my woman straight," he growled. She got up and gave me a kiss on the cheek then went to the door. When she passed him, she whispered something to him before she left and closed the door. I stood up. I wasn't going to cower.

Pitbull: Chapter 22

I'm not ashamed that I'd stood outside the door and listened to her talk to Sara. I needed to know where her head was at, because there was no way in the world, I was going to lose her. Hearing her say what she did and hearing the pain and grief in her voice killed me. When she said I'd find what kind of woman I wanted someday, I couldn't take it. I'd barged in and sent Sara away. However, I'd seen Luciana flinch when I came in. That was the first thing we were going to get cleared up. She stood there staring at me.

"Luciana, I want you to listen to me and hear this. You never, and I repeat never, have to worry about me hitting you or laying a finger on you in anger. You flinched when I came in. Yes, I'm angry, but I wouldn't ever hurt you. I'm angry because you think you're not what I want or need."

"You were listening!"

"Yeah. I had to know what I could do to make this right. I love you. I never want to control you or treat you like a servant. I'm proud as hell of what you've been able to live through for the last five years. You protected Lila and her baby when you knew what Juan would do to you. You're a strong woman. I don't doubt that, but I want to carry that weight for you. You've had no one to help carry that burden and load all this time. I'm an alpha and that's my automatic response to problems." She opened her mouth like she was going to say that was the issue. I didn't let her.

"I know that's why you got so upset. I didn't know what to say when you insisted you wanted to be the one to question Barbie. I saw it as my job. The guys saw it that way too. We want to protect all of our women and children from having to do things like that. It could get ugly before she talks. I don't know what we'll have to do to get her to tell us what she knows. I don't want you to see that."

"And I don't want to be unable to protect myself or my children. You need to hear this. I'll steal, beg, and kill for my children and those I love which includes you. I'm not asking to do it all the time. Hell no, I don't want that. But this time I need to do it. I can't explain it any better. It feels like my whole future and self-worth is hanging in the balance. If I have to learn to let you in and to bend at times, you have to do the same, or this will never work and we'll both be miserable," she pleaded.

I sat down beside her. I could hear the need and pain in her voice. She needed this. It wasn't a matter of wanting it. "I hear you. I know if you meet me halfway then we can make this work and be so fucking happy. I need you like I need oxygen. Without you, I have no future. But Luciana, you can never, I mean never, threaten to take your own life again! Do you hear me? That scared me so badly, I'm gonna have nightmares for a long time. If you feel like you want to take your own life or hurt yourself, please tell me or someone right away." This time I was the one pleading. The image of her holding that knife to her throat kept playing like a movie through my brain.

She laid her head on my shoulder. I wrapped her tightly against my side. "I promise, Cole. Just promise to listen and take my side into consideration. I didn't know any other way at that moment to show you how much I needed to do this. It was wrong and I'm sorry. I don't really want to kill myself. I have to have honesty between us, and no secrets if it affects me or our kids, if we have them."

"Oh, we'll have them, I promise you that. And I promise I'll not be such an alphahole, however you have to cut me some slack. I'm used to being in control." She nodded. I lifted her chin up with a finger and kissed her. I couldn't wait any longer to taste her, to feel how alive she still was.

The kiss lasted for a long time as we both explored each other's mouths. When we finally did stop, we were both breathing raggedly. "We can't get sidetracked just yet. There's something else we need to talk about. It's not pretty, and I wanted to wait, but I'll tell you now, so there are no more secrets." I hated to break up what seemed like our makeup sex.

"Tell me. Then we can take care of Barbie and see what else we might want to do to make things up to each other." She gave me a smile and laid her hand on my hardness, pressing against my zipper. Even if we'd been talking about serious stuff, the touch of her mouth had made me hard. Hell, seeing her did that.

I laughed. "Okay, deal."

"Do the guys already know what you're gonna tell me?"

"Yes, they do. It was actually due to Phantom, Wrecker, and Cuffs that we discovered it. I want you to keep in mind, it's only a theory. We don't have proof yet, but the things they did find out are damning. It's about your mom and dad."

"My mom and dad? What do you mean?" She looked scared and anxious. I hauled her up on my lap.

"It's about the night they were killed. You said you weren't home. What did the cops tell you?"

"They said someone broke in and must have thought the house was empty. It looked like a struggle had happened, which I know must have been dad. They'd both been shot, and some minor valuable stuff was missing. We didn't have a lot of fancy, expensive stuff. They had no leads on who did it and the case went unsolved. Do you know who killed them?" She was looking at me with hope.

"I don't know for sure. God, *bebé*, I don't know how else to say this, so forgive me for just saying it. The investigation wasn't much of one. Wrecker and Cuffs, as well as Boss, believe it was covered up by the old chief of police and the investigating detective. They knew more than they reported."

She sat up straighter. "Why would they do that?"

"Because they're dirty. We haven't proved it yet, but we will. The old chief no longer lives here in Texas. But if we find proof, we'll make sure his ass is brought back.

The detective is still with the department. I think someone paid them off. Did you know that your parents had a will and a life insurance policy?"

Her mouth fell open and she shook her head. "No, I had no idea. That wasn't something they would have talked about. At least not to me. What happened to it?"

"Juan got control of it because they didn't change the will to exclude him or name another guardian for you. Maybe they had hoped he'd turn himself around. Anyway, he was to oversee your portion until you turned eighteen. The house was included in the will and was to be equally shared."

"How much was it?" she asked quietly.

"The life insurance would have given both of you fifty thousand each plus the profit from the sale of the house added another twenty-five after the mortgage was paid off for each of you." She jumped up off my lap and faced me with her hands clenched in front of her.

"So you mean to tell me, he stole my money and used it for God knows what? That he screwed me out of going to school and being able to support myself all these years? Who do you think paid the chief and the detective off?" She was breathing hard and shaking. I need to get this over with. I stood up and went to her. I tugged her close again.

"I think your brother was involved. I don't know if he was there or just set it up, but it looks suspicious. I'm sorry."

A god-awful wail burst out of her. She sobbed and

tears poured down her face. She beat on my chest with her fists as she kept saying, "No, no, he couldn't have been that evil." I could hear the doubt in her voice. She knew deep down that Juan was evil enough to have killed their parents.

I held her and whispered my love to her and let her cry. It took a long time for her to get it all out. When she finally got quiet, I'd already taken her back to the bed and had her cuddled up with me. She was hiccupping. She looked at me. "I'm sorry, I did that. I think you're right. Juan did have something to do with this. I no longer think anything is beneath him. The desire for power and the drugs has eaten everything that was my brother away. There's no going back. He needs to be taken care of as soon as we find him. Let me talk to Barbie."

"No, not tonight. Hell, it's after one in the morning. Let's get some sleep and then if you feel like it, we can talk to her."

"No, we do it now. I won't be able to rest until I do. Please, Cole, take me to her. You and the guys can be there, but I want to know what she knows." I reluctantly nodded. I'd give her this even if I thought she should wait. It would show her I was going to stick to my promise to listen and let her have some control.

"Okay, if you're sure. Why don't you wash your face then we'll go find the guys?" I gave her one more kiss before letting her up. While she did her business, I paced. I was thinking of what we might have to do to get Barbie to talk. I texted the guys to meet us in the common room. I doubted any of them were sleeping. It was going to be one helluva long night.

When we made it to the common room, the last of the guys were coming in the door. They looked hard at Luciana. I knew they were trying to see how she was. I'd told them in the text we'd be talking to Barbie. I got to the point. "Luciana wants to talk to Barbie tonight. She can't rest until she does. She wants us to let her ask the questions. I'm giving this to her." They slowly nodded. They got that this was something I had to do, or I'd lose my woman. I turned to her.

"*Bebé*, I need you to tell us immediately if you want to stop, leave, or take a break. You have nothing to prove to us by doing this. It's solely to get information. Will you promise to do that?"

"I promise. Thank you, guys, for letting me do this."

"You don't have to thank us. We wish you didn't have to do it, but we understand what it would be like if we were in your shoes. Tell us what you need," Sin told her gruffly.

"I need my knife. And I want to know who or what hit me earlier?" Shit, I'd forgotten she'd asked me that. I opened my mouth to tell her, but Omen beat me to it.

"That was me. I hope I didn't hurt you. I just needed to get that knife away from your throat. You were making Pitbull over there nervous. He was about to faint," he teased. She laughed.

"That would have been worth seeing but thank you. I lost my mind for a few minutes. I would never actually take my own life. It was a shitty thing to do. Can we put that behind us and get on with the questioning?"

"We can. Let's go. We have her out in the Gallows. It's an old slaughterhouse on the property from when it was a cattle ranch. Come with us. We'll ride out there," Sin offered. I led her out to the bikes. It was walkable, but it was quicker to ride. She got on my bike. I pulled her tight against me and made sure her feet were in the right place. We fired up them up and rode to the back of the compound. When we got to the Gallows, she was quick to get off. Her eyes wouldn't leave the building. I took her hand and slipped the knife into it. She slid it into her waistband sheath.

"You ready?"

"I'm ready."

I took the lead and the guys fell in behind us. When we opened the door, Brennan was sitting there. He had guard duty. He stood up and raised his eyebrows at Luciana. Our entry woke up Barbie. She raced to the door of the cell we had her in. "You came. Please, let me out."

"Let her out, Brennan," Sin told him. He quickly unlocked her cell door. Barbie came rushing over to us.

"Thank you. I knew you'd realize it was all a misunderstanding." She gave Luciana a small smirk. I waited to see what Luciana would do. I didn't have to wait long. I was stunned when she hauled back her fist and let it fly. She connected with Barbie's face, causing the blood to fly and Barbie to scream when her nose broke. We all heard the bone break.

"What the fuck? She hit me. Do something!" Barbie

screamed as she held her nose.

"We are. We're watching the show. Luciana, honey, you do what you want and tell us what you need," Saint said as he leaned against the table we had in the center of the building.

Luciana grabbed Barbie by the hair and marched her over to where there was a chair with restraints on the arms and legs. She shoved her down in it. After her ass hit the seat, Luciana began to secure her wrists. Barbie tried to get up.

"Let me go!" she yelled.

"Barbie, I suggest you shut the hell up. You're gonna sit there and tell me what I want to know. Every time you don't, every time you fight or argue, I'm gonna leave another mark on you. If you want to leave here looking like you did when you came in—minus the nose—I'd talk," Luciana told her calmly and quietly. It was kind of chilling. Barbie stilled and looked at her stunned. This allowed my woman to secure the other arm and then her legs.

"Now, we can talk. Tell me about my brother. Where is he? When did you first meet him? How long have you been spying for him?"

"I don't know what you're talking about. I don't know your brother; other than the rumors I've heard."

Luciana didn't say a word, she just punched her again in the face. This time it was in her mouth. I had to admit, I was a little amazed she could be that fierce. There was a lot I still had to learn about my woman.

"I think I must have a hearing problem. I swear you just told me you don't know Juan, but in the pantry last night, you said you did. That you get your drugs from him, and you warm his bed sometimes. Wanna try again?"

Barbie looked at me and the guys. She put on such a pathetic look, if I didn't know better, I'd have fallen for it. "Please, she's crazy. I don't know what she's talking about. You saw her. She had me on the floor with a knife to my throat when you came in. I didn't do anything other than come to get my stuff."

I walked closer to her. I saw hope flare in her eyes. She thought she'd convinced me. "Barbie, you're the one who's crazy. You're crazy if you think we'd believe you over her. You're not leaving here until you tell us everything you know. It's in your best interest to do it. Answer her."

I saw the moment she decided she'd rather lie than tell the truth. She really was a vindictive bitch. It made me wonder if it was just her or were the other bunnies waiting to be just as bad. It was a sobering thought. I had to believe they weren't all like this. I could understand being disappointed when things didn't go the way you wanted, but she'd essentially sold Luciana out to her brother, knowing what he had planned for her. That was cold-blooded.

I stepped back to stand with the other guys and let Luciana continue. We watched as she repeated her questions and Barbie remained mute. Luciana hit her a few more times, only this time it was in the stomach and then the ribs.

"See, Barbie, there are a lot of things I can hold against my brother and even hate him for, but right now, I am thankful for one thing. All the times I took a beating, I learned what hurts the most, which spots make you want to curl up and die. The last time he beat me was the worst, however, it wasn't the first time." I jerked after hearing her say that. I suspected he'd beaten her before the night he left her for dead. The guys sucked in shocked breaths.

"There comes a point you kind of go numb. I think you're gonna get there soon. When that happens, I'll have to move on to something else. Just tell me what I need to know."

"Fuck you. He's gonna kill you. And if he doesn't, that insane bastard he sold you to will. You'll be used until there's nothing left. If you're lucky, he'll just kill you. Or maybe he'll give you to some of his friends," Barbie hissed on a pained breath.

I was seething and desperately wanting to wrap my hands around her throat. In a move like a cat, Luciana was up in her face and had her hands around her neck. She squeezed. Barbie gasped and tried to shake her loose, but without the use of her hands, she couldn't. She was bright red before Luciana let go of her. We watched as Barbie sputtered and coughed for a minute or so. When she could speak, Luciana asked her again the same questions.

"Go to hell. They might let you hurt me, but they won't let you kill me. I mean too much to them," she rasped. How she thought that I had no clue. Luciana smiled at her. The look in her eyes, I recognized. It was one I'd seen soldiers get when they prepared to do something they'd have to live with. Before I could tell her I'd do it, she struck. She pulled her knife and stabbed it deep into Barbie's thigh. Barbie screamed. Luciana twisted it a little bit as she leaned in close to Barbie.

"This is your last chance. I have no love or liking for you. Don't think I won't kill you. I will. It won't be with pleasure, but I will do it. Tell me where he is, and everything you know about his drug business along with Hector and the trafficking of women."

I glanced at my brothers. All of them appeared a tad shocked. I think after today, we'd have to reconsider what we thought of all our women and those who could be strong enough to be with one of us. I think all were more like Jenn, Paula, Blue, and Brea than we'd ever thought.

"I met Juan about six months ago. I went to a party with some friends, not the bunnies. It was at someone's house in town. It got wild and the next thing I knew, I was snorting cocaine. That's when it all started. After that, Juan came to see me a few times and brought me more Coke. We had fun. He was different."

"He got you hooked on the drugs then used you," Luciana said.

"Yeah, though I didn't know it. Then things got crazy around here with Sin finding a woman and siding with her over us and Vonnie. After V left, I hoped things would go back to normal, but it didn't. Almost immediately, Executioner came in with Skye and introduced her as his old lady. He even moved her mom and brothers on to the compound. We weren't allowed to have people come stay with us without permission, but he could bring her and her whole family here? That was bullshit."

"We know you're the one who told Juan I was still alive and living here. What did he say?"

"He wanted to know if there was a way to get inside. I told him the place had gates and shit. He'd have to get you when the gate was open, or you were outside of here. That's when he sent Miguel and Jesús. They failed. He was pissed. So he waited, but you never left."

"How did you find out he sold me to Hector?"

"I was over there with him. He thought I was asleep, but I heard him talking. He said he'd sold you off to Hector, who'd been bugging him forever to have you. He laughed about how he'd wished he'd done it a long time ago. And he bitched about the old bartender at the Hangout. If he hadn't been dipping into the product, he wouldn't have had to have him taken out. Then you wouldn't have gone to the Hangout to take his place dealing. Things would have stayed perfect."

I stiffened. That explained why the old bartender had up and left without a word. He'd been dealing. How in the hell had I missed that? As much as I hated he was dead, I was thankful it had allowed me to find Luciana, fucked up though it was.

"Where is my brother, Barbie? Don't make me hurt you more." She put her hand on the knife she'd left in her leg. It was bleeding, but not enough to endanger her life.

Barbie sobbed. "He's in a house out in the country on the northside of town—the old Crocket place. He's been staying there with his closest guys."

"You said Miguel and Jesús were waiting for me down the road. Is that where they were supposed to take me?" Luciana asked.

"I think so. Juan is pissed. You brought all this down on him. Plus, you helped that bitch, Lila, get away. He's done. As soon as he got you, he was going to call Hector to arrange the pickup."

I interrupted at this point. "If you didn't come back, was there a place you were supposed to meet at later?"

"No. Though I told him I might have to wait awhile to get her alone, so no one knew I had anything to do with it. He gave me until tomorrow at noon to get her out of here." I relaxed. That meant they most likely hadn't panicked and ran.

Luciana turned to me. "Do what you want with her. I'm done." She walked out without another word. I couldn't tell if she was upset, shutting down, or really done.

"Make sure she doesn't know anything else. We'll decide what to do after we get Juan." As I left to go after Luciana, I could hear Barbie screaming my name. She wasn't my problem anymore.

Pitbull: Chapter 23

I caught up to Luciana as she walked back to the clubhouse. When I stopped my bike beside her, she never said a word. She just swung up behind me and wrapped herself around me. I took her to the trailer. When we got inside, she collapsed. I swept her up and took her to the bedroom. I laid her on the bed then lay down beside her. "I'm so damn sorry. I knew I shouldn't have let you do that," I whispered.

She shook her head. "I'm not upset about that. I should be, but I'm not. I'm upset at everything I've discovered over the last few hours. Wondering how things could have gone so wrong as to have my brother involved in killing our parents and doing everything he's done to me."

"We don't know for sure he did have anything to do with your parents' deaths, Luciana," I cautioned her, though my gut told me he did.

"I do. After you told me, I got to thinking. He made some weird remarks shortly after I came to live with him. And I swear there was more than once, he fought not to smile when he talked about them dying. He did this. I want you to promise me something, Cole."

"Anything."

"He'll pay and suffer, like they did. I'm not totally sure I can kill him. So you have to make sure of it. And take as many of those bastards he works with down with him. They've ruined enough lives, not just mine."

I kissed her tenderly. Her mouth clung to mine. When we stopped, I told her, "I promise. And your life isn't ruined. I promise I'll make it the best it can be. I can't make up for you losing them, but I can make sure the rest of your life is a beautiful one." She kissed me back. Soon, we were removing each other's clothes. We couldn't get them off fast enough. Our hands were frantically touching everywhere we could reach. I was instantly desperate to be inside of her, to make her feel alive and loved.

I slipped my hand between her legs and felt her slickness. There was no time for slow and easy. We needed hard and fast. I rolled her onto her back, pulled her thighs apart, then drove into her. She wailed and her nails bit into my back. I didn't stop or slow down. I held on to her hips and pounded in and out of her. All I knew was, if I didn't make both of us come within the next five minutes, we might die.

Luciana met every one of my thrusts with thrusts of her own. We were panting and our bodies were coated in sweat. The slap of skin on skin only made me harder and more desperate to come. Her breathing hitched, and I felt her pussy gripping me tighter. I leaned down and bit her nipple. She froze, screamed, and then came, her pussy squeezing the life out of me. I thrust one more time, then roared out my release as I came over and over. I felt like my soul had been ripped out of my body, which was often how I felt when I was with her.

When we finally regained our senses, she was yawning. I kissed her. "*Bebé*, don't go to sleep yet. We need to clean up. Then I want you to take a nap. You need to rest." She sighed but let me help her up off the bed and into the bathroom. As we showered, I told her what we were going to have to do.

"I'm gonna have to go meet with the guys. After that, we'll most likely have to go after Juan and the others. I want Sara or one of the others to come over, just in case you need anything," I told her quickly when I saw she was about to protest. "I'll be back as soon as I can. You'll be safe here. Some of our guys and likely some of Boss' will be here."

"Okay, I understand, but you have to come back to me, Cole. I can't lose you too. If I do, I'm done for." She sobbed. I held her and let her cry as the hot water rained down on us. After she calmed, I got us out of the shower, dried off and tucked her into bed. I sent a text off to Sin and then to Sara.

She'd just drifted off when I heard a soft knock at the front door. I quietly got up and went to answer it. I found Sara, Lyric, Skye, and Jackie standing there. They came inside without a word. My phone pinged. I looked at it. Sin had told me to come to the clubhouse. "I need to go. Make sure she rests and if possible, eats something. She might have some nightmares. Just do what you can, and I'll be back as fast as I can."

"You go take care of business. We'll watch your girl.

Pitbull make them bleed and suffer," Sara hissed. Right then, I could see where Sin got some of his strength.

"Oh, you can be sure of that. Thank you." I gave them all a quick hug and grabbed my go-bag out of the hall closet before racing to the back door of the club-house. Time to go on the hunt. Inside, I found all my brothers gathered in church. I took my seat.

"I called Boss. He's on his way with his guys. We patched up Barbie. She didn't know anything else. We'll deal with her later. Right now, we need to make a move before they get spooked and run again. Ex, why don't you tell us what you know?" Sin said with a scowl on his face. I looked at Ex. What the hell did he know?

"When Barbie told us where Juan is hiding out, that area rang a bell. So, I checked with Skye. That property is one of the ones that is owned and rented out by Bentley Real Estate. It's one of the properties that looks aban-doned. One of the ones Skye questioned. Shit, taking that and the fact Jon Bentley acted like he did with Skye and then Luciana at the wedding, I know there's a lot of shady shit going down on those properties. What it is, we'll have to find out. I'm telling you all this because when we get done with Juan and Hector, we'll most likely be having a talk with Jon. God, I hope it's all noth-ing. If it's not, it might kill Jack."

I knew what he meant. Jack thought the world of his sons, even Jon with all his screwups. I prayed we were wrong, but it fit like so many other things did. "Okay, thanks for checking with her. What's the plan?" Before anyone could answer, there was a knock at the door and Talon got up and opened it. In came Boss and his crew. Time to plan our attack.

In the end, we spent a good two hours going over the plan. Since we had the military training, we'd be the ones going in and bringing out Juan and anyone else we could get our hands on. Boss was having some of his guys stay behind here and the others to run point from outside. He, Wrecker, and Cuffs would handle anything that required the real law. We were going to run it similar to what we did when we had to go in and rescue Paula.

We left in unmarked vehicles. They were ones Boss got from Pop at Yardbirds, his junkyard. They had no plates and were unregistered to us. Boss said if anyone reported seeing them, Pop would say they had been stolen. We'd make it look like a drug gang war. As we got our guns and equipment ready to go, Boss and his guys watched us. I caught him shaking his head. "What's wrong?"

"Nothing. I just still get surprised at seeing you go in like a military assault team with bulletproof vests, dressed to blend in, and hell, night vision goggles and other shit, I have no experience with. I'm thinking you and the guys need to train my club and the cops we do trust in tactics. We don't have a SWAT team, but the way shit is going here, we might need to consider it."

"Boss, I know Sin would say the same. We'd be happy to help you, your brothers, and your department in any way we can. We all want the same thing, to make Tenillo a safe and happy place to live. Hell, that would be fun. We keep up our skills, but it's been a long time since we've trained people. You know we appreciate the hell out of all the help you're giving us."

"You've done the same for us. We're in this together. Let's get this show on the road." He clapped me on the back. I wanted to go check on Luciana before we left, but I didn't want to chance waking her if she was asleep. I got into one of the vehicles with a few of the others. As we rode out to the country, I cleared my mind. I had to be in total battle mode.

In the end, the whole mission was anticlimactic. It was done and over within two hours. We'd parked off the road and out of sight, less than a mile down the road from the Crocket place. We went in quick and quiet. When we burst into the place, we found Juan, Miguel, Jesús, and two other guys. They were all in the living room, watching porn, drinking, and snorting cocaine.

They were so messed up; they couldn't get to their guns before we had them on the ground. I made sure I was the one to handle Juan. It took all I had, not to start beating his ass right there. It was the thought that I didn't want to leave evidence that held me back and the need to make it a slow and painful process.

The drive back was done mainly in silence. Juan and his guys were between two vehicles. I made sure to ride in the one he was in. He glared at me the whole way back. He couldn't say anything since we had his and the others' mouths duct taped shut. They were trussed up like cattle with their wrists and ankles bound in zip ties. I never took my eyes off him.

I breathed a sigh of relief when we pulled through

the gates of the compound. Stamp and Captain stopped the vehicles with the prisoners in them at the club-house. I got out with most of the guys. "Take them to the Gallows. Brennan and Omen will be there to watch them. Then come back and we'll debrief and decide when we start stage two," Sin told Captain. Boss was talking to Stamp. They drove off with Boomer and Ram-page a couple of minutes later.

"Sin, I need to go check on Luciana for a minute. I'll be back."

"Take a few minutes. We'll wait on you. We have time now. Let us know if she needs anything," he told me. I gave him a fist bump then hurried to my trailer. I quietly entered to find the ladies all in the living room. Sara stood up and hurried over to me.

"She's sleeping. She's been out the whole time. She did cry out a couple of times, but she never fully woke up. I assume it went well. No one got hurt?"

I nodded. "It did. We're gonna meet in a few minutes. I hate to ask, but we're gonna be working on this for several more hours. Can you take turns sitting with her? Even if she's awake, I'd like her not to be alone."

"Sure. I know these three want to check that the others are fine. I'll let them go and then we'll arrange the schedule. Take your time. We don't want anyone to be overlooked." I gave her a hug and kiss as I whispered, "Thank you," to all of them. Jackie, Skye, and Lyric hur-ried out the door. I went to the bedroom.

I found her still asleep. I sat on the edge of the bed

and lightly ran my finger along a strand of her hair. *"Mi alma*, we got them. I need to take care of this, but as soon as I'm done, I'll be back here and holding you again." Her eyelids fluttered open. She gave me a sleepy smile then her eyes got wide. She abruptly sat up.

"Did you get them? Is everyone alright? Did he say anything?"

I hushed her by taking her mouth. I tasted her for several seconds before I answered her. "We did get them. Juan, Jesús, Miguel and two others. None of us even got a scratch. We haven't started questioning them yet. We just got back. I know you're anxious. We are too, but I need you to stay with the ladies. I'll be working for a while. As soon as we have what we need, I'll let you know."

She tugged my hand to her chest. She placed it over her heart. "I love you, Cole. Thank you. I'll try to be patient. Not sure if I'll stay here the whole time. I might have to hang at the clubhouse. This might get too claustrophobic."

"I'd like it if you'd rest here, but if you need to go to the clubhouse or even to one of the other houses, that's fine. Just keep your phone on you, okay?"

"I promise. Go take care of this." She gave me a kiss this time. It was all I could do not to strip and make love to her, but this wasn't the time for that. I'd do that later when we could celebrate.

"Bye, *bebé*, I love you." She smiled as I left the room. I felt the answering smile on my face slide away as I got back into the right frame of mind. I entered the clubhouse and went straight to church. I saw Stamp, Captain, Boomer, and Rampage were back. I sat down.

"I don't want to wait. They're high and half drunk. I think we should start on them now. The sooner we do, the sooner we can get the answers we need. If we need to let them stew, we can always stop later and put them on ice. Anyone disagree?" I asked. All of them shook their heads.

"I presume you want to take the lead, brother. I'm fine with that. You let us know if you need a break or want one of us to step in and work on them. Do you want to start with Juan or one of his minions?" Sin asked me.

"I think we start low and work our way up. He's gonna try and act like a badass. I want him to see what will be only a portion of what's in store for him. We'll start with the two we don't know. I figure they're low-level street peddlers. After them, we'll hit his enforcers then finish off with him. Hook, I hate to ask it, but will you have Frankie and Paula on standby, in case they need medical help to keep them going until we get everything we can out of them?" I hated to involve the women, but they were both doctors.

"Already thought of it, and they and the other ladies are on their way. We might have to hold them back from doing it themselves. Hell, we might want to sit this out and just let them and your Luciana loose on them. I hear she's a badass in pint-sized form," Hook said with a grin. That made me smile and got a lot of chuckles out of the others.

"Yeah, she is. Okay, who's ready to have some fun?" All of them gave a thumbs up then stood up. We silently filed out. The short ride out I thought of what all I would do to get the information we needed.

Luciana:

I paced around the clubhouse. The guys had been gone for hours. Jenn, Paula, Brea, Sis, Blue, and Frankie had all come over. They were doing their best to distract me. I loved them for it, but I wanted to know what the guys had found out. I came to a stop when Jenn came up to me.

"Come here. Sit and we're gonna talk. I wanna hear about this awesome wedding theme. We need to make sure we got everything ordered and planned. Are you having it here or somewhere else?"

I let her take me to the table where the other women were waiting. I had to admit, an hour later, her idea had been a good one. We'd talked, and they gave input on things I thought would be great for the wedding. We'd decided to have it here at the compound. It didn't make sense to spend money on a venue when we had one more than big enough here. After that, we got on the topic of me questioning Barbie. Skye, Jackie, Sara, and Lyric didn't know the details of what I did. I shared it with all of them. I saw a few open mouths, but I think it was mainly because they thought I was too nice to act like that.

When the men hadn't come back by dinnertime, we put on a movie. I tried to pay attention, but all I could

329

think about was them. I got a couple of text messages from Pitbull, checking on me and telling me they were making progress and not to stress. That was easier said than done. By eleven o'clock, I called it a night. The ladies all tried to get me to allow one of them to stay at the trailer with me, but I told them I needed to be alone.

Pitbull: Chapter 24

I stared at Juan. It had been hours. We'd started the whole session like I'd planned. We talked to the two guys we'd assumed were dealers or street soldiers for Juan. We found out their names were Tito and Paco. They were brothers and were low-level thugs. They weren't able to tell us much, other than how they intimidated people they were ordered to intimidate. They had no idea who the dealers were or even how the drugs were brought in. They were also cowards. They started singing as soon as they saw the pliers I held up. I didn't even get to hurt them much. We dispatched them quickly with a bullet to each of their heads.

Jesús and Miguel were a little more of a challenge. I worked on Miguel while Executioner worked on Jesús. Whatever I chose as the method of my interrogation, Ex did the same with his guy. They were doubly scared, seeing what was done to his cousin, while having to worry about the same happening to himself at the same time. It also cut down on the time we had to spend.

The standard beating and nail pulling they seemed to be able to tolerate well. They were less happy with the cutting we did. None of the cuts were life threatening, only painful, especially when we got done making dozens of them then rubbing alcohol into them. That had them screaming and swearing at us.

While we worked on them, we made sure Juan was front and center, so he could see everything we did to them. I wanted him to wonder and worry about which of those things we'd do to him. It also helped to see if there were particular things that had him looking or acting more nervous or scared. Everyone had secret fears. For some, it was to be cut or teeth pulled. Others might fear fire or being blindfolded and left in total sensory deprivation. It was finding the right combo. Something my days in the military had helped me and my brothers to learn. We might not have all been interrogators, but we knew enough to inflict mental and physical pain.

After working on them for an hour and a half, we stumbled onto their fears. Interestingly enough, it was the same one. I don't know what they'd had happen in their past, but these two ended up terrified of having the soles of their feet beaten with a bamboo cane. Caning was terribly painful and was used in many Middle Eastern countries. A skilled person could inflict maximum pain without permanent damage, or they could make sure the person could never walk again.

Since these two were never walking again, we didn't worry about that. Their screams filled the air as they sobbed and then begged us to stop. I held up my hand and Ex stopped hitting his guy. "If you want it to stop, Miguel, tell me what it is I want to know. Because if you don't, I'm gonna have my brother take Jesús out of here. He'll deal with him how he sees fit, while I do the same with you." His eyes got wide. He glanced at Jesús then back at me. He hung his head.

"Okay, I'll tell you. Just don't hurt us anymore. You need to know. We didn't have a choice. If we didn't do what Juan wanted, he'd have killed us." Juan tried to yell from behind his duct taped mouth. The hate in his eyes was almost scary.

"I thought you were all friends since you were kids. That's what Luciana told me."

"We were, but that changed, and he started to threaten us after he got into drugs."

"You mean using or using and selling them?"

"It started a little when he got to using them a lot."

"You're his bodyguards. That means you go with him almost everywhere if not everywhere. Who does he get his supply of drugs from? Why were you staying out at that house? I want names of the other dealers, drop points, and supply schedules for picking up more drugs and dropping off the money," I barked.

"Yeah, we go most places with him, but not everywhere. He wouldn't let us go with him when he went to talk to his supplier. He never even told us the name. Said we didn't need to know that. It was for upper management like him. If we had to do a pickup, the drugs were always dropped somewhere, and no one was there." He gave Juan a pissed look.

"How did you come to stay at that house? We know it's a rental property. It's been rented for months. Was that to you guys? Or is it just recently?"

"We've been out there a lot of times over the last

year, so I assume it's been rented to Juan or someone else all this time. We used it as a place to party sometimes."

"Is that where you stored your stash?" I knew it was. We'd found several kilos of cocaine, though no sign of them doing more than cutting it and packaging it there.

"Yeah."

"Who are the dealers? I know he forced Luciana to do it and the bartender at the Hangout before her. How many others does he have? I want names." He gave Jesús a nervous look. I didn't wait, I hit the soles of his feet again in three quick, hard lashes. Executioner did the same to Jesús. Both of them screamed. Jesús was the one to speak this time.

"Okay! Stop, we'll tell you. He has a dozen main dealers. We cover the southwest part of Tenillo. They use others to help them deal. That number changes all the time. They come to us to get their portion. It's on a different day every week and the time varies. We tell them where and when to meet. Juan has the names of all of them on a jump drive he carries around his neck on a chain."

This time, I thought Juan was going to burst a vein. He struggled so hard to get loose. Jesús flinched. "Ignore him. He can't hurt you. I can. We know Barbie told you that Luciana was here, and that she was sent to get her yesterday. As you can see, she failed." I pointed to Barbie. She was curled up in another cell. She was alive but seemed to have checked out. That happened a few hours ago.

"I want to ask you something else." He gulped then nodded. "I want to know if you laid a hand on her the night she was almost beaten and choked to death?"

Both of them adamantly shook their heads no. "No! No, we didn't. He went crazy that night. He screamed and just went off the deep end. We tried to tell him to stop, but he wouldn't listen. When he got done choking her, we thought she was dead. He made us take her and dump her body."

"What about months ago when he thought she helped his girlfriend, Lila, escape? I heard he lost it then too. That he had you strip her and take photos. He threatened to sell her."

"Yeah, he did. We didn't want to help him."

I slammed my fist into Jesús' jaw. You could hear the crack. He screamed. Executioner left Miguel alone. "You're a goddamn liar. You enjoyed it. She told me how you begged him to let you both rape her! You touched her while you laughed and took the photos. We know he's sold her to Hector DeLeón. I want to know what you can tell us about him and Juan's part in trafficking women."

Miguel started to talk again. "He wasn't trafficking women. Yes, he sold Ana to Hector. We all knew of Hector and his business. A couple of times, we'd helped him acquire new merchandise, but we weren't trafficking."

"Cocksucker, you sold women to Hector. That's trafficking, you stupid fucker! Tell us where we can find Hector. Where were you supposed to take Luciana when you got your hands on her?" I yelled. I was fast becoming less removed. The more they talked about how they didn't want to do what they did to her and those other women, the more I wanted to slit their fucking throats.

"I don't know. Juan is the only one who ever spoke to Hector. He was supposed to call him, I think to set up a meeting."

"Where did you deliver the other women you helped him get?"

"We met out back of the Liar's Lair and the truck stop next door. No one pays attention over there. We'd do it late at night when most people were asleep. Listen, Hector is crazy. He's been obsessed with Luciana ever since he saw her. He was going to get his hands on her eventually," he rationalized. At his calm dismissal, I broke. I started to rain hit after hit down on him. The rest of the information we needed to get was from Juan.

After beating him and watching Executioner beat his cousin, I pulled out my knife and slit Miguel's throat. Jesús screamed then Ex did the same to him. I wiped my bloody knife on my shirt to clean it off. I turned to Juan and pointed it at him. "You're next, motherfucker. And I promise you, what I do to you will make this look like child's play." I stalked outside. I needed to take a break.

I leaned against the building. I looked up when the door opened and Sin and Boss walked out.
"I know. I should have stayed calm," I told them.

"Hell, we'd have done the same. Just don't lose it on Juan until we get all of the information we can out of him. Then you can do whatever you want. How do you want to handle Juan? Let him wait or get back to business. You might need a break. Let us work him over to soften him up. That'll let you catch your breath. Then when we get down to the nitty-gritty, you take over and make him hurt."

"Sounds like a plan. I'd hate to not let you guys get a little payback." We both laughed. After about twenty minutes, I went back inside. The first thing I heard was Barbie sobbing. She'd now seen four men killed. She had to know what was coming for her. No way we'd have let her see this then let her go. I tried to feel bad about killing a woman, but in this case, I couldn't. She would've given Luciana to Juan and then over to a life of hell that would have ended in her death. She was getting what she deserved. I detoured over to her cell.

She looked up with hope in her eyes. When she saw my face, that hope died. "You're gonna kill me, aren't you?" she whispered.

"Hell yeah. What did you expect, Barbie? That we'd give you a slap on the wrist and say have a nice life. If that had been enough, we wouldn't have let you watch this."

"Why make me watch? Why didn't you just kill me?"

"Because I want you to know what you were truly going to do to Luciana by turning her over to them. You're not innocent in this, so don't act like it. Be glad you had very little pain inflicted. It'll be over soon." She curled up in the corner and kept crying. I went over to where Juan was now in a chair. I nodded to the guys.

Saint tore off the duct tape from his mouth.

I watched as they worked him for over an hour. I had to give him credit, he didn't break right away. I was tired of waiting. I came over to stand in front of him, and the guys all stepped back. "It's my turn now, Juan. You know the drill. You know the questions I want the answers to. Start talking or I'll make things really unbearable for you."

He spit blood at me from his mangled mouth. His face looked like he'd been through twenty rounds with a prize fighter. Bruises marred a large portion of his body. His fingers were all broken, and cuts decorated his skin all over. He glared at me through the slit of his left eye. I grinned. He was taking the hard road, just what I wanted. I picked up a pair of pliers off the nearby table. We'd used those same pliers much earlier. I held them up.

"Time to loosen your tongue." Only I didn't pull out his nails. I held up another object. It was a dental guard. I gave Executioner a chin lift. He jerked back Juan's head and forced his mouth open and the guard into it. This would prevent him from closing his mouth. I tore out four of his molars before I stopped and took out the guard.

"Ready to tell me something? We'll start with the easy one. How did you get that property on Crockett? What's Jon Bentley's involvement with you and your business?"

"I don't know him. I just found this place for rent," Juan lied. I knew he lied because of the way he shifted his eyes to the left. I casually twisted his broken fingers. He screamed.

"Wanna try again?"

"Okay, okay, we heard Jon rents out his properties on that end of town and doesn't ask questions or bother people. As long as you don't cause trouble or the law gets involved and you pay on time, he's hands off."

"Is that all he does or is there more?"

"That's it for me, though I've heard he might help clean your money if you need it. I've never done that."

I glanced at Phantom. He nodded. I knew he'd dig more into the finances of Jon Bentley. Juan had just confirmed what we'd started to suspect. Those rentals were being used for criminal activity and he was likely not innocent to it. "Any idea who he might clean money for?" I asked. He shook his head no. I grabbed his other hand.

"No! I swear. I don't know. Knowing too much in this town will get you killed. I worry about myself and that's it. People who get too nosy end up dead or disappearing. You wanna survive, only know and stick to your business." I dropped his hand.

"Before I forget, here." I reached up and pulled off the necklace around his neck—the one with the USB on it. I gave it to Phantom. "Fire this up. Make sure you can get into everything. Hate to kill him then find out we need a damn password or something."

"Sure thing, brother," Phantom said as he took it and went to the desk in the office area. He and Preacher both had laptops with them. They'd let me know if they needed more.

"The next question I know you can answer. Tell us who your drug supplier is." He stared at me without saying a word. "Come on, Juan. You don't need to worry about them killing you, I'm gonna do that, but you could lessen the pain I inflict. No reason to protect them."

He didn't say a word for a minute. I got tired of waiting and walked back to the cabinet with a lot of our equipment. He started to sputter. "O-okay, don't do that. I get all of my stuff from a woman. She meets with me when I call a burner. The number is in my phone. Look for the contact named H."

I worked not to look at my brothers or Boss' men. Was he talking about Hannigan? "Go on."

"I'm expected to move a certain amount of product every week. If I don't, then I'm held accountable. That's why I was so pissed when you took that money and the drugs from Luciana. I had to be the one to make up for the shortfall."

"Does H have a name? Where does H get her supply?"

"I only know her as H. She's in her late thirties, heavy set with short blond hair. Kind of a rough-looking woman if you know what I mean." He'd just described Hannigan. He continued, "She never told me where she gets her stuff, but I saw her a couple of times, going in and coming out of two places. She always had something with her she didn't go inside with. Might be nothing, but one is the Sudz laundromat over on Walnut and the other is Trapz, the gym on Brighten Court. She's been there several times a week. No one wears that many clothes or works out that much."

This time, I did look at the guys. We all exchanged satisfied looks. He'd confirmed what we thought was happening at the gym and the laundromat. We'd have to find her inside person or persons, but that would be something we'd get out of her.

"Why'd you kill your parents, Juan? You wanted that money so badly, you couldn't wait?" I asked him abruptly. He jerked in surprise at my sudden attack.

"What makes you think I did?"

"I don't think it. I know it. I'm just not sure why. From what Luciana said, they were great parents to both of you."

"Oh yeah, she'd say that because she was Miss Perfect! Never did anything wrong. All I did was go have some fun and they decided not only to kick me out, but to disown me!" he shouted.

"But you made sure to get them before they made a change to the will, didn't you? Sick son of a bitch that you are. Bet you loved that."

"Damn right I did! Having that little bitch under my thumb was the best," he said with a grin. I picked up a metal pipe and slammed it into both of his shins as hard as I could. He shrieked in agony.

"Did that hurt? Bet it's nothing to what you did to them and your sister. I'd refrain from calling my woman names or showing how happy you are over her suffering. I want to know. Were you there that night? If you were, did you participate?"

"Hell yeah I was there, and I enjoyed watching them die. The looks on their faces were priceless. I was the one who did the final deed," he said as he laughed maniacally. The fucker was truly a psychopath. I couldn't stop from slamming that pipe into both of his arms. As he screamed more, I got satisfaction that he now had four broken limbs. I'd read what had been done to their parents. I was taking it easy on him.

"Phantom, is everything going okay? Need anything?" I called over to him.

"It's all here, Pitbull. Fucker was too stupid to password protect it. He has it all—drops, amounts, dealers, pushers, you name it. He even noted when he had someone disciplined or taken out. Stupid fucker," he grumbled.

"Good. Then that only leaves one more thing. Hector DeLeón. Where can I find him? I know you sold Luciana to him. He has to be getting impatient. I know he's involved in the missing women around here. I doubt he'd tell a dumbass like you much, but you have to at least have a way to contact him when you finally get your hands on her."

"Fuck you, I'm done talking."

I didn't argue. I went to the cabinet and got out the next two pieces of equipment. Luciana had mentioned something to me one day. It was how Juan had always had this nightmare growing up. I was about to bring it to life. As I walked back to him, he watched my every move, his eyes going round when he saw what I had. But he didn't say anything even when I asked Chef, "Mind holding his head?"

Chef got a grip on his head. I placed the first tool. It was a round device used during eye surgery. Like the dental guard, this held open the intended area. When it was in the place, I showed him the last piece I'd held behind my back. It was a tiny blowtorch. He thrashed his head side to side, but Chef tightened his hold. I fired it up and struck. I placed it right on his right eye. The screams and smell were horrible. It only took seconds to destroy his sight in that eye. Yeah, big old Juan was afraid of being blind.

"Wanna talk or do I do the other one?" It was hard to hear him through the sobs, but he talked.

"Hector gave me a phone number to call. It's not in my phone. I memorized it. It's eight-eight-eight-five-five-five-one-seven-six- three. I'm supposed to call it when I get her, and he'll send men to pick her up. As for the other women disappearing, he's involved, though I don't think he's the only one. He travels all over Texas. Rumor is he has contacts in Mexico. He has guys who work for him along the whole route. He bragged about it. I've only ever seen him with three of his bodyguards. He supposedly has a place outside of Dallas and another down in Mexico. That's all I know."

"Is there anything else?" He shook his head no. I gave Chef a chin lift. He removed the eye guard then started to put it on the other eye. This made Juan piss himself and I swear, by the smell, he shit himself too.

"I swear! That's all I know. Listen, I can help you get him. Let me live and I'll help you get your hands on him. I'll call him and arrange a meeting to pick up Luciana. Only it'll be you guys waiting when he gets there." He was bartering hard.

"Sorry, Juan, I can't do that. See, I have an unrelenting need to rid the earth of vermin like you. If I let you live, I could never face my woman. Besides, she asked me to make sure you paid and that it hurt. I do think it has hurt. Now, all that's left is the final payment. I'll be taking your worthless fucking life."

His face showed his horror as I inflicted the final strike. His mouth was hanging open, his eyes wide and darting from side to side. I didn't shoot him in the head, slit his throat, or stab him in the heart. All of those would be too quick. I sliced across his stomach and let his guts spill out on the floor. He gazed down in horror. A man could live for hours sometimes longer with a wound like that. Juan would have a front-row seat to his own death. As he wailed, I turned to the others. They all wore satisfied looks. Boss mumbled, "They said I was sick for feeding someone his fingers. Damn."

"I'm done. Let him finish up and then we can get rid of the bodies. Let me finish one more thing." Before I could say or do more, a shot rang out. I saw Barbie fall to the floor in the cell, a nice hole between her eyes. I looked around and saw Captain holstering his gun. He shrugged.

"I thought I'd save you a bullet."

"Thanks, Cap. Okay, who's ready for a beer and

maybe a shower?" It was quickly decided who'd take care of the bodies and who would go back to the clubhouse. I wanted to go get my arms around Luciana. She had to be crazy, wondering what was taking so long.

Luciana: Epilogue- Three and a half months later

These last few months have been some of the best and most nerve-racking of my life. The worst was waiting as the guys tried to find and eliminate Hector. He was still off the radar, though Pitbull assured me they were getting close. They had found and eliminated the dealers and other people in my brother's gang. The supplier had been taken care of as well. I heard there had been arrests in some cases, but in others, people were rumored to have just vanished. I didn't ask Pitbull if they had anything to do with those.

Even though there were those things, a lot more positives had happened. I started nursing classes last month. I'd been so nervous that first day. Pitbull had been a rock and so supportive of my education. Another great thing was that with Juan and his minions gone, Lila could come back to Tenillo. She was due in a month. I was going to have a niece. I couldn't be more excited. We were helping her to get settled and on her feet.

The guys had somehow confiscated the money Juan had. Not only did I get my share of my parent's inheritance, but the rest went to Lila and the baby. Some good could come of all that ugly is how I saw it. I had a family again and a load of brothers and sisters. I had friends for the first time in years.

However, the best thing of all was about to happen. I was marrying my best friend today. My new mother-in-law, and sisters-in-law along with Pitbull's stepdad came into town last week. I'd gotten to know them and loved them already. His mom had helped us get the last of the wedding plans in place.

I held onto Omen's arm. We'd gotten close, and he was like the big brother I wished for. I was happy that things were finally straightening out for him. Just after getting rid of Juan, he'd gotten into a huge fight with Captain. There had been punches thrown and pissed brothers in both clubs. Omen had been in trouble with the club. Things have been resolved now, but that's a story for another time. Today, I was only going to think about marrying my man.

Everything turned out better than I could have imagined. Everywhere I looked was red, black and white. I'd taken that gothic theme and made it sophisticated and slightly sexy. Pitbull was dressed all in black and he took my breath away as I walked to the altar. His eyes were eating me up and I could tell he appreciated my dress. It was a white underlay that bled into red at the bottom. Over top of it was a black lace flower overlay.

It was strapless and dipped down between my breasts. My bridesmaids were dressed all in red, and the groomsmen in black and red. It was like a cross between a gothic vampire and Mexican wedding. Sounds crazy, but it turned out gorgeous. Now all I had to do was get through our vows and the reception, so I could then get down to the business of seducing my husband for the first time.

Pitbull: Epilogue - Three and a half months later

There were times I'd feared this day would never get here. Even though we hadn't eliminated all the threats to Luciana and our town, we'd made progress. A few days after killing Juan and the others, we'd made our move on Hannigan. I'd wanted to take Hector out first, but the phone number Juan had given us was to a burner phone. It was taking time to find him, but we were getting closer every day. He'd made sure to stay the hell away from Tenillo and us.

When we got our hands on Hannigan, we found out she was dealing mainly with Juan. Her boss only ever communicated through anonymous calls and notes. Nothing we could trace. She had been supplying the high school and Juan. When we took her out of the school, she increased the demands on Juan to sell more. It all ran downhill from the top. If you didn't make your quota, you were expected to make it up or suffer the consequences.

I was kind of disappointed that she couldn't tell us more than her dealers. We were able to get her guy at the gym. He was arrested by Boss. We couldn't kill everyone, though we'd thought about it. Some of the lesser people we reluctantly decided to let them live and go to jail. Hopefully they'd learn their lesson. The one at the laundromat was harder. It was the owner, and we found he was being blackmailed to do it. They had taken his daughter and promised to give her back if he did as they asked. We were now looking for her. He was more than thankful to us. He'd come to realize they would never let him stop or give him back his daughter. I prayed we'd find her alive.

One thing I was thankful for was that Hannigan was a coward. We didn't need to torture her to get her to talk. Maybe the fact people were speculating on what had happened to Juan and his guys helped. She sang like a canary. In the end, she quickly disappeared. The word was she quit the force and decided to move across the country to Maryland. She left no forwarding address.

As for Jon Bentley and his properties, we were still watching him. We knew he was laundering money for a lot of people. It was finding who that we had trouble with. Until we knew who all of them were, we couldn't afford to tip them off. We had to be content, knowing when we took out someone like Juan, that was one less person he was laundering for or helping in some other way. I couldn't wait until the day his ass went down, though I hated to think what it would do to Jack and Ben.

But all of that paled into comparison as I looked at my wife on the dance floor. She was dancing with her girls and laughing. The wedding and the reception had been perfect and beyond anything I'd imagined when she told me her idea. We'd had fun today with our friends and family, but now it was time to take her back to our place and start the rest of our lives. The first thing on the agenda was to make love to Mrs. Cole Landis, several times.

Pitbull: Epilogue- Two years later

The last two years had flown by. We'd gotten most of Tenillo cleaned up. My brothers had found their own happily ever after. Or at least most of them had; I still had a few who were searching. I was clapping as I watched my wife accept her diploma for graduating her nursing program. I couldn't be prouder of her. She'd come such a long way from that scared woman in my office at the Hangout. I was hoping she'd soon be ready for us to take on a family. I knew she'd want to get started with her career first, and I was okay with that.

Later at the clubhouse, we all celebrated into the night with our family. Both clubs had thrown her a surprise graduation party. She was glowing with happiness. I went up and wrapped my arm around her. She was talking to Paula. She turned and gave me a smile then a kiss. "Hi, honey. I was just telling Paula. I was going to find you. Do you have a minute?"

I nodded as she said goodbye to Paula and walked off with me. She led me out of the clubhouse. When we got to where we were going, we were outside our house. "What's going on, Luciana?"

"I wanted to give you a present. It wasn't something I could do there." I grinned. It sounded like my wife was about to get naked and let me feast on her body.

"Well, don't let me stop you." I led her into the house and up to our bedroom.

As soon as we got there, she told me, "Wait here, I'll be back." She went into the bathroom. I hurried to strip. I wondered what outfit she had this time. *Mi alma* liked to wear sexy things which drove me wild. I lay down on the bed as soon as I was bare and waited. A couple of minutes later, she came out. I saw she was still clothed. I frowned as she laughed.

"Did I get the surprise wrong?" I asked her. She shook her head as she came to the bed and crawled up next to me.

"No, that part is definitely happening. But first I have something else for you. Here." She held out her hand. It was a small box. I took it and unwrapped it. She was the one who was supposed to get the gifts on her graduation day, not me. Once it was undone, I opened the lid and stared at what she'd given me. Lying inside in a bed of tissue paper was a stick. What caught my eye was the word on it, *pregnant*.

I looked at her in disbelief. "Are you saying—"

"Yep, I'm saying in seven and a half months, you're gonna be a daddy. How's that for a surprise?" I crowed with happiness and then attacked her mouth, as I took her down to the mattress. This was one of the best surprises ever. Second to the day I met and fell at her feet as her most willing slave. I made sure to show her over and over how much I loved her.

The End Until Book 4:Omen's Entrapment

Made in United States
Orlando, FL
17 July 2025

63059881R00193